BROKEN ROSE OF TEXAS

AUSTIN AFTER DARK BOOK 2

Alexa Padgett

ISBN-978-1-945090-26-4

Edited by Sarah Allan
Cover Design by Covers by Combs

For Sarah. Your insights for these characters were spot-on.

CHAPTER ONE | Regan

I glared at the glowing neon rocket with building trepidation. My body hummed with a restless energy that shimmied through my nerve endings, making me jumpy.

"You sure about this?" I asked.

I mean, I'd heard of The Blue Bar and wanted to attend one of the live shows for ages, but the crowded parking lot and long entrance line worried me.

So did the clench low in my gut.

That feeling I hadn't been able to shake since my father's message two days earlier. The one I ignored—just like the message before, and the message before that.

"You said you wanted to kick back with some great tunes. This is the place to do that in Denver."

I turned my head to study Mindy. Her short, dark ringlets rioted around her head in that sexy, I-just-got-out-of-bed look men adored. Thanks to the smoky shadow her large hazel eyes popped more than usual, and her glossed lips turned up in happiness.

Mindy deserved happy. I sighed, knowing I was going to end up wishing I'd stayed in the hotel room. Not even the lure of fantastic music could allay the fear that something…something terrible would happen tonight.

We walked in, getting the typical VIP treatment that made me cringe even as it made Mindy preen. Sometimes I wondered why she couldn't be the performer and I the assistant.

But Mindy didn't have the compulsion to lay all her pain out in lyrics, set to throbbing beats. No, that was *my* way of handling my formative years.

Not sure my type of therapy was healthy, but there you go. And lots of people were willing to pay to hear more about my pre-pop-queen life.

I smiled and posed for about twenty selfies before we made it into the actual bar. A waitress met us and led the way to a nice table stationed off to one side. Yeah, The Blue Bar staff were professionals when it came to the glitterati.

I hated my tiny space in the group.

But I did want to see the act. Not an easy feat—going to live shows. I nodded to Darryl, my bodyguard, and a new guy…I think his name was John. They stood off to the side but near enough to intervene if necessary.

I would have preferred them to sit with me, but they refused. While I loved the guys, they tended to be a bit gruff and stand-offish. I wasn't sure if that was because of my age—all twenty-five years of it—or the fact I'd overheard Darryl and John talking about my smokin' hotness. When I called them out on it, not liking, what, in my mind, seemed like a lack of professionalism, they both clammed up and backed off.

I glanced down, as unimpressed as I normally was by myself. Sure, I kept in shape. I liked to do Krav Maga. It gave me a sense of independence, and I spent at least two hours working out in the discipline each day. That didn't count the time I did yoga, which I also loved. But that was for relaxation and focus, not strength and kicking booty.

I understood my features classified me as pretty, but people got caught up in my stardom and forgot I was a person who liked to veg out in sweats and watch movies, same as the next woman. Maybe more because it was so rare now.

Not that my short jean skirt and scuffed, ten-year-old cowboy boots screamed sexy, but I did like looking nice. For myself, sure, but also because anytime I left the security of my hotel room or house, someone was going to take a picture, and it was easier to look put-together rather than face the rumors about my impending drug overdose or pregnancy.

I settled into my chair and took in the stage. A rich red light slashed across The Blue Bar's coat of arms at the back, giving the space an eerie, cold feel. The stage was shallower than most of the ones I performed on and raised only a couple feet off the ground.

While I liked the intimacy of the space, the red lights reminded me of the night my mother died.

Deep breath in, then out. Again, just as I did each day in yoga. Okay, so not the stage on which I wanted to perform, but then, the world considered me a pop princess. Everyone assumed I loved synchronized, heavy beats, not the light instrumental touch and intimate space of tonight's singer-songwriter.

Fact was, I liked both. After this tour ended, I planned to end my relationship with my current label and strike out in a more artistic fashion. Sure, I knew that was a risk. But it was one I felt compelled to take.

That's part of why I was there tonight. I wanted to see Janie Thorpe in action. If we got along as well as I hoped we would in our lunch meeting scheduled in Austin later in the week, I wanted to talk with her about a collaboration for my next EP. If she chose to see me as anything other than the airhead sexpot the media regarded me as, anyway. I hated that more than my fans' belief of the pop princess persona, an image my own father helped create.

A waitress waited patiently at my elbow, and I realized she wanted to take my drink order. I flushed, thankful I'd picked up the menu before I'd zoned out.

"Sad Panda Coffee Stout," I said, because I just had to try a beer with a name like that. I wasn't much of a beer drinker— drinker at all—so I added, "And a water, please."

The waitress must have already taken Mindy's order because she scurried off.

I blew out a breath.

"Well, I hope tonight's fun," I said.

"Relax, Regan," Mindy said, face lit with pleasure. "It will be. I have a good feeling about this."

At least one of us did.

———————— ★ ————————

I was bored and had heard enough to know that Janie Thorpe's studio albums would always be her bestsellers. I grimaced as she hit another flat note. This was why she played small clubs.

I texted Mindy, asking her if this performance was as bad as I thought. Mindy grabbed her phone, checked her message and shot me a glance. She typed something.

My phone beeped.

Worse.

I rolled my eyes. Mindy kept working on her phone, dismissing the bar and the tunes. Her ability to focus with such intensity left me awed. But that's why I'd hired her, and she did her job with an ease I'd never match.

I caught him staring at me sometime during Janie's second set. His eyes penetrated my every pore, even from across the room, heating me up and making my skin plump.

Whoa. I'd never had that kind of a reaction, especially from a man's look.

But there was something about him. Sexy, of course, and, well…hmmm. Predatory. Primal. Yeah, that was the right word. His desire was primal, and his face was stamped with sex and sin.

I wanted him to keep looking. Wanted him to touch me.

That freaked me out.

Maybe that's why I paused, beer raised halfway to my mouth, and I gawped like an idiot.

"What are you looking at?" Mindy asked, craning her head. She couldn't see him from her angle, thanks to the people milling between us and his table.

"N-nothing," I managed to stutter. "I just need to use the restroom. Be right back."

I hurried off before Mindy managed to open her mouth. Darryl would follow—that's just how my life worked, and no, it wasn't all due to my fame. Nope, some of it was my own stupidity in getting mixed up with the wrong guy.

After using the facilities, I washed my hands and let the cold water run over my wrists, cooling me further. I shut off the tap and looked in the mirror.

I shook my head, thankful for the momentary quiet to calm myself. I dried my hands and opened the door, nodding to Darryl who stood off to the left. I stepped forward, but then immediately darted into a small alcove when a herd of women scuttled past me.

A large hand gripped my waist as one of the women nearly mowed me down, pulling me snug against a muscular chest. I craned my head back to look up into clear gray-blue eyes. A gasp fell from my lips. It was *him*. He'd been potent across the room, but up close and this personal, my pulse quickened and my body hummed to life.

My reaction baffled me. I wasn't one to take undue risks—I knew the pain and fear that could swiftly come because of them. So why was my body, my freaking heart, so interested in this man?

"Hope you didn't get trampled."

The man had an accent. Softly Southern. Combined with that deep voice washing over my sensitized skin and holy cow!

"No. I'm fine."

"Glad to hear that, sweetheart. Wouldn't want anything to muss such a special package. My name's Carter. What's yours?"

Oh. He didn't recognize me. I blinked up at him, waiting for him to laugh at the joke. But I tended to be most popular with the under-thirty female crowd, so it was possible Carter didn't recognize me without my stage costumes and big hair.

"Regan." I gave him my real name. For some unknown reason, I wanted to keep the energy between us even.

"Regan. Lovely name for a lovely face."

His lips turned up but his eyes remained firmly trained on mine.

Something clicked—that stranger danger my mother warned me about way back in first grade.

"Wait. Did you follow me back here?" I asked.

He nodded.

I stepped away. "All right. Well, thanks for the save from the ladies. Bye."

"You're just going to walk away?" he asked, surprise flaring in his eyes.

"Yep." Keep it simple, signal Darryl to leave. Get out fast.

"May I ask why?"

The gaggle of women shuffled out of the bathroom *en masse*. As I turned to face him, this time my chest pressed to his. My pulse slammed in my neck. His gaze dropped there and he chuckled lightly.

"I don't bite," he whispered. "Not unless you want me to."

"I don't." But the words came out breathy. Like I did. Except I didn't. *I didn't.*

The music started up again, the crowd louder now that they had some drinks in them, and Janie was into her dance hall blues tunes.

"I have to go," I said.

"What if I took you somewhere quieter? Offered you a nightcap? Coffee?"

My brow wrinkled. "Why?"

He reached up and gently brushed a dark brown curl from my

cheek. "Because I like looking at you, and I think I'll like talking to you even more. Can't really do that here."

Even though he'd leaned down toward me, his voice was loud—almost a yell. Speaking here would be difficult.

But did that mean I wanted to go somewhere with him?

I analyzed my body's reaction. I trusted it more than my mind–unlike my mind, the prey buried deep within my genetics still knew when to run. But right now, all my inner prey wanted to do was rub against this man's hard chest and purr.

I glanced over at the entrance to the dance hall and considered my options: sitting at the table while Mindy continued to work; take a million more selfies; maybe get asked to come up on stage to perform. Janie had noticed me earlier and winked. That was usually code for "I'll call on you to entertain my crowd later."

I didn't want to after listening to the last hour of missed cues and notes. I winced as Janie's voice shrilled. No way could I get mixed up in this hot mess.

I had to cancel the meeting with Janie. For my reputation, sure, but also for my ears.

"Okay," I said. "Just let me tell my friend where I'm going."

"What about your bodyguard?" he asked.

Observant. I liked that. I also liked the fact that he didn't seem overly fazed by my personal protection.

I wanted to get to know him better, but I wasn't sure going anywhere with him was smart.

He must have seen my hesitation. "Live a little, Regan." His voice was low, soft, and eyes held mine.

I bit my lip.

A couple of women stumbled back into the hallway, laughing as they fell against each other. One stopped to blink at me, her mouth opening as recognition dawned. I turned away quickly, the sick feeling in my gut lingering as tightness built in my shoulders and neck.

I didn't want to have to play the part. Not tonight. My head began to ache as tension coiled up my spine. Carter touched my cheek again and my good sense crumbled.

"If you promise to play nice, Darryl can have the rest of the evening off." Oh my…*what* was I saying?

Carter smiled, his eyes dancing with pleasure.

He rubbed his callused thumb down my cheek to the edge of my lip. My breathing stopped. He dropped his hand and I shivered, thankful he hadn't pushed me further. Because, much as I was attracted to him, there was no way I could offer him more than my company.

"I'd be honored to get you home later."

I smiled more brightly than I had in months. After texting Mindy to let her know I was heading out and to ask her to gracefully extricate me from the meeting with Janie, I faced Carter. My phone buzzed, but I ignored it. Mindy would do her best not to hurt Janie's feelings, which would be easier to do if I wasn't here.

"I'm ready."

"So am I," Carter said, his voice softer than spun sugar and twice as yummy.

CHAPTER TWO | Carter

We spoke about bits and pieces in the car. I told her I lived in Wyoming most of the year on the vast ranch I'd purchased after completing my computer science degree at the University of Texas. I didn't mention I owned another place near San Francisco for when I needed to geek out with the biggest names in the industry, or that I'd just decided to move back to Austin to spend time with my family now that my twin and I had mended our relationship.

Until Cam and I hashed out the issues that led to me cutting off contact, I hadn't realized how much I'd missed him—like one misses a lost limb, I'd expect. Cam would understand that metaphor better than I, having some army buddies who'd been through horrific accidents and firefights that cost them arms, legs, eyes. Sanity.

I shook off that melancholy, trying once again to focus on the lovely young woman next to me. But that proved hard—for years, I'd second-guessed my decision to get a degree and not follow my brother into the military.

I didn't want glory or have the warrior mentality; I'd let Cam go because I was pissed he'd married Kim. I was even more pissed off when he left that succubus on our family's ranch and decided to become a badass Army Ranger.

Then, Kim died in an unspeakable disaster. Cam's injury a few months later led to his medical discharge and an extra pile of guilt because I hadn't saved my brother from any of the demons that tried to take him down.

They'd nearly succeeded, and that was on me.

Going back home proved hard, but I'd found I enjoyed Austin's charm more than San Francisco's tech-heavy charisma, or even the vast openness of Wyoming's ranch land, the place I'd needed so desperately in order to heal.

Just something about the vibe in Austin—the cross between frenetic and easy-going, eclectic and cutting edge, appealed to me. That's why I'd built a tech empire based, most recently, on independent authors who sold me the rights to construct choose-your-own-adventure stories in a fun little app I put together over a three-year span. The version before my current work in progress focused on simple graphics and addictive gaming. Thankfully, I enjoyed the challenge and already had a few other apps in the works to further my portfolio. But I'd also enjoyed working my spread. The vastness of the sky as I rode across the land, checking on my cattle, always calmed me.

"How long are you in town?" I asked to be polite, but also to get out of my head.

"Um. A few days."

"For work."

"Yes."

"Me, too. Where are you off to next?"

Regan hesitated, nibbling at that luscious lower lip. I wouldn't mind biting it myself.

"A few places. My calendar's booked solid through the end of the year."

"Oh? You headed out to, I don't know, San Francisco or Austin any time soon?"

Again, Regan hesitated. The street lamps flashed light into the car, casting her face into sharp relief. She reminded me of that new American/British princess. The one my sister was so gaga over. Meghan something.

Except Regan's hair was curlier and longer and she was an inch, maybe two, taller. In her heels, she came to my chin, and I stood over six feet tall. And her eyes. They were a rare, deep sky-blue. Arresting, especially against the warm skin tone and surrounded by her long dark lashes.

The light slid past and we were cast in shadow. I didn't get the sense she needed to consult her calendar to give me details, simply that she chose not to share with me.

"I'd need to check with my assistant about the exact timing."

"She handles your travel?"

"Among other things," Regan said.

I frowned, not liking how evasive she was being. With bodyguards and an assistant, Regan was rich, probably famous. While she looked familiar enough to tickle a memory, I'd clearly buried myself way too deep in my tech company and cattle if I couldn't place a woman as beautiful as Regan.

We parked in the underground garage, and I led her to the elevator, both of us ignoring the heat of the Colorado evening.

I inserted my keycard and pressed the floor to the penthouse. Regan didn't even raise an eyebrow.

Huh. I always got a response when I pressed the penthouse button, no matter where I was staying.

I shifted, starting to wonder just who Regan was. She turned toward me, raising those striking eyes to mine, and I decided who she was didn't matter. She was beautiful and the chemistry sizzling between us was undeniable.

Anticipation began a slow, steady drip through my tightening body.

Once the doors opened and I led her into the suite's large living room, she glanced around the vast, airy space.

"What do you want to drink?" I asked, moving closer and running my hands over her hips. The denim skirt she wore was short enough to give me a good idea of the suppleness of her tanned thighs. I wanted to drag my fingers up the inner side to see if they were as soft as I imagined.

She stepped back, out of my embrace.

"You brought me here to seduce me," she said, her voice hinting at a huskiness that made my pants less comfortable.

"And if I did?" I asked, once again shifting closer to her, but I didn't touch her again. Not yet. Just let the heat between us build, swirl, intoxicate.

She smiled. Not the smile of a sultry witch I wanted under me. Hell, over me worked, too. No, this smile was sad—as if she were disappointed in me.

The last woman to look at me like that broke my heart.

"May I ask you something?" Regan asked.

I blinked, shoving the hot anger in those brown eyes and stiff lips from my memory. I was alive, standing next to a beautiful woman.

All was right in my world.

"Sure." I didn't lean back, but I didn't lean in closer. Something told me now wasn't the time to push her.

"Is this an every-night experience?"

I rolled back on my heels, nonplussed and unsure of how to answer.

"What do you mean?" I hedged.

But I knew what she was asking. And, dammit, my erection died because any answer I gave her now would destroy my evening plans.

Her lips flipped up again. "Every night. You bring a different woman back here and screw them, don't you?"

"No, not every night," I mumbled. I'd spent weeks on this newest update to my software. "Not here." Because I didn't actually live in this city. This was a stopover on my way home, to Austin.

Wait. Why was me wanting companionship—wanting a chance to forget—wrong?

She turned her back toward me, and I swallowed the groan working its way through my gut, up my chest. The skirt slithered over her hips, cupping her ass. I wanted my hands there, fingers digging into the supple flesh, as I pounded into her body. And forget…

Whoa. Not going there. Especially twice in under five minutes.

Thankfully, she spoke, breaking my near-trance.

"I'm going to have to pass," she said over her shoulder.

I crowded her a little. Her pupils dilated and her delicate nostrils flared. I lifted my hands, prepared to run my palms down her bare arms.

She walked back in clear dismissal.

"There's one thing you didn't ask me," she snapped.

I dropped my hands. "Fine. I'll bite. What's that?"

"If I was interested in a one-night stand."

"Who doesn't like pleasure?" I growled. She was as into me down at the bar as I was into her.

She cocked her head, all that long, luscious dark hair spilling across her neck and down her back. "You're sexy. You're charismatic. Unfortunately, your reasoning that I would fall into bed with you after having a fifteen-minute conversation is unacceptable."

A live wire zipping up my spine wouldn't have hurt anymore. "Unacceptable?"

She slid her purse strap back on her shoulder but continued to face me, her eyes filled with such disappointment—in me—that I looked down at the floor.

"You use sex. For pleasure. Nothing wrong with that, I guess, if both people are okay with it." Her tone said there was a lot wrong with my choices. She stepped in closer, her rich voice caressing my skin, causing a ripple over my flesh. "But, see, I'm *not* okay with that."

My chest ached at the weary sadness that filtered into her eyes.

"Did someone…" I didn't know how to ask—*what* I wanted to ask—but it was evident from her bleak expression that she'd seen sex used as a weapon. That realization made my heart stutter.

She brushed off my question with a flip of her hair. That silky, shiny hair I really wanted to pet. Not in a sexual way, not now.

I just…shit. I wanted to hold her close and tell her everything would be okay.

We both knew that was a lie.

"You want to do intimate things to my body without understanding my mind, my feelings."

"What does sex have to do with feelings?" I asked, my voice harsh because these emotions she'd churned up inside me *hurt*.

Her expression held no amusement. What had happened to her?

"For many men and women, but most importantly, for *me*, everything."

"You're saying you've never fucked for the sake of the release?" I asked. No, I couldn't have heard her response right.

"I don't fuck." Her voice was as flat as her expression.

The word fell, hard and ugly between us. I shivered. When she said it, it sounded…well, bad. Everything about this evening had taken a nose-dive into unfamiliar and painful territory. I didn't know how to respond.

"I'll take you home."

She pursed her plump lips. "No."

"No?" I asked. I was so out of my depth.

"No. Me coming here was insanity." Her delicate throat convulsed and her eyes filled with tears that she ruthlessly blinked back.

She was ripping my heart out. Bringing her here had been an epic mistake.

"I have one very simple rule." Her voice broke but she kept her gaze locked on mine and her back straighter than a flagpole.

"You don't get in here without getting in here first." She tapped her chest, then her temple.

Her words settled against my skin like acid rain.

"You expect me to…what? Love you? I don't even know you."

And this time she didn't even smile. Her gaze remained steady, true as I met it.

"Exactly."

Her next words, spoken in that rich voice that wrapped around me like a mug of hot chocolate, stopped both my heart *and* my desire to comfort her.

"I don't think you can love a woman."

With effort, I managed not to stagger. My body turned stiff as I shut each emotion down. She was right—I didn't. Well, not the kind of relationship she meant. I mean, I loved my mama and my sister, but not wanting emotional entanglements with other women? That was a choice. One I'd made because… I shook my head, trying to force the memories from my mind.

She turned on her cowboy boots and walked to the door. Hand on the knob, she glanced back at me. The light set her hair aglow.

"Good luck with the seducing."

CHAPTER THREE | Regan

"Wait."

I tried to keep walking away from the beautiful, sleek male in his beautiful, sleek penthouse.

"Please."

His voice cracked on the word, and I stopped but stood still, quivering.

"What if we...played chess?"

I turned but left my hand on the doorknob. "You want to play *chess*?"

His cheeks burned a dull red and his lips twisted downward. I expected him to shoo me off. "That's what Miranda and the prince-dude do in *The Tempest*."

A startled laugh burst past my lips. "Ferdinand."

He frowned. "What?"

"Her love interest—her fiancé—his name is Ferdinand. I loved that play because she asks him..." The giggle continued to bubble up my throat. "You were forced to read that play, weren't you?"

"Tenth grade English class. Mrs. Montgomery was a Shakespeare fanatic. We also read *King Henry IV, Part 1* and *Macbeth*."

I should leave. I needed to get out of here, escape Carter's pull over me.

"While I liked the fight scenes in *Macbeth*—that dude was badass, stealing the throne, well, until he went crazy, but Mrs. Montgomery preferred *The Tempest*. She focused on what she saw was the empowering feminism of Miranda and how she directed the relationship with Ferdinand and her father."

I pursed my lips as I considered Carter's statement. He shoved his hands in his pockets and appeared much like a lost little boy. That look—gah! I was such a sucker.

"I think I like your teacher."

Carter's smile lit me up with its brilliance and white teeth. "We didn't. And we got even madder when we found out the rival school got to act out all the bloody battles in *Macbeth*." He shook his head, causing his too-long hair to flutter around his head. "We had to settle for shipwrecks, a wizard, and weird sprites."

Warmth tingled up from my chest. I liked this—the back and forth that came with such ease.

"I just bet you would have preferred to play Macbeth to Ariel. Swordplay would have been fun."

His look turned scorching and I flushed, realizing how he chose to interpret my words.

"Do you have chess?" I rushed to ask, already castigating my poor decision-making.

"I can call down for a set. Or…" He whirled on his heel and I bit my lip, taking in the gorgeous view from the back.

"Ah ha!" He pulled out a dusty box from a cabinet with some exotic wood door. The box looked older than the two of us, combined, and definitely older than the luxury suite we were in.

He shook it, pieces banging against the edges.

"Scrabble?" I said.

"Yeah. My friend knows I like the game. He must have brought up the box. We'll have…um…tea. And play."

"Why?" His friend, the game, tea…so many questions I needed answered.

He tilted his head, studying me for a long moment. "I'm not sure yet. Just…talking to you matters. I like hearing what you have to say. I haven't liked spending time with a gal in…" He trailed off and busied himself with opening the box.

Something about his words, the catch in his voice, cinched my decision. I hoped I didn't regret it—even as I knew I would. I stepped away from the door on shaky legs. "How about you get me that beer instead?"

His hands stopped, hovering over the box. His blinding smile lit into my chest, warming me. "I'll order a six-pack. And a pizza."

I sighed, knowing I shouldn't eat that—it was *so* against my diet. But, then again, I shouldn't be in this room with this sexy man.

"Make my part double cheese," I said as I slid into one of the sumptuous leather Parsons chairs at the table. My smirk turned into a full-blown smile as I pulled the small tile bag toward me.

"What's that look for?" Carter asked as he hung up the phone.

I blinked up at him, all innocence. "I like Scrabble," I said.

He slid into the chair across from me. "That sounds kind of dire. Like you know your way around those Qs and Ps."

"I might." He didn't know the half of it, and I wasn't going to tell him—yet—that I was the former fourth and fifth-grade spelling champion for my entire school district.

Carter groaned, and I belly laughed. When was the last time I managed that? Not sure, but boy did I enjoy the freedom and giddy bubbles of happiness bursting through me.

I shook the tile bag. Carter stuck his hand into the bag and pulled one out. He flipped it to show me a K. I rummaged through and held up an E.

"Something tells me that's pretty much going to be the way the night goes," he grumbled.

I set out the first word, using only six of my letters but earning a nice double-word score. Carter shook his head, causing his thick, dark hair to ruffle. He clenched his jaw in concentration and I wanted to run my fingertip along its edge, see if it was as smooth as I anticipated. Press my thumb to his lips to feel the plumpness there.

He huffed out a laugh as he spelled his word: AMOK

"Not as many points as yours," he said, preening at my open-mouthed expression.

He was smart. Probably a brilliant brain behind those pretty eyes. And he was clearly well-read. I clenched my thighs together because, really, was there anything sexier than a learned man who enjoyed books?

Maybe I should have taken him up on the acting naughty.

A series of no-nonsense knocking sounded on the door. I inhaled as I studied my letters, trying to get my libido wrestled back into its normal cage. I hadn't wanted anyone—hadn't considered a relationship with a man since James broke my heart.

"Pizza and beer and a pretty lady who's going to kick my ass at Scrabble. I'll call that a fun Friday night."

I laughed again, the rest of the tension unwinding from my neck and shoulders. Carter brought over the box and some napkins, then opened us each a beer. He handed me a slice of pizza before settling into his chair to study the board.

"Damn, girl, you got fifty extra points for using all your letters."

"Sure did." I bit into the pizza and stifled my groan of pleasure. Tight clothes would not be happening tomorrow, but this pizza tasted divine.

Carter dropped his tiles on the board. "Only six. You really are going to kick my ass."

"I was two-time spelling champ in grade school," I said, setting my pizza on a napkin and using another to wipe the grease from my fingers as I assessed the board. "Whew. This isn't going to be pretty."

Carter kicked back, taking a large bite out of his pie. "I got nothing but time tonight, sweetheart."

The endearment caused a fizzle of contentment to burst in my belly. I sipped my beer in an effort to show nonchalance I wasn't feeling. Crap. This was nice, maybe too nice. But I wasn't going to leave, nor was I going to give up my time with this enigma who managed to be infuriatingly sexy and sweet.

The longer I spent with him, the more I realized Carter might just be the man I hadn't known I wanted.

CHAPTER FOUR | Carter

She was a spelling phenom. I should have guessed by the sly smile as she sat down at the table at the start of the game. But I was having fun, the entire night relaxing and pleasant in a way I hadn't realized I missed—or needed. And I didn't want it to end.

Thoughts of Dianna and the hours we used to spend together ran through my head. We'd never played Scrabble—or played cards, anything where we faced each other and talked like I did now with Regan. No, we ran together on the indoor track because she liked to run but *only* indoors.

I'd always been an out-of-doors man, and I'd hated the stale air and lack of interesting things to look at as we paced around the track. She insisted we go to basketball games and sit courtside, but then she'd spend the whole game waving at friends or on her phone.

We rarely, if ever, accommodated my passions for poetry and plays. Or even for the rodeo, which was rougher and more in-line with what Dianna thought a man should like to watch. I did like the rodeo, had even flirted with the idea of going onto the bull-riding circuit after high school. But I liked reading and words more than the thrill of sitting on a bucking brute for eight seconds. And, truth be told, the idea of broken bones never appealed. Hence, my career path in tech and as a ranch owner, not into the military or PBR circuit.

I took another long swig of beer, hoping it would wash down the thoughts running through my head. Regan laid down the last of her tiles with a flourish, a wide grin blooming across her face, her white teeth and a slight dimple in her left cheek adding to her girl-next-door charm.

I wondered again who she was. An heiress, maybe. Though, she didn't act like the women I'd met over the years. I liked that.

"Twenty-six points," she crowed.

She was real in a hesitant way, as if someone was always trying to restrain her enthusiasm. Who would want to?

Not me.

Never me. In fact, the next time we hung out...

Whoa. Slow that crazy roll. We were having wholesome fun, but that didn't mean I was going to make a habit of playing family board games or seeing this woman. She'd go her way and I'd go mine.

The thought depressed me, so I shut it down.

"Watch from the master and learn," I said, pulling out all my tiles as fast as I could. All seven. "That's right, baby! Seventy-two points." I would have fist-pumped but that seemed excessive. And I was still losing by twelve, even with my monster score.

I mulled over what she'd said earlier. Of course I didn't love Regan. I barely knew her. I shuddered at the word—at the pain it had cut so deep into my heart all those years ago. Regan was correct in her belief I didn't *want* to love anyone. But that didn't mean her company tonight didn't make me happy because it did. She did.

She pursed her lips and stared at her letters, then at the board. She swept her hair back from her cheek.

"I have the best proper name," she muttered.

"Against the rules," I said with a smirk.

She rolled her eyes and went back to studying the board. Her face brightened and she pushed her pieces between a few other letters to make the word CLOTHES. She gave me a long side-eye.

"Clothes make the man. Naked people—"

"Have little or no influence in society." I smiled as I leaned back in my chair. "A reader of Twain and good ole Willy."

"And the former spelling bee champion." Regan laughed.

"Makes me think you must be a naughty librarian." I leaned in, forearms on either side of the board. "You're not a librarian, are you, Miss Regan?"

She shook her head, eyes bright.

"Now, that's a real shame. If you'd been the librarian when I was growing up, I would've spent more time reading."

She collapsed back in her chair with a deep guffaw.

Now that I knew her a little more, I wished I'd handled the beginning of our time together, here in the penthouse, better. Because Regan was a gal I'd like to know. Intimately, of course, but also for more evenings like this.

I refused to think of why that could be.

She polished off her beer and a second slice of pizza, eating with a relish that I hadn't seen in many of my dates. I liked that. Hell, I liked Regan.

I laid down my next word, counting up the points and writing the new total.

Too bad she'd disappear tomorrow. Worse, that she didn't want to tell me more about her life. But I let her set the framework for tonight—I had to after I messed up so badly by trying to rush her into my bed.

She slid her fingers together and pushed her hands outward. "Oh, this is *on*," she muttered.

———————— ★ ————————

Time slid away during our second game. I had another beer while Regan switched to the sparkling water we found in the fridge. We laughed at the stupid words we managed to create, not bothering with normal Scrabble rules any longer—not after Regan was able to create CALLIOPE.

I taught her an alternate version called Take-Two and we played that a couple of times, though I kept getting distracted by the cute way she pursed her lips as she tried to use up all her tiles.

After she beat me yet again, Regan laid her head on the table.

"I'm sleepy," she said with a yawn.

I glanced over at the clock and gasped.

"Well, you should be. It's after three in the morning."

"What?" she squealed.

I pointed. She ran her fingers down her face and groaned. "I don't want to call my security detail," she mumbled. "It's not nice of me to get them out of bed."

"Then don't. This is a big place. Lots of bedrooms. Three, maybe?" I hadn't bothered to count them all because I was only staying a couple of nights and the extra space was meaningless for me. I hadn't cared what room I stayed in—that was the benefit of growing up with a no-nonsense mama and a struggling ranch.

A soft bed and locked door were the pinnacles of comfort far as I was concerned. But my buddy, Pete, who happened to own the hotel, wanted to impress me into parting with a larger portion of my cash when we met tomorrow. After spending the last couple of nights here, I just might let him talk me into a substantial increase in the shares I planned to purchase.

Regan yawned again, her eyes tearing. She was cute with droopy eyelids. I doubted there was a time in her life when she wasn't one of the most beautiful women in a room.

Those thoughts were not part of our agreement for the night. I cleared my throat and tried to focus on something less sexy than her soft, warm skin.

"I can give you something to sleep in. And there have to be extra toothbrushes around here, somewhere."

Yeah, those words didn't lessen my interest in seeing her change. Bad Carter. We were…friends, I guessed.

"Yeah. Okay."

Regan yawned again, so hard her entire body vibrated. She blinked at me much like a newborn calf. My damn heart squeezed with a painful thrum.

"That sounds good."

Her voice was huskier with exhaustion. I liked knowing that about her.

I led her to my room to grab a shirt but she must have misunderstood because Regan made a beeline for the bed and collapsed onto it. I shook my head with a chuckle because, damn, if she wasn't already out.

Like my little sister used to do, years ago. My twin or I could pick her up and she'd lay her head against our shoulder and be asleep before we could blink. I missed those days with Katie Rose. Life had been so simple then. When I'd thought I knew who my family was and my place in it.

Something soft and warm blossomed in my chest as I took in Regan's sprawled, sleeping form. I bent down and pulled off her boots, grunting as I worked them off her toes. She promptly rolled over with a grumble, pulling her knees to her chest and sighing as she snuggled deeper into the pillows.

I pulled a blanket over her and tried not to ogle the extended view of thigh brought about by her hiked-up skirt. With a sigh of relief for actually being the gentleman I'd promised her I could be, I went to the bathroom to brush my teeth. I dug around in the drawers and found an extra, which I laid out for Regan next to a clean washcloth. I splashed water on my face and stared at my dripping visage in the mirror. I wanted to sleep with Regan. Yes, sexually, but also just…just to be near a person, to keep a connection for a little while longer.

I bit my lip, considering if that was creepy. Probably was.

But the desire welled up from somewhere deep inside. A place either I'd buried years ago or that hadn't existed before Regan. More than likely, the answer was a combination of both.

I sighed and toweled my face. I stripped down to my T-shirt and underwear before padding into the bedroom to grab a pair of thin sweat pants I'd brought. I pulled them up my legs and over my hips when I heard Regan stand from the bed and shuffle to the bathroom.

In the doorway, she turned back toward me, and for the

second time since I met her, I was reminded of an angel surrounded by a soft glowing light.

"Can I stay in here with you?" she asked in a husky tone that definitely tightened my groin.

Guess her mind wanted the same thing mine did. Maybe she was as concerned about people using her as I was. If she were an heiress, that would make sense. Whatever the reason, I didn't want our time cut any shorter than it had to be.

"Sure."

She nodded before closing the door, but not before I saw the sadness and fear in her eyes.

CHAPTER FIVE | Regan

I woke to streaming sun and a relaxed body. Carter's heavy arm lay across my waist, his hand tucked underneath, keeping my back cinched in close to his chest. I liked this position, just as I enjoyed his scent and how his knees tucked just so under mine.

Staying with Carter, in his bed, overnight had been even stupider than agreeing to come to his suite in the first place. For some reason, I couldn't regret the decision.

Carter's breath was even and deep, a light puff against my neck. For the first time in years, maybe since my parents' problems began, I felt cherished.

But that train of thought, of *wishing*, was stupid and would only end up hurting me. The disgust on Carter's face when I mentioned the word "love" told me everything I needed to know—this man would never love me. Simply the idea of such a notion revolted him. So, my emotional response to him was ridiculous.

Carter wanted company for an evening. Clearly, he'd been hurt before, deeply if I had to guess, and the best choice I could make was to leave before he woke. While our night together remained untainted by the weirdness of this morning-after.

My heart ached at the thought he might want me gone, but it also spurred me into action. I edged out from under his arm in slow increments, holding my breath, desperate now to make my getaway before the awkwardness could set in.

He nuzzled into my hair, sighing my name, which made me want to melt back into him. Whatever else Carter was, he seemed to care enough to remember who he slept with. That *had* to mean something.

I bit my lip, refusing to cave to my desire to turn our night into something more than it was. I needed to get out of here, get back to the relative safety of my hotel before the paparazzi found out where I was and could catch me looking like I'd…well, done a lot more than play Scrabble and eat pizza.

I smiled. Last night ended up being so much like a high school date. Not that I had many of those thanks to my hours on the set for the TV show my dad contracted me to do. But, still, my time with Carter I would cherish for many, many nights to come. First, though, I needed to leave.

I made it out from under Carter's arm and to the edge of the bed. I eased upward, careful to move slowly. He continued to sleep.

As soon as my feet hit the floor, I grabbed my boots and hustled out into the living room, closing the bedroom door behind me. I slid my feet into my boots and grabbed my purse. I pulled out my phone to see seventeen missed calls. I grimaced at the notices from my father.

Every choice had a cost, and my night of freedom just called in its price.

I pulled up my Uber app but paused. Leaving this hotel at…I glanced at the clock on my phone and winced harder. Seven-thirty in the morning. Calling an Uber to pick me up this early

was not going to win me any points with the tabloids. Or
my father.

I texted Mindy. *Pick me up, please? ASAP.*

Kick-ass assistant she was, she responded instantly. *Where?*

I gave her the address I'd pulled up from Google. Then, to my
surprise, I hesitated next to the dining table for a long moment. I
needed to repair my appearance and get the hell out of there, but
simply leaving without a note turned my fun evening with Carter
into something sordid and ugly. I was unwilling to cheapen the
time I'd spent with him. I grabbed the paper and pen he'd used
last night to keep score and scribbled out a note.

I also snagged a bottle of water off the table and downed it in
one long drink, smacking my lips. Not the caffeine shot I needed,
but at least my mouth didn't feel gross. I grabbed a comb from
my purse and ran it through my hair, twisting it up into a chic
knot as I headed to the nearest bathroom where I washed my face
and reapplied my makeup with the emergency bag of cosmetics
I'd learned to keep with me at all times.

Because celebrity was *always* about the face I presented the world.

I tried to smooth the rumples from my clothes. My phone
pinged with a message from Mindy letting me know she was in the
underground garage near the elevator bank at the back side of the
level, farthest from prying eyes. I heaved a huge sigh of relief that
she hadn't mentioned my father insisting on riding over with her.

I sucked in a deep breath and straightened my shoulders.
Walking out the door and the relative safety of Carter's penthouse
took more courage than it should have. The last story written
about me was nasty.

I just wanted to make music. To sing like I used to with my mother. As the elevator doors slid shut, I closed my eyes for a moment, remembering the pleasure of our simple concerts, the joy of being with her, doing something we both loved.

That wasn't my life but that didn't stop me from yearning for the simpler days when no one noticed my hair or clothes or the extra few period pounds.

Didn't matter I never actually signed up for this life—when I was just fifteen, fame seduced my father with its wealth. He claimed to be "between businesses at the time" and more than ready to manage my career, spending the money I made long before I understood the price required for its caustic glittering world.

The elevator doors slid open, and I thanked Carter for his penthouse upgrade. The elevator never stopped on another floor, meaning I didn't have to interact with another person. Maybe this would work out.

Spotting the SUV, I beelined to the back door, looking straight ahead—just in case there were paparazzi around. The door opened, and I slid into the seat.

Only Mindy sat in the back. Thank goodness.

"Hey, Darryl."

"Miss Leroux."

"Did you have a nice evening off?"

"I was worried about you," he rumbled.

Well, hell. "Nothing to worry about. I had a nice time with Carter."

"You should know your father arrived last night. He wanted

to talk to you. Mindy told him you weren't available."

I inhaled sharply. "Bet he didn't like that."

I pretended not to see the scowl Darryl shot at me via the rearview mirror. No reason to make the situation worse. Instead, I returned my focus to the topic at the top of my mind: how to pivot my career. I'd hoped I'd get my first attempt last night, but Janie's messy performance wasn't the correct time or place. Unfortunately.

"You touched base with Janie?" I asked my assistant.

Mindy grimaced as she nodded. I reached over and grabbed Mindy's hand. "Thank you for dealing with that unpleasantness."

Mindy's phone pinged and she extricated her hand. "That's what you pay me for."

I frowned, not liking the implication, but her tone remained chipper. Maybe I was just overtired and, yes, worried about my future.

I wanted to move into more mature music—the kind I preferred to listen to myself. I would have pushed for that years before, but my father cajoled me into sticking with the sweeter pop sound. Then, he fought my switch from TV glam girl into full-time performer, stating that giving up my position might well crater my burgeoning empire.

That alone wouldn't have stopped me from trying to forge the path both my mother and I saw for myself. My plans collapsed when my father went to the label behind my back to keep me in the television show contract longer than I'd planned. Since I was still a few months from my eighteenth birthday when he signed the multi-year contract, I had no choice but to honor it. Well, I

could have fought him in court, but I didn't have the energy...
and I couldn't do that to my father. Not then, so soon after my
mother's death.

I looked out the window. Seven years of my life down the
drain on a show I *never* wanted to participate in. Not that I wasn't
thankful for the opportunities—I was, deeply.

I dropped my gaze to my clasped hands, feeling like the
petulant child my father claimed I was. That conversation—
really, my father's chastisement—stuck in my mind and caused
the same shivers of disgust at my selfishness now that they had
when he'd spoken the words then.

"Your mother would love to see you so successful, Regan. This
was always her dream, you know. This level of success, the fans,
the write-ups."

When I'd said nothing, he continued, "So it's not your
absolute favorite type of music to sing? You have enough fans to
fill up, like, China or something. You're wildly successful, thanks
to the deals I've cut for you. All you have to do is sing some songs
and dance a little, show some skin. Smile. Why can't you just be
happy with this easy money?"

Because it *wasn't* easy. The longer I spent on the television
series, the more I dreaded the hours, my co-stars' misbehavior,
the drugs and alcohol and sex that numbed everyone enough to
get up and do another sweet, peppy scene the next day.

And then there was James.

He'd been a disaster of my own making, one I chose toward
the end of my tenure with the show. I shook my head, wishing I'd
been smarter then as I tried to be smarter now.

Another one of the other actors and singers on the show, James seemed so exciting and fun. He'd been nearly four years older than me and entrenched in the Hollywood lifestyle before we started dating. He never was willing to give up his pills or his other women, as I'd later discovered, but in the beginning I'd been so flattered by his attention, unaware he lavished it on all his costars, looking for the next one to boost his career.

When he and I imploded, I flat-out refused to go back on the set. We'd just wrapped the season's final episode, which, thanks to an addition to the contract I stipulated, became the series finale.

I walked away with great relief, both from James and the destructive lifestyle I'd been struggling to avoid for much too long, but with a deep regret that I stayed with him so long, ignoring the rumors of his other women—of his other woman, specifically.

The tabloids ripped me to shreds in article after article for my diva behavior, for my father's overprotectiveness, for not thinking of others, and many other less-kind sentiments.

But I did not sever the business relationship with my father that Mindy and even my label suggested might be beneficial then. He was holding me back, they said, not seeing my full potential.

I'd ignored them. For what I told myself were good reasons.

I rubbed my temples, trying to stave off the headache building there.

I had ten more concerts to figure out how to fix the growing tension between not just my father and me, but my father and my staff, and my father and the companies I worked with. I'd spent the last four months seeking a solution, and I was no closer now than I was when we started.

But I did know I wasn't signing a contract for another pop album, no matter what my father wanted.

CHAPTER SIX | Carter

As I woke, I knew I was alone. I'd held Regan in my arms the short night, waking at intervals to enjoy the feel of her body pressed to mine. As I came to full alertness, I missed her warmth and the tickle of her hair against my neck and chin. Her pillow was cool and the room quiet.

I sat up and yawned. Just before eight. I grabbed my phone off the nightstand where the alarm blared. I turned it off—just as I realized I didn't have Regan's number.

"You're a goddamn idiot." I tossed my phone back on the nightstand and stood, stretching, before I padded into the living room and kitchen area of the suite. As I expected, Regan's purse no longer sat on the dining table.

She left.

A deep well of something that felt an awful lot like sadness rose in my chest. *Stupid.* Such a stupid reaction. I didn't know her, and I sure shouldn't miss a woman I didn't know.

But I wouldn't get to know her *unless* I saw her again. Frowning at the direction of my thoughts, I went into the kitchen and made myself a cup of coffee. Espresso roast. Black. I slugged it back, ignoring the heat biting into my tongue and throat. Maybe now that my brain was awake, I'd be able to stop thinking such sappy thoughts.

And, anyway, I had a lot to do today, not least of which was pick up my new Land Rover. I'd been eying the vehicle for months and now that I planned to move back to Austin, I'd made the purchase, finally turning in my beat-up work truck to the salvage yard near my ranch. I'd taken that Ford pickup to university and then on to San Francisco before buying my own spread when the city life got too hectic for my country-boy roots.

I set my coffee mug on the table next to the Scrabble box. My wistfulness for the game—my companion—last night turned into a full-blown grin. My cheeks ached as brutal happiness surged through me.

Regan wrote a note.

I snatched it up, reading the words faster than my brain could process. Digits—yes! She left me her number.

Hot damn. I set the paper down and made a second cup of coffee that I sipped more slowly, the outlook for today turning brighter than the morning star.

———— ★ ————

After putting Regan's number into my phone, I resisted the urge to contact her. While she'd given me her number, that didn't mean she wanted to hear from me. Instead, I texted my brother, Cam. We communicated multiple times a day, something I would never take for granted again. Talking to my twin might not solve problems, but the connection with him made me more able to take on the world.

He replied within a couple of minutes, which let me know he'd been as happy to hear from me as I was to touch base with him. I chuckled at his long-winded explanation of his fiancée's latest antics. Jenna said crazy shit, but I loved her, mainly because she made Cam happy. He deserved this level of contentment, especially after what he'd been willing to give up to get it.

I, on the other hand, had been equally unlucky in my love life as my brother, but had no desire to seek out the emotion again. For some reason, Regan's sky-blue eyes flashed through my mind. The way the left side of her mouth hitched up more than the right. That off-kilter smile made me grin in response more than once last night.

But I didn't really want to pursue something with Regan... did I?

Is it worth the risk? I texted Cam before I thought it through.

What?

Falling in love. Being with someone like that.

My phone rang, startling me. I took a sip of my tepid coffee before I answered. "Yeah?"

"If you're asking, it means you met someone."

The response was knee-jerk. "No, it doesn't."

"Carter," Cam said with a sigh.

"Fine. I met a gal last night." I couldn't help but smile. "She's a helluva Scrabble player."

Cam's laugh boomed into the speaker. "Y'all played Scrabble?"

"Mmm hmm. She kicked my ass."

"Jenna cheats words. She likes to use proper names and slang."

"Regan would be all over her. She's strict about the rules."

Cam chuckled. "Sounds like an interesting lady. Are you gonna see her again?"

I hesitated. "I..." I never told my brother how badly my

relationship with Dianna ended. In part because I was ashamed of my role in the final showdown.

The mortification I carried didn't forgive her for cheating with my friend and former suitemate. I winced as I remembered finding them together on the couch in our dorm. But, worse, was the scene between Dianna and me afterward. I scrubbed my free hand over my eyes, banishing the images. I just wished I could do the same with the memories.

"I like her," I finally said.

"But?" Cam hummed. "This got something to do with the girl you dated in college? Dianna, right?"

Hearing her name out loud made my stomach ache. "That didn't end on a high note."

Massive understatement.

"You planning to finally give me the details?" Cam asked.

"Prefer not to."

"All right. Just…don't let something that happened a long time ago mess up your chance at happy now."

Cam's voice changed, getting softer, which told me Jenna was nearby. I smiled for Cam even as my stomach iced over at the thought of giving someone that much control of my happiness. No, no way would I ever hand over my heart again. I wasn't sure I even had the whole of it left after Dianna pulverized it.

"Love isn't something you seek out, Carter. It finds you and smacks you hard in the gut. The question I had to ask myself was if I was man enough to accept those feelings even if Jen didn't feel the same. Lucky for me she did."

I heard Jenna's voice but not the words. Cam grunted.

"You all right?" he asked.

"Yep," I replied.

No. Cam's words twisted me even further into knots because I wanted to be man enough…except I didn't. I wanted to go back to last night and not walk into that bar. Then I wouldn't be all twisted around and asking my little brother for love advice.

"Gotta go, bro," Cam said.

Course he did. He had a gal to keep happy.

I ignored the part of me that reared up and roared that I, too, needed love and happiness in my life. Problem was, I thought I'd had it. The deep, satisfying kind that would last through any adversity.

Instead, I spent these last ten years trying and failing to forget the ugly end of my last relationship.

CHAPTER SEVEN | Regan

I should have been more prepared, but maybe it was the few hours of sleep, or the euphoria I still felt from my date night with Carter. Whatever the reason, I wasn't ready for the shit-show that developed within moments of Darryl delivering me back to the hotel. At least I managed to sneak up to my room to shower and change clothes before my father sought me out for breakfast.

"I heard you weren't well last night," he said, his narrow gaze sliding over me.

"I'm fine now," I said.

"We should talk about what the label wants on your next album."

My shoulders stiffened. "I've let them know I plan to record in Austin," I said as I poked at my egg-white omelet.

I hated eggs. The smell, the texture. Everything about them was nasty. Mindy kept ordering them for me, telling me they were healthy. I set down my fork and instead picked up my toast. Then I remembered the pizza I'd eaten last night and set the warm bread down with a sigh, settling for a long sip of my coffee.

Breakfast of champions. Or at least skinny people.

"I told them you'd given up that nonsense for a better tour package, and they're expecting you back in L.A. next month."

My hand convulsed around my mug, but I managed to take another sip as I made a noncommittal sound in the back of my throat.

I was going to Austin, and I planned to record the album I wanted there. Thankfully, my father didn't know the arrangements I'd made, and I wasn't going to tell him.

"Since you didn't sign the documents I sent you, I assumed you didn't get them. I brought a copy with me."

He placed them on the table, peering at me intently from beneath his graying eyebrows and over his bifocals. As usual, he was dressed in that older gentlemen uniform of pleated khaki slacks, a polo shirt, and, inexplicably, boat shoes. I'd given up telling him pleats were not flattering to his midsection. And the boat shoes were such a strange fashion choice, I ignored them.

"I'll look it over," I said.

"I already did," he said, frowning. "Don't you trust me?"

"It's not about trust. I need to take more control of my career. Understand the nuances."

Mostly, I needed to get through these next few weeks of not signing so that I could pursue the record I wanted to make. If I slipped and mentioned any of the details I'd already set into motion—like the type of music I planned to record—Dad would start ripping apart my plans, telling me how I was throwing away everything I'd built over the past decade.

I almost wished I could.

I stared down into my mug. That sounded so selfish. Maybe I was acting like the diva I'd been called. Maybe I should just continue to make the music my current fans expected.

My hands shook and my chest ached because I just…couldn't anymore. I'd rather quit making music entirely.

That was the thought that cinched my decision.

I just wanted to make music I could be proud of. Music that reflected the intrinsic me I'd bottled up inside for far too long.

"You don't think I negotiated you a good enough deal," my dad said, the beginnings of a pout pulling at his lips.

"It's not about trust, Dad. I'm twenty-five. You're sixty-one and you are going to retire one day. I need to be ready when that happens."

He finally sat back in his chair with a muttered agreement.

I sighed into my coffee, my fingers relaxing their death grip on the mug. That standoff had been close.

Too close.

———— ★ ————

Now, an hour after my non-breakfast, we were back in the SUV; this time I shared the back seat with my father and Mindy.

My phone pinged. I listened with half an ear to their discussion about the bus positioning that would allow us the best opportunity to exit Denver later tonight and get to Colorado Springs with plenty of time for my first round of interviews tomorrow. I grimaced. Late travel meant I didn't sleep well.

Considering my minimal hours of shuteye last night, I was going to need to get serious about my pillow time.

My phone pinged again, so I pulled it out of my pocket. A message from a number I didn't recognize or have programmed into my phone. I wrinkled my brow. 307 area code. I lifted the phone to my face, and the message popped up.

This is Carter. Your Scrabble buddy.

I had a great time last night. I was very disappointed that you were gone when I woke up.

I smiled, warmed by the message. That he'd contacted me. I typed out a quick reply.

Regan: *I didn't want to leave. That hotel bed was comfy.*

That was the truth. I'd slept better in the bed last night with Carter than I had in weeks. Insomnia was becoming a real problem and was part of the reason I wanted to slow my tour schedule.

Carter: *I worried.*

I typed back. *About what?*

That you wouldn't leave me a way to contact you, was his reply.

"Are you listening, Everly?"

My dad's irritation slammed into me, and I sighed. Dad no longer called me Regan. Once I landed the role on the television show, he told me I was Everly both to him and the world. He'd never understood how heavy the weight of that mantle weighed—how I wanted to snuggle up next to him and just have him love me, the scared little girl who lost her mother too soon.

But that wasn't my father's way. He embraced my fame with an intensity that frightened me. Like it defined *him*.

Only late at night, after the whole James blow-up, did I realize it was because Dad didn't care if *Regan* disappeared. He wanted me to be Everly Leroux and all that entailed. He wanted that because *Everly* was his creation whereas Regan had always been close with her cheating mother.

"Yes. I have to be on the bus by twelve thirty in order to get to the venue by two thirty so that we can keep on schedule tomorrow.

Really, Dad, I have all this down. I managed to get where I'm expected while you were in L.A., and I can continue to do so."

Dad frowned at the phone in my hand but managed a brief nod. Mindy glanced over and began talking about the food the venue planned to cater. I was thankful for her redirection. I responded to his last message.

Talking to Carter was much better than dealing with my father.

Regan: *I'm glad you did. Contact me. And I had fun, too.*

I held my breath, waiting for his reply.

Carter: *What are you up to today?*

How to explain to someone outside the industry the grind of the press, the sound check, the makeup and hair and costuming? I was down to the tail end of the shows. Much as my father kept pushing, pushing, pushing for me to add more, I'd refused.

Making new music was more important to keep me on top of my game, I'd told him.

Not that he had read or approved any of my new songs. I didn't plan to show them to him, which would be hard if he found out I refused to sign the contract extension he'd spent the past five days working on. No way I could allow him to stick around Austin.

That's why I'd asked Mindy to book him an expensive, month-long vacation in Fiji, a place he'd always wanted to visit. It started in just a couple of weeks. I needed to hold out, stay strong, until then.

That worry was for another day. Right now, I needed to answer Carter.

Regan: *On my way to work.*

Carter: *You never told me what you do.*

I hadn't because it almost always led to more questions or people seeing me differently. I didn't want that with Carter, but was it worth telling the truth?

Yes, because I wasn't going into another relationship with anything less than full disclosure. Just the thought of James' angry face as he watched me nominated for a Grammy was enough to make me shudder. It wasn't the award nom he disliked. No, James played that up to the media, and even to me and my father.

It was the nasty things he said to me later in the privacy of my room that caused the hurt to burrow in deep. How I didn't deserve the recognition, that I was nothing more than a cute pawn to the label—replaceable, expendable—and not even a good singer since I lost. Or a good girlfriend if I was busy running around after my dreams and not helping James achieve his.

I'd bought that; I'd apologized and asked how to make James' day better.

I took a deep breath and began to reply to Carter's text, unwilling to remember the rest of that hurtful, demeaning night.

Regan: *I'm going to a music venue. I have a concert there tonight.*

This time, Carter was slower to respond. I licked my lip, wondering if he was Googling me.

You're a singer? he asked.

Regan: *Yeah. Though we use the word "performer".*

I'd like to see one of your shows.

No, he wouldn't. My core audience was tween and teen girls, thanks to my years on the television series and the songs the men in suits curated for my albums.

But that was going to change. Once this tour ended, I was no longer under a label contract, though they had first rights to decline my new album.

I hoped they would. I wanted to explore and branch out, and everyone else seemed motivated and dedicated to keeping me in the tiny box they'd built around me.

The one tonight in Denver sold out, but I'll have another in Colorado Springs, then Wichita on Monday.

And another two days after that, then another…I closed my eyes as I considered the grueling schedule in place. I hated it.

"Everly? Are you listening to me?"

"Yeah." I opened my eyes and focused on my father.

"So you agree?" he asked.

I glanced over at Mindy, not wanting to admit I'd zoned out on their conversation again because then I'd get an earful about respect. I just didn't have the energy to hear his lecture. She gave a small shake of her head.

"I'll talk it over with Mindy to make sure it's feasible."

Thankfully, the vehicle slid to a stop and voices grew outside the doors. We were at the venue, which meant my father wouldn't berate me further. At least I hoped that still held true.

It was only later, after my interviews and sound check, that I was able to check my phone again.

Carter: *I take it you're a pretty well-known and well-loved performer, then. I guess I should look you up, but I won't. I like the mystery.*

My heart settled into a better rhythm. I didn't want Carter

digging into my bubblegum past or the juicy tabloid covers that came from my break with James.

Carter: *I'm guessing you're on the stage, so I'll just tell you to break a leg. And, Regan? Next time we get together I'm kicking your ass at chess. That's always been my best game.*

I couldn't help the chuckle that slid from my lips. But then I frowned. I was leaving after my show tonight. The tour buses would take us across another two states before we headed down into Texas for my final leg through Dallas, Houston, San Antonio, and Austin, where the tour ended and I'd set aside nine weeks to work on my new album.

Soon…

Well, sooner than it had been last night, anyway.

About a month left to go. I could handle that long. I had to.

I closed my eyes, soaking up the idea of a few weeks without riding in buses and changing locations each day. Of being able to have a favorite place to eat out and listen to lots of good bands. To soak up Austin's ambiance and its incredible talent.

I already had meetings booked with some of the people I wanted to work with, but I hadn't yet heard back from Camden Grace's people. He'd spent the second half of the summer and fall touring for his last album, selling out packed stadiums much like the one I sat in now. Word trickled back that he, too, planned to be in a local Austin studio to finish his upcoming album.

If he planned to be in the studio while I was working on my album, I wanted to be there. I wanted to get his input on a few songs. But, more, I wanted him to produce my newest album. That would be a hard sell—not just because Camden was as busy as I was, but because my current music sounded nothing like the bluesy country and western I'd written for this new LP.

One I hoped would silence the voices that kept encroaching. The ones James set to wagging about my lack of actual talent.

I bit my lip. If I really played my cards right, I hoped Cam would agree to sing for two, maybe even three of the songs. I'd written them for his voice and making that collaboration a reality was one of my biggest goals.

The more I thought about the partnership, the more I considered it a pipe dream. I was a sugar-pop princess and Camden Grace was country royalty, anointed through the trials of his relationship with Jenna Olsen and fed to every red-blooded American via every social media outlet for a solid two-week period. His willingness to walk away from his career last Fourth of July proved the impetus I needed to make my own leap of faith.

Plus, that moment caused me to sigh and my heart to pitter-pat in longing. He'd been willing to give up his career for Jenna. Totally swoon-worthy moment. Thank goodness Camden's fans came to their senses and realized the world would be a much bleaker place without his genius.

Since that video went viral, Camden hopped to the absolute pinnacle of his career.

I, on the other hand, was the good girl turning bad. Like Lindsey Lohan but without some of the really crazy antics. Maybe more like Britney back fifteen years ago. Whatever. Who I behaved like was irrelevant, though the media viewed me through that lens no matter how much distance I tried to put between myself and James and his drug-laced period. Worse were the salacious articles about the love triangle between James, my best friend Savannah, and me.

My mistakes were mounting, and if I couldn't get a contract from a touring company to set me up with a new, lavish set of concerts like these on my pop world tour, the entire singer/song-writer, down-home bluegrass project could be a complete flop. Big time.

And I'd be a has-been. The girl who thought she had talent until the industry trampled her and left her on the ground, bruised and bleeding. I slid my trembling hands under my thighs and tried to still my bouncing knee.

I'd lived through that hellscape one too many times already. My thoughts drifted back to Savannah. I missed her. And I struggled to understand her choice to end her life rather than admit she'd had an affair with my boyfriend.

I closed my eyes and brought up her gorgeous smile. Her Asian heritage shone through her dark eyes and complexion. I used to tease her that her dark hair was a sheet of silk, while she told me mine was a mass of corkscrews.

Mindy took the call. It was the only time I ever saw Mindy fall apart. She'd collapsed onto the sofa and bawled her eyes out right along with me. James found us there. I frowned, hating how he'd told us we looked ugly with our red-rimmed eyes and dripping noses.

"I don't get what you're so upset about," James said. "I mean, she admitted in her note that she fucked me a bunch of times. Cuz, you know, she was jealous of how good our relationship was."

I should have told him then to get out.

But I didn't.

At first, I simply didn't believe the media accounts or James' recitation of all the times he'd screwed my bestie behind my back.

Mindy never mentioned Vannah again. We'd missed her funeral because I'd promised to go to a premiere for James' movie that weekend in L.A. The movie flopped and James said part of the reason was because I hadn't shown enthusiasm for his project—or the proper level of affection for him. I'd been stunned, still reeling from the latest interview I read, featuring both James and another mutual friend about James' affair with Savannah.

After seeing how devastated I was by the news, my father began spouting off about how James was a liar and a drug addict, showing the world the ugly split between my boyfriend and my dad. James lapped up the bad press with the same intensity as he did the good.

I'm not sure he knew the difference.

I blew out a breath. No. More. James. Or thoughts of Savannah.

I needed to focus on tonight's concert and my future. I wanted this album so badly to finish the transition from teen TV star who'd gotten more than her share of bad-girl press to respected musician.

If that happened to me—the lack of touring options and flat record sales—I'd have alienated my current fan base and destroyed my chances to build a strong first impression with the fans I really wanted. Which was why working with multi-platinum performer Camden Grace was the linchpin of my new plan.

I just needed to talk the multi-Grammy winner into helping me.

CHAPTER EIGHT | Carter

She was a singer. A *performer*. Who the hell could she be? I typed in Regan…and realized I didn't know her last name. I winced. Much as I wanted to ask, that seemed ungentlemanly. We spent the night together, and I hadn't bothered to ask such a basic question.

I frowned. Granted, she hadn't asked my last name either. That seemed like an intentional decision. But she'd told me the truth just now.

At least I believed she had. How was I to know? The thoughts ran around and around in my head, making it impossible to concentrate on my business interests. Dianna taught me to be leery of any type of mind games, of lies, and of omissions.

Dianna also said that I…

I tossed my phone on the table and strode into the large bathroom with its luxury features, determined to forget anything Dianna ever said to me.

———— ★ ————

After showering and dressing, I raced down to the hotel offices for my meeting, showing up a few minutes late, thanks to my continued fixation on a beautiful performer I knew as Regan. I gritted my teeth, frustration boiling up in my guts at my wayward thoughts.

I hated that she continued to invade my mind. I detested how my heart skipped a beat when I remembered her sparkling eyes as she spelled out a word I'd never heard—and had to look up on my phone to make sure it was real—while she laughed in delight.

Regan struck a chord last night when she talked about love because I certainly didn't have relationships. I didn't *want* to do relationships. Except…except I definitely wanted to see Regan again, even if it was just to play chess or cards or Boggle. Maybe we could switch it up and watch a movie. Hell, talking to her via text was delightful. She was smart, a little flirty behind that guarded exterior.

Cam's words from earlier rolled through my head and my heart whispered that whatever I started with Regan last night didn't have to end. Thanks to my position and my company's success, my schedule was flexible. Really, I could work from anywhere.

I *must* stop thinking about Regan. We'd had a fun night together. She left this morning because our night was over.

A petite brunette smiled at me from her position at an elaborate reception desk as I strode into the lobby of the hotel's business offices.

"Mr. Grace?" she asked.

"Yes."

She stood. "Mr. Harris is handling a PR situation at the moment, but he is expecting you. He asked me to settle you in the conference room while he finishes up his calls. This way, please."

I followed her down a long hallway, decorated with black and white prints of Denver and the surrounding areas. The carpet was plush and muffled our footfalls. Pete always did have an eye for pulling together a space.

The receptionist opened a door and waved me in. A carafe of coffee and some bottles of water were situated in the middle of the gleaming table. I wandered around the room, enjoying the view from the large windows.

"Carter," Pete Harris said, striding into the room moments later, hand extended. "Glad to see you, man."

Pete was a few years older than me—thick-waisted and tall with sloping shoulders, bushy reddish-blond hair, and a neat goatee. We'd met in San Francisco years before at a college alumni mixer. He, too, enjoyed the wide-open spaces of the West, and we'd talked about the ranch I was considering purchasing after my first app blew up. At the next meeting, he sought me out to see what I'd decided to do.

After a few more mixers and a couple of beers in which we both growled at the terrible showing in the big Texas-OU football game, I decided Pete was a good guy.

So when he'd started his first glamping hotel in Wyoming a few years back, I'd been more than happy to invest in the property, which had made me a tidy profit in the five years since.

I shook his hand. "Heard you're having a tough morning," I said.

Pete scowled. "Publicity issue. Actually, it may well be to our benefit." He waved away my concern. "I'll handle it."

I nodded but my mind immediately turned to Regan. That couldn't be what he was talking about, though. We hadn't attracted any paparazzi at the bar. She might be famous but she couldn't be as big a name as my brother if we managed to get in and out of the honkytonk without being mobbed. Cam was *always* mobbed and going anywhere with him required patience and a lot of security.

"Got my contract?" I asked.

Pete smiled, the corners of his mouth crinkling. "You are the easiest of my investors. Need me to sweet-talk you into more shares?"

I shook my head with a chuckle. "Sixteen percent of this place is plenty. I just need to look over the final documents to make sure you received all of Remy's changes."

Remy, one of my college buddies, now worked for me full-time. I'd lured him away from a big law firm with a larger financial package and fewer hours. I didn't really need Remy full time, but I liked to be ahead of the curve as my holdings continued to grow. And I liked surrounding myself with people I could trust.

Pete handed me a file filled with a thick stack of papers. Never say contracts, even between buddies, weren't arduous to plow through. He poured himself a cup of coffee while I opened the folder.

"Want one?" he asked, gesturing toward me with his mug.

"Sure," I said. "Black, thanks."

I began to read. Pete settled the coffee next to my hand and went back to his office. He returned a few minutes later with a shiny laptop and settled into a chair a few down from mine.

Pete's computer started to ping with incoming messages. I flipped through the pages, reading over the contract I'd already read twice before. All the final details appeared to be in order. I glanced up at him after a few minutes of consistent alerts.

"Everything okay there?"

Pete shook his head, stress lines forming between his eyebrows. "I had no idea Everly Leroux was on the premises early this morning, and now all the publications and even some of the tawdry rags are asking for information."

My shoulders knotted further, building on the tension I'd been carrying since Regan's text about a sold-out venue. But the woman Pete mentioned couldn't be the woman I spent the night with. I set down the document.

"Who's Everly Leroux?" I asked.

Pete waved his hand. "A pop princess. Huge in her industry. She's got a show in Denver tonight."

I really wanted that to be a coincidence, but I didn't believe in them. "Huh. And she stayed here last night?" I asked.

Pete shook his head, scowling. "That's the thing. We have no record of her booking rooms or anything. The senior staff have to know because of the security such high-profile celebs require."

I knew this from my brother's experience with touring. "So how'd she get here?"

Pete raised a thick eyebrow. "We don't know. But from the pictures I've just seen it looks like she came down from the main elevator straight into the garage around seven thirty this morning."

That uncomfortable feeling fluttered in my stomach. If Regan was Everly...then she'd lied not just about her name but also about who she was. Like Dianna. Only so much worse. She'd given me a false name.

"Mind if I see those pictures?"

Pete shrugged. He opened the laptop he'd carried into the

room and turned the screen toward me. My throat went dry and my palms started to sweat. "That's Regan...what's her name?"

"Everly Leroux."

I sighed, my good humor crashing the longer I looked at Regan striding across the parking garage toward a large SUV with dark, tinted windows.

"Well, I can tell you how she got to the hotel."

Pete waited, his eyes narrowing.

"I brought her." I raised both hands, palms out flat. "I had no idea she was someone famous."

Pete hung his head and ran his fingers through his tousled locks. "Shit, Carter. You do end up with all the damn luck."

"I don't get why her being here is a press issue." I settled into the soft leather seat next to his. "I mean, if she's patronizing the place, that has to be good for business."

"Her, yes, absolutely. I have no problem with her in my hotel. That's a huge boon PR will lap up." His gaze turned shrewd. "I'll see if we can get a statement from her camp about the luxury of the penthouse suite."

He raised an eyebrow.

"Yes, she was in my room, but—"

"You just slept with her, didn't bother to get so far as names?"

He chuckled, shaking his head as pride in my supposed antics lit his eyes. For the first time in my life, I didn't like the implication I'd seduced a woman into a one-night stand. Not Regan—*Everly*.

No wonder Regan acted the way she had when I suggested just that. Pete might be my friend, but right now, he was acting like Regan was simply a…a…trophy, not a warm, smart, fun woman who I'd enjoyed spending time with.

But wasn't that how I normally acted? Screw a pretty lady and move on?

I was so confused by these protective emotions, by the shift in my thought process—because of Regan?—that I missed whatever Pete said next. All I knew was I couldn't let him keep thinking of Regan as a conquest.

I didn't want her to be one. I wanted…hell. I flattened my hands on the table so my palms were flush against the cool wood. No, it wasn't as satisfying as slamming a fist against it, causing the coffee mugs to jump and the papers to slide to the floor, but it showed I had control of my emotions and the situation.

"It wasn't like that," I said.

He raised an eyebrow. "It wasn't like you had a wild romp with a sexy singer?"

I shook my head, so angry at Pete's speculative look that my throat seemed to swell shut.

"So, you're telling me…what?" he asked, almost incredulous.

I gathered the papers back into a neat stack with just the final one awaiting my signature. Part of me wanted to fling them at Pete and storm out without executing the deal. But doing so would jeopardize a long-term relationship, and Pete wasn't acting differently.

I was. Over a woman.

Regan had lied about her name. *She'd lied to me.*

I picked up the pen from the folder and scrawled my name on the specified line.

"What's going on, Carter? Please tell me this isn't going to turn into a shit storm."

And the ache in my stomach built. "Why would you assume that?"

Pete shook his head, lips flattening. "I don't know. Because you're acting weird."

I blew out a breath. "I like her."

Pete leaned back in his chair, fingers clasped over his chest. "You like her?"

"Yeah. We made plans to see each other again."

Well, we hadn't, really. But she hadn't said no when I told her I wanted another round of board-game fun. Without really thinking it over, I'd taken her non-answer as a yes. That Regan would give me the chance to get to know her, to explain to me why she'd neglected to tell me who she was, really.

Those omissions really should give me greater pause. I'd been down this road of lies before. I needed to put the brakes on my emotions. Hard.

Instead, I wanted to focus on eventually taking our relationship to the physical place neither of us could deny.

"So…are you dating the pop princess?" Pete asked, eyes wide.

I shook my head. "Too early to say."

But as soon as Pete said it, I turned keen on the idea. I liked the look on Pete's face—one of shocked admiration. What would Dianna and Dean think if I was in a relationship with one of the world's hottest acts? They couldn't call me a loser, second to my twin.

I wasn't—not anymore, anyway. I had more money than my

brother, and I already owned more than forty percent of the shares of Dean's entertainment company that I had planned to sell off in painful chunks as soon as I returned to Austin.

I hadn't told anyone that was the impetus for my move home because I knew, deep down, wanting to watch Dean struggle to hold his company together only to flounder thanks to the bad deals he'd made these past few years, wouldn't be met with as much relish by my mother or brother. Only Remy understood.

Pete's computer continued to beep. He cursed softly as he leaned forward, his expression full of concern as he read some new message.

"I guess I better tell you there's a bunch of questions brewing about Everly being here," he said slowly.

"What?" I asked, yanked out of my pleasant daydream that had both Dean and Dianna tearfully apologizing for hurting both my heart and my pride all those years ago. "Show me."

Pete shook his head. "It's nothing more than inquiries at this point. Not in photo form. But…the questions are bad."

I stood as I handed the documents to Pete. Normally, I'd offer to take him to lunch, but concern for Regan ate at me.

"I need to find out what's going on with Re—Everly."

"I don't get it, Carter." Pete asked. His brow wrinkled. "Why didn't you just let me know she was here?"

Not like he was going to believe me this time if he hadn't before.

I scrubbed my hands over my face, up through my hair. "I didn't know she was a celeb."

At Pete's nonplussed expression, I shrugged. His response was to be expected.

"I don't really do all that pop culture crap, which you know. I like to read. I ranch. I work."

"Fine," Pete said, clearly annoyed. "But *everyone's* heard of Everly Leroux."

"I've heard one of her songs, I'd bet, but it's not like I go to gossip sites or pick up those magazines by the grocery checkout."

Pete swiped at the folder. "If you want to play that angle, whatever. But you better hope the leads the journalists mentioned don't pan out."

Shock slammed through me at Pete's comments. "What leads?"

Pete hesitated. "One asked me if we had a party here last night. A rager." He raised his eyebrows and spoke the word slowly.

Yeah, I got what he was saying.

"She didn't take drugs." Well, not that I saw. She drank a beer. I drank two. Not that I knew what she did when she woke this morning before I did. Still, the idea of Regan shooting up or popping pills didn't square with the slightly nerdy and utterly adorable woman I'd spent the evening with.

Pete closed his laptop. "Look, her last boyfriend has been in rehab a bunch of times. She has quite a history."

"Don't we all?" I shot back.

Pete smoothed his hair. "If you can make a statement, even if it's just to me, then great. If not, well. I'm in for a long day."

"I'll see what I can do," I said. I turned to go but I spun back. "She's a smart, funny, fun woman. I happened to enjoy her company as just that—her company."

Shit. I sounded like her now. What was happening to me?

"And she didn't take any drugs," I continued. "It was just us from about ten until this morning. Whatever source they have is lying. Flat out. To get attention, no doubt. You know that's happened to my brother."

Pete still appeared annoyed, but he also had the good grace to drop his gaze as contrition slid over his features. "I'm sorry I had the wrong idea. Just…I'm stressed, Carter. This hotel hasn't had the best bookings, which you knew, so we have to keep the image and message right on point. A celeb overdose or something won't do that."

I narrowed my eyes, irritation at the entire situation reverberating through me. "Why are you so fixated on drugs?"

"The journalist—a real journalist from a major industry publication—he said he had an insider in Regan's entourage who told him she'd been here last night and returned to her hotel higher than a kite."

CHAPTER NINE | Regan

I opened Carter's last message to respond when a new message popped up.

We need to talk. Now.

I blinked at his words.

I can't. I'm about to start my final sound check.

The phone was ringing before I hit *Send*. I licked my lip as I stared at the screen, my stomach rolling with nerves. I didn't have time for whatever Carter wanted to say.

"Hello?" I said, dread pooling in my stomach.

"Regan."

I thrilled at the sound of my name. So few people used it now, and I hadn't realized how much I missed it. I shouldn't because I didn't really even know Carter. Just knew that I liked the way he said my name.

"Or should I call you Everly?" His voice turned cooler as he said my stage name.

"No. Please." I cleared my throat on the catch there. "My first name is Regan, and I…I like you calling me that."

He waited for a beat before saying, "All right." His voice softened with those words.

I squeezed my free hand into a fist in my lap, thankful I was alone for these few moments. Taking this call in front of Mindy would be mortifying. In front of my dad…he'd gotten so weird about me being near men ever since my breakup with James and all the speculation about me popping pills right along with my ex. I wasn't sure how my father would react to Carter.

I wasn't ready to find out.

"What's going on?" I asked.

"Well, first, I need to ask you something."

Dread pooled in my belly. This was the side to fame people didn't understand. How no one could just hang out with me, get to know *me*—Regan. "Um. Sure."

"Will you be honest with me?"

I heard the pain in his words, and my heart cracked open. Whatever his past, it was filled with a deep hurt—a betrayal, I'd guess. Because only someone who'd been lied to would ask that question.

"Yes. I promise," I said immediately.

"All right. All right," he mumbled.

"Are you okay?" I asked.

"A bit discombobulated to learn I spent last night with one of the biggest names in pop-dom," he said, his tone dry.

"That word's more than seven letters. You could have beat me by a mile with a word like 'discombobulated'."

"Didn't have the right letter sequence, as you know. Look, I need to tell you something, and I'm trying to figure out how's best."

"You don't want to see me again," I whispered.

"What? No. I was meeting with Pete. He owns the hotel where we stayed last night."

"Okay," I said. But already I could feel my stomach sinking.

"He's been getting calls from journalists."

"Trash mags, no doubt," I said, anger filling my belly. "I'll get my PR team on it. So they won't bother you."

"I'm not worried about me, Regan. I have a pretty good set up myself."

Right. I might not know what Carter did for a living, but he stayed in penthouses and met with luxury hoteliers. Safe to say, he knew a thing or three about business and publicity. "So then why did you call?"

Mindy stuck her head in. "We need you back out here," she chirped.

"Sure," I said as I pointed at my phone. "Just finishing this call."

She nodded but concern flitted over her face. "Be quick."

"I heard that and know you need to go," Carter said. "It wasn't trash mags. It was one of your industry publications. A well-known journalist."

When Carter gave me the name, my mouth dried out. Crap. If John Mitchell was going to do a story about me, I wanted it on my terms—to show me as a serious musician.

"What did he want?" I asked, pleased with the levelness of my tone.

"Pete said this John guy's got a source. An insider in your entourage. The person said you were at a rager last night. And that you're popping something. That you were high when you got back to your hotel."

"Well, isn't that peachy," I murmured. Carter remained silent for a long moment and my stomach rolled. "You know that's not true."

"I know it wasn't true when you were with me," Carter countered.

I sucked in a deep breath as anger sparked in my chest. "My mother overdosed, Carter. Well, technically, she drove her car into a pylon exiting the freeway, but that's because she was high. I'm not about to follow in her footsteps."

"Why the hell are you talking about your mother?" my dad roared as he slammed into the room, eyes wide and nostrils flaring like an angry bull.

Well, double shit.

CHAPTER TEN | Carter

She hung up but not before I heard the words hurled at her. I winced, wondering if I'd made the PR situation worse for Regan. That hadn't been my intention, but intent and reality tended to diverge.

I'd been frustrated she hadn't told me her career. I'd been upset about the possibility of drugs. Instead of clarifying the situation, I managed to muddy it further.

I groaned. She needed to perform. I needed to let her. Calling back would not help now, but that didn't mean I could leave the situation alone. Before I thought the details through, I texted Cam and asked him for a favor. He responded twenty minutes later with the details.

Cam: *Guess you've decided you're jumping in. Everly Leroux, huh?*

Carter: *I didn't know who she was when we met,* I typed back. Cam would understand. He knew I didn't follow his industry.

Cam: *Katie Rose adores her music.*

Katie was our sister, and that didn't surprise me. While our tastes diverged, Katie was known for choosing quality.

Carter: *I'll have to download some of Regan's music.*

I leaned more toward singer-songwriters and independent bands, not the sweet pop that my sister seemed to prefer.

Cam responded a few minutes later.

Cam: *Jen likes her stuff, too. Just got word through my people (when I was getting you the VIP passes) that Everly—should I call her Regan?*

Carter: *Yeah. Call her Regan.*

I'd already picked up on the realization she didn't love her stage name.

Cam: *Cool. Got it. Regan wants to meet up with me in Austin next week. Tell her HELL YES! I'm hoping to talk her over to the dark side. Aka country.*

Of course Cam did. He was always expounding on the greatness of his preferred music. He'd talked his fiancée over to his way of thinking, but then, Cam's talent oozed out of his voice and every pore, and Jenna was a sucker for anything Cam wanted. In fact, part of the reason I liked her so much was the way she looked at Cam—with such faith in his ability, as if he was the center of her world.

They'd made their relationship flourish despite his fans concerns and his label's demands. If Cam could get there, maybe I could, too.

I shook my head, shocked by the wayward stupidity of my thoughts. I'd make sure Regan was okay and see if I could lend my company's PR machine to help silence her critics. That was the gentlemanly choice. And a stand I needed to take to make sure being with me didn't get her into trouble.

Carter: *We'll see. I need to smooth my most recent screw-up before you try wooing her.*

Cam: *I have faith in you.*

At least one of us had some confidence in my abilities. I stared at the message with grim determination. My stomach rolled at the thought of going to her concert. But my heart ached at the disappointment and worry she must be going through based on the questions John Mitchell was tossing out.

In twenty-four hours, Regan had managed to tie me up in knots.

Cam*: And don't mess this up for me! I really want to work with her. She may have the perfect voice for one of the songs on my next album. Jenna agrees. Well, that's if she's the one actually singing.*

That was a strange comment.

She doesn't sing her own songs? I asked. *How's that possible?*

Cam: *I don't know. There's been talk she lip syncs. Hey…send me her number. I'll contact her directly.*

I sent Cam another text: *I need to ask her if that's okay.* I hesitated, then typed the message I needed an answer to most: *Is me pursuing a relationship with her smart?*

Cam: *Depends. Do you care?*

Therein lay the rub. I did care. How I could care this much in so short a time baffled me.

Carter: *Apparently not.*

———— ★ ————

Time to find out who--and what--I was dealing with. I pulled up my web browser and typed in "Everly Leroux". A million pictures of Regan popped up, but Regan as a performer. On the stage with a microphone. Next one was her with…wow! The woman sang with some of the best-known performers in the world. How could people question her talent if she was mixing company with these types of celebrities?

I sank to the side of my bed and pulled up more details. Her name was Regan Everly Leroux. She was twenty-five. Lots and lots of articles of her breakup from some dude named James Peele.

Another singer. Not as famous. Currently in rehab for drugs and anger management related to his substance abuse. I scowled at the pictures of the two of them holding hands on a red carpet. The date stamp was nearly two years ago.

Lots of articles about James' love triangle with Regan and another singer/TV actress from their show named Savannah Liu. I frowned when I read Savannah committed suicide. That sounded…intense. Poor Savannah.

I scrolled through more. Seemed that James was the "source" that Regan didn't sing her own music. That guy was clearly a d-hole.

I clicked over to images, needing a break from the heaviness of the stories about Regan.

She was *gorgeous* in every picture. Poised, elegant and apparently at ease with the public scrutiny.

Of course she was. And she might well be in trouble right now, thanks to my conversation. I needed to make sure she was safe.

Nerves skittered across my shoulders and down my back as I closed the browser and all the way to the stadium. I pulled my new Land Rover into the packed lot. Groups of boisterous people streamed toward the entrances, calling to each other and singing lyrics from what I assumed were Regan's songs. Thanks to Cam's connections, I had VIP treatment, getting into the spaces closest to the venue, which was a good thing because I'd passed probably a few hundred cars idling as they waited for their chance to pull into a spot.

I stepped out of my vehicle and looked up at the stadium. With a shake of my head, I told myself not to be intimidated by Regan's obvious popularity. I liked her; she seemed to like me. I'd make sure she was okay, then be on my way. She had my phone number and could contact me anytime she wanted.

I pressed the lock button on my key fob and patted the gleaming door handle of my new baby. Half-wishing I'd never come, I strode forward, listening to the screaming crowd and the throbbing bass from within as I flashed my phone and its all-access pass to whoever stopped me. Cam sure had the right way of dealing with other celebrities. I'd have to thank him again for using his connections.

The doors that led to the inner sanctum proved harder to breach, but the people in uniform there, too, allowed me through. I sucked in a deep breath as I began to understand the life Regan lived, full of checks and vetting and a careful layer of curation that removed her further from reality. No wonder she came with me so willingly last night. Regan must crave normalcy just as much as the rest of the world craved the wealth and prestige Regan enjoyed.

I frowned, glancing around the space. Moderation. Compromise. Over the years I'd worked hard to build my business and my wealth. And as I'd watched my parents' relationship destruct and then my brother's with his first wife, I'd realized that the only way to move forward, to not lose the people we needed in our lives, was through some levels of compromise.

Granted, I'd tried that with Dianna, and our relationship still blew up.

"She's on stage." The guard from the bar stepped next to me as I glanced around. "Just...don't mess with her head. She's had a rough day."

"Darryl, right?" I asked.

He grunted.

"Is she okay?"

Darryl shrugged.

I rocked back on my heels. "All right. I don't want to mess up her concert. Why don't you take me to the green room or whatever you call it?"

Darryl motioned for me to follow him.

"Thanks for showing me back," I tried again.

He grunted again, refusing to turn to face me.

"Is it me, specifically, that you don't like?" I asked. "Because I'd understand you wanting her yourself."

Darryl turned, the scowl etched deep into his forehead. "I'm her main guard. That's it." He didn't like it, but I'd bet the edict came specifically from Regan. "She's dealing with a lot."

"You said that."

I stepped in closer, up to his side, though I shimmied around a group of people who ran toward us. Were they performers? Their sequins made me think yes. Regan probably had dancers and back-up singers—the whole entourage.

"When I was on the phone with her earlier, a man yelled at her. That's why I'm here. I'm concerned."

Darryl's eyes flared with the same concern I felt and his lips pressed together into a tight line. "It's getting worse."

"Who treats her like that? Why doesn't she get rid of him?"

Darryl stopped and apprised me, not so much as a competitor but as a man worried about a woman's safety. That I could get behind.

Darryl motioned for me to follow, then strode down a corridor and opened the door to the lounge space where Regan's entourage must hang out before and after the show. The room was large, with high ceilings. Multiple couch groupings made the space seem cozier and gave the impression of private conversation nooks. A long table lined the back wall, covered in a large array of foods and bottles of drinks. I counted ten different types of water and sports drinks and an even number of beers.

Darryl checked out the room before turning back to me. He crossed his arms over his chest. "If someone was yelling, then you probably heard her father. He's been her manager since the beginning—before I came on board. I've been with her for five years."

He said the last part with pride.

I nodded, letting him know I understood. "What I heard…is that normal? It sounded intense." The reason I stood there, now, was because the anger in the tone reminded me of my stepfather, especially in those last years after Cam married Kim. Just before my family unraveled, imploded, and I hightailed it as far away from the wreckage and guilt as I could.

Darryl leaned in closer. "I haven't seen him cross a line. It's my job to keep her safe."

"And you're worried about him…crossing the line?" I cut

in. Darryl confided more in me than I expected, and none of it sounded good. In fact, the situation was already a lot more complicated than I'd guessed.

Darryl seemed unaware of my growing agitation, or maybe he just really needed someone to listen to his fears.

Darryl's eyes darkened with anger. "He's only sticking around to get more money out of her. From what I gathered, he did okay—he was some kind of importer before he took over as Regan's manager. But…this is just between us, right?" Darryl shifted, like the conversation made him uncomfortable.

"Of course, man. I…" I blew out a breath. Might as well just man up and admit the truth. "I care about her."

That wasn't so hard. In fact, saying the words felt…good. Right.

Darryl dipped his chin toward his chest. "I don't want this getting out. Someone's talking about her, and that's upset her."

I nodded but remained silent.

Darryl seemed at war with himself. Finally, he blurted, "Her father…he doesn't care about her, you know?"

I nodded again. I did know that pathetic story far too well. Cam and I had learned recently that the man we'd considered our father wasn't—and he'd only stayed married to our mother because he wanted the family ranch.

I hated men who used women like that. Sure, because of my mama, but also because those men showed how weak they were. Instead of using their own damn mind and skills and hands to better their own position in the world, they sweet-talked, schmoozed, and bullied the women in their lives to do what they wanted for them.

Darryl breathed out a thick rush of air. "I want her to be happy." He grimaced. "She isn't. She hasn't been the whole time I've known her, but the last few months, she's pulled in. After that fiasco with her last boyfriend…"

Whatever Darryl planned to say, he managed to stop. He rolled back on his heels and pressed his lips together.

Share time was over.

This time, I studied him. Mid-thirties, so just a few years older than me. Dark skin, dark eyes, close-cropped hair. He worked out, probably every day. I wondered what types of weight training he preferred, but tucked that into the back of my mind for another conversation because I had other, more pressing issues.

"So, her dad…you're telling me he'll stick around as long as Regan's pulling in shows like this?"

Darryl nodded. "Definitely."

Which meant getting close and remaining in Regan's inner circle would be difficult. Not just because of her father but because of the time pressures she dealt with each day.

CHAPTER ELEVEN | Regan

Weariness settled over me like a cloak, thankfully drowning out my father's words about tonight's performance.

"Seriously? That's the best you can offer these people? They spent a lot of money on these tickets and deserve your *full focus*, young lady."

He'd thrown that tidbit of criticism at me before I even managed to step off the stage. Tonight hadn't been my best showing. My legs felt like jelly and my vocal cords quivered with the need for rest.

Darryl met me at the edge of the stage where the curtains began. From the moment my father appeared, Darryl watched me. He didn't think I was aware of how closely, but I cataloged his reactions, just as I did Mindy's and the rest of my staff—and six of the people I paid to help me in some way, not including my dancers and the musicians. Putting on a performance like this took hordes of people. Last count, I employed thirty-seven people full-time while on tour.

That seemed ridiculous, excessive, but my staff remained smaller than a lot of the acts I'd met, and I planned to keep it that way.

I took the towel Mindy offered and dried my face and neck, dipping the terrycloth between my breasts with a grimace. So gross.

Carter's comment about a spy in my midst—someone handing over information to the press—wasn't a surprise. The larger my entourage, the more likely that situation became. It was part of why I didn't hire more people. With each new hire, I left myself open to that person's greed or desire for the limelight, and I just wasn't sure who would sell me out. Someone created a direct line to the media, more than willing to hurt me both professionally and personally.

I needed to get the leaker off my payroll, and quickly. But trying to pinpoint the person was proving exhausting and fruitless.

I made my way to the meet-and-greet room, wishing I could shower and sleep instead of chatting with fans and taking selfies for the next hour or so. But I'd have to spend extra time with my fans and lavish them with attention if I wanted to keep them happy—especially after my performance tonight. It hadn't been bad, but neither had I performed with my normal energy.

My late night with Carter had caught up with me. The entire time I worked through these thoughts in my head, my father kept pace beside me. At least he'd stopped commenting on my sad efforts with the night's dance routine.

Darryl fell in step next to me, subtly moving my father farther away. I silently mouthed, "*Thank you*." He dipped his head.

"Got a surprise for you," he muttered. "Hope you like Mr. Tall, Dark, and Into You."

I stumbled in the stiletto boots I wore on stage, which reminded me that my feet ached. "Carter?" I managed to gasp.

"In the flesh," Darryl said with a small smile.

I licked my lower lip. "Can you keep my dad out?"

Darryl raised an eyebrow before nodding. "I'll take care of it."

He allowed me to walk in front as he once again managed to cut my father off from direct access to me. I beelined into the room, shutting the door behind me.

Carter rose from one of the couches, looking just as delectable as he had last night—almost as yummy as he appeared asleep this morning. So far, sleeping Carter was my favorite. His face relaxed and his mouth parted enough for me to see the soft pink on the inner part of his lips. Something about that delicate skin seemed so intimate. I wanted to kiss him to see if he tasted as good as I imagined.

I stepped forward, reminding myself there were many nuances to him I'd yet to learn—like the dress shirt and slacks that were obviously tailored to fit his physique.

I hummed in approval. The jeans and the button-down rolled up at the forearms he'd worn last night looked fabulous on him, but the world seemed to underestimate the sexy factor of a man in dress clothes.

"Hi," I breathed. My fatigued legs still ached but my heart raced with excitement. What this man's mere presence did to me.

"Is it okay I'm here?" he asked with obvious concern. "I heard yelling when we were on the phone, and I worried."

"That was my dad." I tried and failed to suppress the grimace of distaste. "And it had nothing to do with you. My mom…"

I shook my head. I liked Carter and the attraction between us seemed to grow with each breath we shared, but I wasn't ready to bare my soul—or my skeletons—to a man I didn't know well. One who'd propositioned me and might well just be interested in a quick lay or some story dirt on me.

I leaned back against the door, my hands on the knob. We wouldn't have long before my band arrived, and then the fans who'd snagged backstage access.

"I'm glad you're here," I said, my voice soft.

"I had to call in a favor, but I needed to make sure." He blew out a long breath as he stepped up in front of me until the tips of our shoes touched. He ran his knuckles down my cheek, his eyes never once dropping from mine, even to check out my low-cut outfit. That warmed me as much as him showing up did.

I nibbled at my lower lip as I realized how much I wanted him to care about me.

"I'm glad I'm here, too. Regan, I have to tell you, I don't like this driving need that's been eating at me since you hung up." He leaned in further so our faces were close enough for me to feel the heat emanating from his skin, to sniff his delicious aftershave and to see the lighter flecks in his brown eyes.

I held my breath as he inched his face closer still to mine.

"I need to protect you. Keep you safe, happy. I haven't wanted that—haven't *needed* to do that for anyone in years. But with you, it's visceral. Not a choice."

He touched his lips to mine. The pressure remained light, as if he were asking permission. I surged up on to my tiptoes and wrapped my arms around his neck. Our lips pressed together, but I didn't part mine and he didn't either. Instead, we enjoyed the soft glide of skin against skin while his scent wrapped around me like a hug.

After another pounding beat of my heart, I slanted my head.

Carter cupped my cheek, and the tip of his tongue touched my lower lip. I moaned. Instead of deepening the kiss as I expected, as I needed him to do, he eased back. His thumbs rubbed up and down my cheekbones.

"I want you to understand I worried. The tone in the man's—your father's voice was unsettling. The anger in it."

He studied my eyes, seeming to ask for answers I didn't have. On one level, his words somehow eased my tension. Sure, he wanted to explore the physical attraction between us. Truth be told, I did, too.

"I'm fine."

"I want you to be more than fine, Regan." His eyes burned with intensity as he kept his gaze focused on mine. "Meeting you—no, spending time with you." He swallowed and his lip trembled just a little. "I think last night changed something for me."

"Yeah?" I whispered, trying to ignore my pounding heart.

He dipped his head, bringing his mouth closer to mine. "You seem to think I don't date."

I arched an eyebrow. "I don't think you date the same woman for long."

Carter flashed a brief grin. "Fair enough. I haven't for a while. Years." He paused, still searching my face. "But I'd like to date you. Very much."

I eased back, aware of the voices getting louder—our time was close to an end.

He seemed to understand that because he pressed his body tightly to mine and kissed me again with a desperate hunger that had me clinging to his shoulders as he ravaged my mouth. Oh, how I wanted more of him. And *more*.

He tasted of mint and something uniquely Carter. I sucked on his tongue and he grunted. He clasped my thigh and brought my leg up to his hip as he ground against me. I mewled my need into his mouth. A laugh and a thump against the wall tore us apart.

He pulled back, eyes bleary. He rested his forehead against mine as he struggled to catch his breath.

"Damn, I want you."

"How could we make this—us—work? I'm touring." For another few weeks. I wasn't sure that Carter knew much about my schedule. "I mean…if that's what you want."

"That's what I want," he said.

The words seemed to echo through the room. Or maybe that was just through me. I'd never wanted a man as much as I wanted Carter. I wasn't sure what to do with the intensity of this attraction.

The voices drew even with the door. With a look of reluctance, Carter let my leg drop. I wanted him to hold me longer even as I appreciated his decision to let me set the tone with my crew.

"I'd like to see you again," I said. "But you're here."

His smile beamed brighter than a cat with a cup full of cream. "Your last stop is in Austin, right?"

I nodded, my heart beating faster because he'd checked out my schedule. That must mean something.

"I happen to be moving back to the city. It'll be my home base."

My belly rolled. I wanted to shift my feet just like a little kid who needed to use the bathroom. Why did the idea of seeing

Carter again make me so nervous? "I hope to record an album there."

Carter nodded, his eyes shining before that smile that caught me in the back of the knees lit up his face.

"I know," he said, tone as smug as his grin. "And I also happen to know how to get you a meeting with Camden Grace, the country star you want to talk to while you're there."

"You do?" I breathed. Then I jumped up and down, clasping my hands under my chin. "How? How do you know him? When can I meet him? What's it going to cost me?"

Carter laughed. The door opened behind me and my band and the dancers poured into the room in a frenzy of voices and limbs, casting a curious gaze at Carter as they raced toward the food table.

Carter leaned in closer so that his lips brushed my ear. "I told you, I'd like to go on a few dates, see if we like each other enough to take it further."

I shivered, loving the intimate moment, but loving his words more. "I'll think about it."

The words tumbled out of my mouth and my cheeks flushed. Oh, my, I was flirting.

Carter's amusement ratcheted up. The jerk knew I wanted to go out with him. That's what I got for kissing him back with enthusiasm. I licked my lips, wanting another, deeper kiss.

His breathing changed, telling me he wanted the same. Now wasn't the time.

"Well, I can promise you I'm the gatekeeper to Camden Grace, so if I don't get my dates, you don't get Cam." His eyes sparkled enough to tell me he was teasing.

Good, because I wasn't in a joking mood about this move I planned to make. I'd worked too hard to orchestrate the opportunity to have anyone mess it up for me.

My hands dropped to my hips. "Really? You know him that well that you can make a blanket statement like that? He might want to meet me, regardless of what you say."

At least, I hoped he would. My next album needed to be stellar. Having a name as big as Camden Grace on it—having his vocals on my lead single—would definitely get me air time and lend to my bona fides as a quality performer. I needed this album to work, desperately, to squelch those nasty rumors James started.

Damn that man and his pettiness. I'd had many people suggest I couldn't hold a note and that all my music was technically enhanced. That I lip-synched every song and someone else recorded my albums.

Those accusations stung. And it's a large part of why I needed this next album to exceed my previous sales. I had to prove my worth, once and for all.

Instead of telling me to get over myself, Carter tilted his head. His next words sent a shock wave through my system.

"Oh, he does. But, see, he's my twin brother, so…if I say no, he'll agree out of solidarity."

CHAPTER TWELVE | Carter

"*Brother?*" she squeaked. Her jaw unlocked and her mouth tumbled open. "Oh my gosh! Oh…I can see it now." She shook her head with a wide grin. "You two look so alike."

My stomach dipped as she continued to rake her gaze over my features. "Thanks, I guess. We're twins. Fraternal, obviously."

Regan's mouth tilted up before she tapped her forefinger to it. This gal got off on teasing me. And I liked it.

Normally I didn't like to be compared to my brother—I was well aware he was an international sex symbol. Really, there was no comparing.

"Hmm. If you say so. Different hairstyles and your eyes are lighter." At my nod, she grinned. "He got the musical talent and you got the looks?"

I winked at her, enjoying her willingness to play along. Cam and I did look very similar, but I didn't have his husky drawl or his gaggle of fans. "That's what Cam says."

She chuckled, and I couldn't help but smile as the delightful sound rippled over me. She had an amazing laugh. I wanted to hear it again. And again. I wanted to be the one who made her laugh and the one who caused her eyes to sparkle.

"How come you don't twang like he does?"

I shrugged. "I still have an accent."

"It's slight. Just the right hint," she said, a bit breathy.

"I lived in San Francisco and Wyoming. People don't speak with strong accents in either place. And…Cam plays his up for the ladies."

She glanced at me from under her lashes. "And you don't need parlor tricks to seduce the ladies."

"Mmm. I'm not so sure about ladies, plural. There's only one I want…" At her parted lips, I smiled and finished, "To play Scrabble with."

She laughed.

Damn, I liked that sound.

I leaned forward, intent on capturing the last of the sound on her lips, but Regan stiffened and backpedaled from me. She seemed to pull back into herself, appearing smaller, her face losing all its joy.

I followed her gaze.

A man stepped into the room and the vibe took a nosedive. About twenty years older than any of the other people there, his hostile pale-blue gaze slammed into me.

"Dad."

She flashed a guilty look in my direction. Almost as if she were begging me to keep quiet. Darryl stood stony-faced at the older man's side. His words from our talk earlier rattled around in my head.

"Who are you and why are you standing so close to my daughter?" the older man asked, belligerence sliding into his stance and tone. From the pictures I'd seen online earlier, I already deduced this must be Olin Leroux, Regan's father.

I gauged the other man's reaction, unsure how best to respond. Should I offer to shake his hand? The hostility in his expression and his puffed out chest suggested I might not like his reaction to my overture. Still, this was Regan's father, and I wanted to make a good impression.

"I'm Carter Grace, and I—"

"Jenna Olsen asked him to stop by to discuss my meeting with her in a few weeks," Regan blurted out.

Again, her eyes begged me to go along with that flat-out lie.

"Huh," he said, still eyeing me like an insect that needed to be squished.

I shoved my hands into my pockets, not wanting her to see them fisted. "Right. Jenna's looking forward to discussing specs with you."

"And I can't wait to get to Austin. So much great stuff happening in that city," Regan gushed.

Darryl caught my eye and shook his head. What was with all this negativity? Olin was a man, not a damn emperor, and he wasn't the famous person in the room, either. *Regan* signed his paychecks.

"Will you be in Austin, Mr. Grace?" Olin asked. He maneuvered so he stood in front of Regan before he shoved out his chest, pushing into my personal space.

I kept my hands in my pockets. I didn't plan to escalate the situation, but I refused to be the one to step back. Regan nibbled at her lower lip. I'd already noticed that habit, which seemed to correlate with how comfortable she felt in a situation.

"I'm in the process of moving back there. My family's been in the area for multiple generations."

"And where is it that you live now?" Olin asked.

While the question might have been innocuous—small talk to break the ice and develop commonality with anyone else, nothing about the way Olin asked made me relax. In fact, his tone caused the fine hairs on the back of my neck to stand at attention.

"Over the past few months, I've split my time between San Francisco and Austin, though I have a ranch near Billings, Wyoming, so I drove down to Denver from there to spend some days completing some business."

"Business." The word sounded like an epithet. Olin's face turned to a mask of disapproval.

"Yes."

"What kind of business?" Olin asked.

"I was buying some shares in a hotel," I said.

Olin's face settled into nonplussed lines. "That doesn't seem related to guitar making," Olin said with an angry glance at Regan. I took that to mean I hadn't fit into his preconceived ideas.

"It's not, directly. Jenna is family."

Olin continued to glare at Regan but with a budding look of triumph building across his features. "So, you buy hotels and show up at concerts to talk to young ladies about guitars they do not need?"

I clenched my jaw. What was up with this guy?

"I'm lucky Jenna is willing to consider making me one of her beautiful instruments," Regan said, stepping back into the conversation.

She straightened to her full height as she sauntered between us, but tension remained around her mouth and her lips were flattened. Nothing remained of the fun-loving young woman I'd been talking to a few moments before.

"Now, I need to finish talking to Carter about this guitar before the fans enter," she said.

Darryl stepped closer to her side, settling on the balls of his feet. Like Cam did when he expected trouble.

"You know when we have to get on the buses," Regan said, a faint tremor in her words. "Why don't you make sure Mindy and Darryl have the scheduling down?"

A low rumble permeated from Olin's chest. All my muscles bunched and I pulled my hands from my pockets. This man wasn't a bantam rooster.

He was much more dangerous. And in the few minutes I'd spent in his company, I'd learned enough to know he would never let Regan make her own choices. Worse was the realization she was completely unaware of just how under his thumb she was. Her team must work hard to minimize Olin's impact, not just on Regan but on her career in general.

Unfortunately, her team was losing to a man Regan clearly feared.

CHAPTER THIRTEEN | Regan

I continued to nibble on the inner part of my lower lip as my father decided whether or not to take the graceful exit I offered. His mouth turned down in that expression I'd come to hate. Yes, I understood where his protectiveness came from, but I wasn't my mother.

Carter resettled his body, somehow appearing more alert and ready for a coming fight.

"I'll be over there," my father said, jerking his thumb to pinpoint a spot across the room. Which meant he'd be watching me. I tried not to let the stifling feeling overwhelm me. I failed.

Still, I didn't want an altercation—not here with journalists and fans milling around backstage, close enough to overhear, and not between Carter and my dad. My father, though, seemed more than happy to pick a fight with everyone these days.

Agitation spread over my skin like a painful rash. After a long, painful moment, Olin spun on his heel and headed off with Darryl trailing him. My father stopped and waited for the bigger man to catch up. From the look on my bodyguard's face, he wasn't pleased with whatever my father was saying.

But then, not many people had been happy with my father's presence, let alone his words, for weeks. Maybe longer and I just never noticed. I'd been so caught up in the fallout from James' departure and his bad behavior thereafter that somehow his fans made out to be my fault, that I'd missed some of the goings-on in my own entourage.

Mindy's dislike for my father solidified when Olin told us both to get over Savannah's death. So much so, Mindy began to broach the idea of me hiring a professional manager, stating my rising international stardom required a greater understanding of the music industry and public relations. But what she meant was my father was in over his head and handled his insecurities by lashing out, which became more consistent and harder to manage after James broke my heart.

That's what the month-long vacation I purchased for my father was for—me to put my life in order the way I wanted it. I just needed to get through the next few weeks so that I could put my dad on a plane and get the headspace to figure out the best strategy forward—not just for my career but to maintain a relationship with my father. My only living relative.

"Are you okay?" Carter asked.

He moved in closer like he wanted to touch me but he didn't. That was my fault. Shame washed over me. No one understood why I put up with Olin Leroux's attitude. Most days, I didn't either except…he was my father. He pushed me in my swing, carried me on his shoulders when I was too small to see the parade or when the water at our beachside bungalow was too cold.

I remembered him reading me books and playing tea parties. Those had been good memories. Such good memories before my mother began to hurt us.

I pushed those thoughts away because they wouldn't solve my

current dilemma but they did make me feel worse, less secure in my decisions to keep my father around.

Carter's concern washed over me like a soothing balm.

"Of course," I said.

He blew out a breath. "You're sure?"

I frowned. "I just said I was."

He eased back, giving me the space my frustration required.

"Jen likes your music and would probably be happy to make you a guitar. Cam told me she's a fan when I talked to him."

I pressed my palms against my stomach and groaned. "I've been hoping to talk to her when I'm in Austin. I'm in love with your sister-in-law's designs and sounds. I'm also in love with your brother's melodies."

Carter's gaze flit to my father and then back to my face. "Cam's interested in the meeting you want. He asked me to give him your number."

"Sure," I said. "I'd love to talk to him directly." I rubbed my arms, telling myself it was the puff of cold air as the air conditioning kicked on.

"Will do. So…I'm going to head out if you're sure you're okay. But, first, I need to know if you'll let me take you on a date," Carter said.

I nodded before I managed to think through my answer. Carter's smile caused one to break out across my own face. "In Austin. Once my father's on his vacation."

"I'm not one for sneaking around," he said. Carter's expression turned hard as he tracked my father's movements. "If you don't want me in your life, it's better you just say so now. I won't make it hard for you to meet my brother. I promise."

I touched his wrist but dropped my hand quickly. "I do want you there. I want to go on that date. I…" I swallowed hard. "I never would have gone home with you if I didn't want that."

He leaned in, causing me to tense. If my father saw this, he might well go ballistic. Carter pressed his lips to my ear. "Then I'll see you in Dallas. Because that's sooner than Austin."

"Okay," I whispered. I could make it ten days until I saw him again.

"I better call you so you don't have to miss me."

"Yes," I whispered. My heart slammed against my ribs and my entire body warmed as his breath tracked across my cheek.

Carter pulled back enough to drag his lips across my cheek. I couldn't draw a breath, couldn't move at all. If I did, I'd once again embarrass myself by throwing myself fully into Carter's arms and damn the consequences. Problem was, the consequences were significant.

CHAPTER FOURTEEN | Carter

Cam sent me the article written about Regan and me. I read it with growing dismay. This John Mitchell character was definitely out for Regan's reputation as he managed to convey a concern about drugs and the fact she latched on to me after my brother rebuffed her attempts to get in touch.

But, the allegations made little—no—sense. Regan hadn't seemed to know I was related to Cam, not until I flat-out told her. Well…she'd been on that TV show. She might well be a great actress. How would I know?

I'd told her Cam wanted to meet her, giving her the opening the journalist said she wanted. But she hadn't pushed for a meeting. She'd been more worried about her father's reaction to me—to us dating than trying to cozy up to me to get to my brother. In fact, if she wanted to make sure I was willing to get her an introduction, why hadn't she had sex with me the first night, when I'd made it clear that's what I wanted?

None of this situation made any sense.

I told Cam as much.

"I don't know what to make of it either," he said. "I believe she's talented. I told you that. I wanna work with her. I told you that, too. And her people already made overtures to mine. So I don't get this 'source'."

I stared at the words, frowning. "The whole situation reeks of something nasty."

"It's always hard when reporters are dogging your every step, but it seems to me she'd be extra careful with how she's portrayed, you being related to me and all."

"I don't think she knew we were."

"Then what's the story here?" Cam asked. "I mean, really? Is there anything to it? Y'all got written up. Happens all the damn time. People think they deserve to know what I ate for dinner and what color Jenna's bra is," Cam growled.

He was fiercely protective of Jenna, and I appreciated that because I wanted to take the same growly tone Cam used and turn it on everybody attacking Regan.

"But then why hasn't Regan called me back?"

"Hell if I understand a woman's mind. Half the time I don't get my own," Cam said.

Cam suffered from PTSD, thanks to the missions he had to lead his men through in Iraq. I couldn't blame him for his head issues.

"If it isn't true, wouldn't she just say so?" I asked.

"I don't know your gal, Carter. I don't know what stress she's under or who's telling her what, or if she's even seen or heard the news. She's on tour, she might be too busy to call you."

"Or she's ignoring me because she feels guilty. Or doesn't want to talk to me."

"Where's all this negativity coming from?" Cam asked, clearly surprised by my lack of confidence.

The brother Cam used to know fell apart when he caught

his girlfriend with a guy he'd considered a friend. Well, no, that wasn't exactly true. It was my reaction to Dianna's words that snapped my self-worth.

I wasn't getting into that now. So, I told Cam I had to go, get some work done. Same excuse I'd used for years because it worked. Even my mama let me off the hook for work, stating she didn't want to get in the way of my livelihood.

I probably should tell my family my net worth, especially now that reporters listed me as a "tech millionaire" and that piece in *Wired* magazine was coming out next week. While Cam knew I'd done well for myself with my tech startup, we never spoke details, which was probably why he'd thanked me so profusely for the check I wrote him to update our family's ranching equipment.

I didn't like to talk about my bank account. I got lucky in business, unlike in my personal life.

I stared at my phone for a long moment, willing it to ring. Maybe Cam was right and I overreacted to Regan's silence. Performers struggled to find personal time. I'd seen first-hand how slammed my brother was during a tour.

I sent Regan another text, deciding not to pressure her with a call: *I miss hearing from you. We need to set up that date.*

Hours later and I was still waiting for a response. All right. Regan planned to ignore my texts, which caused my chest to ache.

Still, now wasn't the time to focus on anything other than my architect's plans for the new headquarters I planned to remodel within a stone's throw of a tech giant's new campus. My building boasted 1950s styling, but it was more than adequate for my ten-year growth plan. The location proved ideal, close to the rest of the growing tech sector moving to the city, but because it was older and not in a style I enjoyed, we needed to do some light cosmetic work to bring it up to my standards. More importantly, I wanted to make the entire property LEED certified.

"Can we get more natural lighting in there?" I asked, pointing to the area where most of the newest hires and interns would work.

Alvin, my architect, scratched his bushy salt-and-pepper beard. "We could, but that'll mean knocking out this wall." He tapped the spot with his blunt thumb. "It's weight-bearing, which means additional supports. That'll take longer to get the building open for occupancy."

"Or making it out of some kind of glass. Like those blocks, so people going past and the workers have a semblance of privacy but also the correct lighting for their health."

Alvin nodded his head before making some notes. "Seems to me you could have re-designed this without my input."

I slapped the older man on the shoulder. "But it wouldn't have been up to code."

Alvin began to roll up the blueprints. "I guess I'm earning my commission, then."

"You know it."

I settled my hip against the conference table in Alvin's trendy office space. It wasn't far from Jenna's shop just off Sixth Street in downtown Austin, about three blocks from my temporary floor in a low-rise building.

"Because I'm not the one who'll be pulling permits, fighting with contractors, and whatever else happens with buildings of this size and scope."

Alvin smiled, causing his double chin to wobble a little. "I'm glad to be working with you, Carter. You're a smart young man who's doing good work. Not only are you revitalizing this old beauty, you're bringing good jobs to the local economy. That's going to mean something for a long time for a lot of families."

I nodded, trying not to squirm. This aspect of my business planned to gobble up Dean's design studio located about ten miles north of downtown. Before that, I intended to hire away some of his key staff, then buy him out and sell off the bits of his company I didn't want or need—the jury was still out on those details because our two industries were merging as video for apps became more mainstream.

With Alvin looking at me with such pride, my plan seemed a bit, well, shady. I tried to shake off the guilt swirling through my stomach. My plan was set into motion more than ten years ago. This was just the pinnacle of my current success. My HR director had already spoken to Dean's key executives, and if they chose to take my company's generous offer, well, then that was business. And if Dean's company couldn't survive his stupidity, well, that was business, too.

Because if you couldn't keep your people satisfied, you didn't deserve to keep them.

I was paraphrasing Dean's words to me then, but the same principle applied to Dianna. I hadn't satisfied some visceral need, which was why she turned to Dean. And now, Regan wouldn't respond to my texts.

Maybe Dianna had been correct when she flung accusations at me all those years ago. Maybe I was defective, unable to connect emotionally. Maybe Regan saw how walled off I'd become and decided I wasn't worth the risk.

She wouldn't be the first. That was part of why I never sought out anything long term. The women I'd tried to date in the ensuing years told me I was like a blank chalkboard, unwilling to write on it because that would make a mess.

The last dating debacle occurred when I lived in San Francisco full-time and ate, drank, and slept in my tiny office space not far from the Embarcadero. Those eighteen months were the most challenging of my professional life, but I'd needed the focus to get over the loss of not just Dianna but the dream of the life I thought we were building together.

And I'd considered her my third strike in the romance department. Why keep trying?

Before I could stop myself, I checked my phone again.

My heart leaped and pounded like I was six years old again.

I miss you, too. And I'm so sorry about the article. I don't understand why he's going after me.

I didn't either, but I wanted to be with Regan to comfort her, to make her smile as she had the night we played Scrabble. I thought about what Cam had said, about taking a leap, and I made a decision that I hoped wouldn't return to bite me in the ass.

———— ★ ————

I booked my flight to Kansas City, anticipation thrumming through my veins. I made it to the hotel before Regan and her crew, so I hung up my clothes in the closet as I called Larissa, my HR director.

"We all set with those potential hires?"

"Yes," she said. "I emailed you a report with details."

I walked out of the dark closet and to the large windows overlooking the high rises of downtown, squinting against the piercing autumn sun.

"Fantastic." But somehow this victory rang hollow. After meeting Regan, I'd come to the conclusion I wanted to leave Dianna where she belonged: in my past. Same with Dean. Unfortunately, the more I looked at the synergies, the smarter buying Dean's company was for my company's continued growth.

"I'll look it over and be in touch," I said, ending the call with Larissa.

I called Remy. "Any word from Dean?"

"None, man, but you can't expect him to make this easy for us. He never has. I'm sure he's pitching an epic temper tantrum."

Much as I wanted to disagree, I couldn't. Dean hated to lose but he sure did gloat when he won.

"And I need to say," Remy continued in a rueful tone, "you saw this connection to the animation Dean's company offers long before I ever did. This is why you have such a stellar reputation in the business, Carter. Making this deal will grow your revenue by at least a quarter."

I considered telling Remy I hadn't thought about potential growth when I started buying up the shares but decided against that much sharing. He knew that, knew my reasons for wanting to quash Dean and even shared some of them.

"We can go with that version," I said.

"I get your desire to ruin him for what he did, Carter. But you're making a better choice here, buying his digital graphics company. Plus, it makes you look better."

Less like a vengeful asshole. Remy didn't say those words, but I still heard them.

A knock sounded on my door, and I headed to answer. I opened it to see Regan's assistant, Mindy, standing there.

"I have to go. Keep me posted on the potential negotiations." I opened my door more widely to let her in, but Mindy shook her head and stepped back, putting more space between us.

"Of course," Remy said. "I'll touch base with you tomorrow."

"Great."

I hung up my phone. "What's up?" I asked.

Mindy twisted her fingers together. "Hey. I got your message." She smirked a little. "Obviously. And I wanted to let you know we're here."

I smiled. "I see that. I can't wait to see Regan."

Mindy blew out a breath. "That's one of the things I needed to talk to you about. John Mitchell is embedded with us this week."

I narrowed my eyes. She didn't deserve to be attacked by a reporter. "Did he write something else?"

Mindy's mouth twisted in a scowl. "I haven't seen anything except the story that came out yesterday. But…" She fidgeted. "You need to understand that Regan's father invited John. This was weeks ago, sure, but having him here is already turning into a disaster."

I frowned. Why would Mindy tell me all this?

She blew out a breath. "Sorry. I shouldn't have said anything. It's just…" She raised her gaze to meet mine. "I'm worried about

Regan. This tour's been hard on her. She wouldn't be the first star to cave under the pressure."

I nodded, still unsettled. "All right. I'll do my best to make sure I don't add to her discomfort or cause anything newsworthy in the wrong way."

Mindy tilted her head. "You really like her."

Since Mindy stated it, I chose not to answer.

"Well, I don't think you'll hurt her," she said. "At least not intentionally. And Regan's been mopey since you left, so I'm glad you're here."

I didn't like the direction of this conversation, so instead of pursuing Mindy's hints, I stepped back into my room and grabbed my key and wallet. I wanted this conversation over and to see Regan for myself. We had a lot to discuss.

Mindy trotted beside me toward the elevator. I needed to go up two levels to get to Regan's room.

Mindy fidgeted even as she entered the elevator. "She hasn't been right since everything went down with Ja…" Mindy looked away. "Something's going to snap."

CHAPTER FIFTEEN | Regan

The knock on my door took me by surprise. I'd asked to be left alone. I needed to read through all the recent news posted about me, and I wanted to develop a plan to take to my label's PR department. That's why I turned off my phone earlier, though Carter's message taunted me.

No, I shook my head. I had to figure out what to do about John.

I walked to the door, pulling the top of my silky robe closed. I flung the door open, prepared to tell whoever was there to take a hike. Instead, I gasped.

Carter stood there, his hands gripping the sides of the door frame. He leaned in until his lips were millimeters from mine.

"You've been ignoring me," he said.

I met his gaze, trying to memorize the flecks of gray and blue and green that splintered out from his irises.

"No, I just..."

Damn, those were pretty peepers. Sure, they looked brown from a distance, but up close, Carter was full of surprises. Like the soft kiss he brushed on my lips.

"I missed you," he said against my mouth.

I rose on my tiptoes as I threw my arms around his neck and kissed him again, deeper and with lots of enthusiasm. "I missed you, too," I murmured against his addictive lips.

His tongue tangled with mine as he dropped his arms to my waist. I jumped up and wrapped my legs around his waist as his hand moved down to cup my bottom.

"Then you should have responded to my messages."

I pulled back a little so that I could make out his features. His eyes were stormy, maybe with irritation or desire, but his lips were damp from our kisses. Oh, I liked that look on him. "I didn't know what to say."

"The truth," he snapped. The fire in his eyes burned bright.

"I'm sorry, Carter." My face flushed. "I didn't mean to shut you out. It's just that I really like you, and that reporter made it sound like I was using you, and I hated that so much but couldn't think of how to prove I wasn't."

Out of air, I snapped my jaw shut and stared at him, heart pounding.

"Okay."

He captured my lips again in a deep drugging kiss that I never wanted to end. He strode into the room and kicked the door shut behind him. And still he kissed me with slow and soft licks and nibbles. I loved the feel of him in my mouth, his large hands gripping my butt cheeks and his growing erection pressing against my center.

He broke off the kiss long enough to glance around, his eyes lighting on the couch. He strode toward it and settled me on it. He kissed me again as he came over me. His chest rubbed against my silk-clad nipples, causing them to pebble in need. His lips moved from mine to trail down my neck and lower to the deep V splitting the emerald silk.

His hand came up to clamp over my breast and my back arched as I pushed into him, my mouth opening wide enough so I could moan with the pleasure of his hands and mouth.

All of a sudden he reared back, eyes wild. "I wanted to see you, but I didn't mean to take this so far so quickly." His gaze dotted down to my thin robe, and he groaned.

I sat up and then stood on shaky legs before settling in his lap.

"Carter?" I whispered, bringing his face close to mine.

He reached up and ran his palms along my ribs, causing my body to heat further.

"I'd really like you to kiss me again."

He cursed as his eyes slid closed. "I can't," he mumbled.

"Sure you can." I brushed my lips over his. He cupped the back of my head as he deepened it. His hips settled between my splayed thigh.

"I don't want to stop," he groaned.

I nibbled at his lower lip before pressing a series of soft kisses there. "I don't want you to stop either."

"This isn't why I came here. I mean, it feels fantastic, and I want to take you to bed—"

"No bed. Here. Now."

I remembered what I'd told him before—not like I was going to forget. But…he'd flown here to see me when I ignored him. He'd tried to protect me in Denver. And I wanted him.

Correction. I *needed* his body to love mine.

I dragged my fingertips down his chest to his belt buckle. Carter rocked dress clothes. The fancier his pants and the more powerful his tie, the more I just *had* to have him naked.

I slid my hands back up his chest and loosened his tie. I unfastened each of his buttons, pressing kisses to his gray T-shirt as more of it was exposed.

He slid his hands inside my robe and tugged on my nipples with gentle pressure. I squirmed in his lap, enjoying the sensations he evoked. I stripped off his shirt, which meant he had to pull away from my warmed flesh.

He undid his cuffs and let the pinstripe dress shirt fall to the side. Then, in one clean move, he tugged his tee over his head.

Sexy. So damn sexy.

And then I got my first look at his chest. I'd seen many shirtless men, either in photo shoots or dancing backup for me. But Carter…he was a class of hot I'd never witnessed before. His muscles were thicker than the gym-going models I'd met. Clearly, there was something to say for hard physical labor.

He obviously spent time riding the lines and whatever else ranchers did because his skin glowed with a light tan. Thick slabs of muscle tensed as he brought his arms back around me.

His arms—was I drooling? Not that I cared enough to look away from the sculpted muscle there.

"Wait. Regan. Wait." He huffed a breath.

"Mindy mentioned something about your ex…"

I reared back, tensing as if I'd been hit. "I don't want to talk about him," I said, annoyance making me short-tempered.

He stared into my eyes for a long moment. He opened his mouth like he wanted to say something more. But I was done talking. I grabbed his large hand and placed it against my breast.

His lips parted, showing a hint of his white teeth. I leaned up and nipped the lower lip before I soothed it with my tongue. Then, I deepened the kiss. He surged up against me until I could feel every ridge and contour of his sleek body. And still we kissed.

His hands disappeared under my robe, callused fingertips running over my skin. I pressed down into his lap as I arched my back, shoving my breasts further into his hands. That also gave him access to my neck, which he took advantage of by nipping and licking his way down to my breasts. This time, he pushed the thin material out of the way and suckled on the taut bud.

"Gorgeous," he said as he sought out the other one.

"Carter," I gasped.

"Shh. I got you."

I wanted him to do more. Faster. Harder. The need for him overtook my better judgment. For tonight, I wanted to let go. The stress of my father's unwillingness to let me lead my life, the relentless press that continued to dog me…It would still be there tomorrow. But, right now, I had Carter here. Carter who desired me and could make me feel good. Feel loved.

Carter savored and took his time. By the time he unbelted my robe and pushed it off my shoulders I was trembling with need and so damn wet I would have been embarrassed if Carter wasn't telling me how hot I was.

When his fingers brushed across my pubis, I lurched against him. Desire strummed through me, lighting up all my nerve endings.

As he let his fingertips drift along the edge of my panties I undid his belt, the button, and lowered the zipper, ready to wrap my hand around his firm flesh.

When I did, he threw his head back and clenched his teeth. But he didn't make a sound. I wanted him to pant and beg for me—just as I was. I nipped his ear as I squeezed his shaft just below the thick head.

I smiled as he arched his spine and groaned into my ear. He shifted the lace covering my groin and traced his fingers across my folds. I kissed him as he sank a finger inside my body.

"Aw. Hell, Regan. You feel amazing."

"So do you," I whispered.

Before I could process what was happening, I was on my back, my panties flung somewhere and Carter's lips trailing a scorching path up my inner thigh.

He licked the seam of my leg where it met my hip and then nosed his way into my center. I cried out again.

His dark chuckle told me how much he enjoyed my reaction. Before I had time to catch my breath, he kissed me.

Like, really kissed me with his tongue. My back bowed at the sensation. He placed one of his big hands on my stomach and I stared at the difference in our coloring. I was a few shades darker and I loved how well we complemented each other—him so large and slightly rough from his ranching; me soft yet firm from years of exercise.

Carter sucked on the bundle of nerves at the top of my folds as he slid his finger back inside me and I forgot to breathe let alone think.

What he was doing felt good. Illegally good, especially when he pressed in with another finger and curled them, hitting that magic spot that had my thighs shivering with pleasure.

I tugged at his hair and twisted, trying to both get closer and slow down the pleasurable assault. But Carter was relentless and he drove me up and over.

He pulled me close and kissed me. Dazed, I found the taste of myself on his lips shocking and sexy.

Slowly, my breathing evened out and I trailed my fingers down his chest to circle his navel. He caught my fingers and squeezed my hand lightly.

"This isn't a tit-for-tat experience, Regan. I wanted to make you come, but I get it if you want to wait. Like you told me before."

I studied him for a long moment, just searching his eyes for a hidden agenda or dishonesty. He stared back, letting me in.

That willingness to bare himself shocked me, especially after my offhanded claims during our initial night together.

Carter, I was learning, was much deeper than I expected. And his innate kindness made me nervous nearly as much as his desire to let me set the pace turned me on.

I licked my lips, unsurprised when he followed the motion, his eyes scorching my skin.

Somehow, this moment seemed poised for something more than another swell of pleasure. Carter shared with me, just as I'd wanted him to that first night. My eyes pricked with tears, but I blinked them back. This was mutual passion between consenting adults.

"I want you," I said, ignoring the alarm bells clanging through my head, reminding me I never did passion for passion's sake.

His body tensed, his fingers digging into my shoulders where he held me. "You're sure?" he asked, his voice deeper than before.

I nodded.

"I need you to say it, Regan. I need you to tell me what you want."

My face flamed. My sexual experience was limited to James and some making out with a couple of boys during my teen years. I'd spent my entire existence hovered over and watched and hadn't yet really had a chance to explore my sensuality.

Carter was offering that to me as well as earth-shattering orgasms and ownership of our relationship. My heart beat a bit faster and I told myself it was because I was in uncharted territory.

"I want you to…" What to say? I cleared my throat. "I want to be with you, Carter."

He smirked, clearly enjoying my hesitancy. The big jerk.

"What does that mean?" he asked. "Tell me *exactly* what you want."

I shifted and felt his erection press against my thigh.

I took a deep breath and said, in a rush, "Fuck me, please."

His smile would have melted my panties off if I had them on. I pressed my thighs together as a fresh ache built there.

He shifted and lifted me into his arms, carrying me with an ease that made me feel more feminine. He laid me out on the bed, spreading my legs as he stood between my knees. His thick cock jutted out from a small nest of hair, bobbing a little as he reached down to fondle my right breast.

"I think I will," he said. "And I'm really going to enjoy it."

He leaned in and kissed me again, all soft and tender enough to make my eyes tear. He used his hands and lips to love his way all over my body. I tried to reciprocate, stopping to flick my fingernail across his flat nipple a second time when he inhaled sharply. He liked my hands on his lower abdomen and me nibbling at his neck and earlobe, so I spent time there as he caressed my ribs and hips.

I pulled him down to me, needing to feel his skin against mine.

"I like your skin touching mine," I murmured against his mouth.

"You're soft, supple," he said.

He tweaked my nipples.

"I want you inside of me," I said.

He smiled as he slid off me and I realized he'd been waiting for me to ask. Once again, this man made something slippery and warm slither in my chest.

He rolled on a condom and then climbed back on the bed, his body moving with predatory grace, intent on joining us together.

He grasped himself in hand and lined us up. I'd never felt anything as good as the thick, heavy slide into me as he rose up over me. I pulled him down, kissing him with the passion that burst between us.

He slid out before his hips snapped back against mine.

"Oh."

"You like that?" he asked. His features were sharper, eyes glazed with pleasure.

"Y-yes."

He groaned as he settled into a smooth, deep rhythm. My

hands fell to the comforter and I grabbed it as I flattened my feet to the mattress, tilting my hips up to take his next thrust deeper. He swore, low and guttural, as he gripped my hips.

Then, he began to really pound into me. I thrashed back and forth, fighting the pleasure even as it built higher than the last time. He continued his deep, heady thrusts as my body began to shake.

He pressed his fingers to my clit and circled. I gasped before my body shuddered with pleasure.

Carter kept up his assault, the smooth in and out, until he, too, stiffened. He hissed out a low curse, then another, as he pressed his groin even tighter to mine. He bit his lip, his eyes closed as his release raged through him. Then, he collapsed on top of me.

I wrapped my arms around him, marveling at his sweat-slicked muscles. I pressed a kiss against his shoulder, as he struggled to regain his breath.

These moments, now, after our craving was sated, frightened me. I'd lied to myself earlier tonight.

I'd been stupid enough to do exactly what I told Carter I would: I let him into my head, then my body. But the worst of it was, even though I didn't know him well enough, even though I worried he might just want me for my fame, he already occupied a place in my heart.

CHAPTER SIXTEEN | Carter

I flew back to Austin late the next morning. Leaving Regan proved hard, which surprised and worried me. Something about those big blue eyes and that tousled morning-after hair made my heart trip. But Regan had a concert tonight, and I had to hammer out more of the details of this hot mess I'd created with my decision to force Dean out of his company.

Remy met me at our cramped, temporary offices four blocks from Sixth Street. Yes, I'd chosen the location based on proximity to my sister and Cam's fiancée. I never wanted them to feel unsafe again. Cam slapped my back in thanks when I showed him my space, but no words were necessary—he'd be in and out of town, and our ladies needed consistent protection. Their guards were a good first line of defense, but for both Cam's and my sake and sanity, I wanted to be available within minutes.

Remy settled into the chair across from me.

"Did you see the new gaming numbers?" he asked.

I nodded. "Choose your own adventure's growth is impressive." I leaned back in my chair. "Makes for another good reason to purchase Dean's company," I said.

Remy shrugged. "You already had enough. And you know I have your back for all of 'em. But, yeah, if you can add the illustration and animation to your pipeline, having it in-house, then

you have a nice built-in advantage over the static app makers.
Even over the full-blown video game producers because you can
get high-quality, graphic-oriented, phone-based games to market
more quickly."

"I have a prototype for a particular app that takes the adven-
turing up a level. Somewhere between the static and full-blown
user immersion. It'd be good for the virtual reality headsets
hitting the market."

Remy whistled.

I shrugged. "I built it about a year ago just to see if I could.
I played with the option to make the images stream more like a
movie, but without a team of animators, it was too choppy." I
twisted in my chair before bringing it back to face front. "So, if we
can get this deal through, finetuning that app is the perfect place
to start. I'm pretty sure the synergies work as well as I suspect they
will. And this particular game is based on a popular book."

"You own those rights?" Remy asked.

"For a few hundred novels that I enjoyed reading. Many of
them are well-positioned to transfer from book to game."

Remy slapped his knee. "You do know how to stay at
the forefront of the industry." Admiration shone in his
eyes. "We need to get you Dean's company so you can stay
top-of-the-heap."

I scowled. "Much as I want it, I'm not sure it's worth it, man."

"What?"

"Dean's going to make this buyout difficult."

Remy nodded. "He always does. Prick only thinks about
himself."

I didn't need to respond because Remy spoke the truth. But I wasn't looking forward to the upcoming battle. Dean never let anything go without a fight. And usually a dirty one. One I wasn't sure I could stomach because I knew what Dean would do. He'd go after my family or, worse, Regan. He'd try to sabotage my ability to buy him out of his executive position by hurting or strong-arming the people I cared about.

I blew out a breath as I thought of the worry in Regan's eyes. Then, there was how much Cam and Jenna had been through these past few months, not to mention the drama with my sister and mama.

Dean would find a weakness in one of the people I loved, and exploit it. That's how he stole Dianna, and, from what Remy and I heard, it's how he continued to do business.

Maybe I should just let Dean, his company—the past—go.

"You're thinking about someone in particular. This got anything to do with your new girlfriend?" Remy asked. "And don't you dare tell me you're not going soft because of her. You totally are."

I pulled myself out of my dark thoughts and focused on my friend. His scowl made it clear he wasn't happy with me.

"What are you talking about?" I asked.

"You, man." Remy's hazel eyes narrowed. "You've always been the shark in the water. You scent blood better than anyone I know. But now, after your overnight party with Everly Leroux, you're willing to drop this deal after spending years putting it together—at a time when it *really* makes sense to close it."

At my look, he waved his hand.

"Your sleepover is all over the net. Media and fans are

lapping up the tech bajillionaire dating the sexy pop diva."

"Really?" I blinked a few times, trying to regain my equilibrium. News of us hit the world fast. We were so new. I wasn't sure how Regan…shit! Her father was not going to like us being linked together. And, now, I had to wonder if Dean had caught wind of the story. Double, triple crap.

Not like I could say anything. I'd been the one to push for transparency, not hiding our relationship. I'd never dated a famous performer before, and clearly Regan had been around this block before. She'd tried to protect herself…and me. And I'd dismissed that concern.

Color me a fool.

"I had no idea there were pictures of us together," I said.

Remy raised an eyebrow. "Not just pics of you, but the writer points out you have a greater net worth than she does. Seems like he's implying your girl is just with you for the bucks."

Remy hesitated for a moment. "As your friend and legal advisor, I feel the need to warn you about the importance of a prenuptial agreement."

God. Who knew money would prove to be such a pain in the ass? I'd gotten lucky, hitting the app store with the right app at the right time. Okay, fine. I'd done that over and over again. And, sure, that luck translated into a cushy lifestyle, but up until my net worth topped the hundreds of millions, most media outlets ignored me. I liked that better.

"Show me," I said.

Remy pulled up a website on his phone and handed it to me. The photo was from yesterday. Regan wore her robe. Her legs were wrapped around my waist. From the background, I deduced the photo was taken in the hallway outside her suite. I frowned. I never saw anyone there.

As far as I knew, Mindy was the only person who knew I'd flown in. But that John Mitchell guy…he'd already written a couple of sleazy pieces about Regan, so I wouldn't doubt him hanging out on her hallway to get just such a picture.

My irritation turned to rage when as I continued to study the photo. Regan's panties peeked out, showcasing the sweet curve of her ass, and most of the inner curve of her breast was visible, thanks to the angle of the shot.

The entire world could be looking at the same picture right now. I gritted my teeth as I handed Remy back his phone, but jealousy continued to flow through me.

What Regan and I had together was *ours*, not something to share with the world.

Remy stood. "I'll let you deal with this." He walked to the door, pausing in the frame. "For the record, I'm real glad you found someone you care about, Carter. It's been too damn long."

I stared at the empty doorway for a long moment before I picked up my phone and texted her, asking if she wanted me to make a statement.

The story's from John Mitchell, she replied. As I'd expected. I hadn't met the man, and I already detested him. *We're pretty sure he camped out in front of my room, hoping for something juicy.*

Which we gave him, dammit.

What can I do? I asked.

I'm handling it, she said.

My phone pinged again a moment later.

I'm sorry.

Fuck texting. I called her.

"I'm not sorry," I said when she answered. "I mean, I am… about the pictures. But I'm not sorry I spent the night with you."

I held my breath, waiting for her response.

I didn't know her well enough yet to properly gauge her reaction. And I didn't like the uncertainty I was feeling. Granted, I liked seeing Regan again way more.

"I'm not sorry for the night either." She paused. "If you're okay with it, I've asked Mindy to put out a statement that we're dating."

"Yes," I said, my tone emphatic. "Exclusively."

"Exclusively," she echoed, a smile filtering through her voice.

———— ★ ————

I texted Regan before I went to bed that night, but I was asleep when she wrote back.

I sent flowers to her next venue, letting her know I was thinking about her, but I was too slammed with working through the legal details of a potential hostile takeover of Dean's company to be able to travel to see her over the next couple of days.

Regan: *Everything is fine with my father. I'm handling it.*

Carter: *You're sure? I'm worried about you. And I miss you.*

I did. Desperately, which was irritating and equally unavoidable.

Regan: *He started to lay into me, but then he received a call from the record execs who were thrilled we're dating. They think it'll keep John Mitchell's articles kinder and my image cleaner for my fans.*

I wasn't sure I believed her response, but I chose not to push her and mess up this relationship.

I sent her a Scrabble app I created for us to play between meetings with Remy.

Regan sent back tons of heart emojis and proceeded to destroy me yet again. Her intelligence was so sexy.

The next day, I finished going over the final permitting with my architect. I was pleased with the progress on the plans and the time frame for moving in. Just three months until I could sit behind my desk and view the city skyline from a building I owned. Who would have thought I'd have such success in business?

I frowned as I walked toward the parking lot behind Jenna's shop, wishing my initial concerns about Dean and his company weren't already proving correct. Remy, Larissa, and the rest of my team wanted to pursue the takeover. I abstained from voting, wanting to get a feel from my brain trust on whether this was a smart buy. All ten of the board voted to move forward with the buyout.

I gave Larissa the green light to continue to contact the company's key employees. While a few of the executives were excited to meet with my HR director, a couple more seemed not just hesitant but hostile, no doubt because of some lies Dean fed them about me.

I didn't need the entire management team, but I liked the idea of keeping as much continuity for the rest of the employees as possible. That kept morale higher and the work at a higher quality.

At least that had been my experience up to this point.

Worse, I hadn't heard back from Regan today, the day after our text conversation about her father. The Google alerts I set up hadn't brought up anything new, which I took as a good sign, but I was worried her father had convinced her to dump me—or worse, he'd hurt her. I was nearly out of my mind with concern, but until she chose to get in touch, I was in the dark.

And I hated feeling unsure.

"Hey, ladies," I said as Jenna let me in the shop's back door. My sister, Katie Rose, didn't bother to look up from her computer, but Jenna beamed at me, wiping her hands on a small, faded piece of flannel that told me she'd been in her workshop.

"Carter," she said with a smile. "Nice of you to pop in. We haven't seen anyone but ourselves all week."

Katie Rose scowled at her computer, still ignoring me. I swept Jenna up into a hug and smacked a kiss on her cheek. "I thought maybe y'all would want to grab a bite. My treat."

"I'm busy," my sister, Katie Rose, grumbled. Wait. No. She preferred us to call her Kate, and in her current mood, I'd do well to remember that.

"All right. I'll just take this pretty gal out, then," I said, forcing a smile even though my heart felt even heavier with my sister's response. I turned to Jenna.

She rearranged her features into neutral lines as she nodded. "I'll grab my purse."

Jenna hurried over to her desk. I slid a sly glance at Katie… *Kate*, who watched me from the corner of her eye.

"I was thinking of hitting up She's Not Here," I said.

Kate shifted. She adored the sushi spot, especially the crab butter. She turned, her mouth set in a firm line. "You talked me into it, like you knew you would."

I shrugged. "You don't have to come, seeing as you're mad at me."

She stood, smoothing down her skirt. "I am mad at you. I'm mad at all of you. Except Jenna," she said, a fond smile tugging at the corners of her lips. "Because she's an awesome boss and an even awesomer friend."

"That I am."

Jenna smiled. But, then, Jenna seemed to glow most of the time now, thanks to my brother putting a ring on her finger. She and Cam faced down not just their demons but the entire music industry and came out the other side not just stronger individually but in their relationship to each other. I'd never given voice to the fact I might just be jealous, but since meeting Regan…

"Now, let's get going," Jenna said, hooking her purse over her shoulder. "I've got a craving for tempura."

We walked down the street making idle chitchat, Kate back to glaring at the side of my head. My mama sure made a mistake in trying to keep secrets. Now everyone was upset with everyone else. Not that I really had room to talk—I'd kept a few too many of my own from my twin and that caused all kinds of problems that he and I were still working through.

"How come you never told us you were rich?" Kate asked.

"You need some money for something?" I asked.

Her back stiffened. "No. I do just fine, thanks. But I wondered what other secrets you were keeping."

She didn't say the rest of what she was thinking: That I'd lied about my reasons for leaving, that she was only my half-sister.

But I hadn't known that truth until our mama told us.

"What do you want to know?" I asked.

Kate grumbled and sped ahead.

Jenna shot me an apologetic look. "She's hurt and feels left out."

I nodded because I understood the feeling since I was living it right now with Regan.

The walk was short and thankfully not too hot. We did look intimidating, thanks to Jenna's two full-time guards, one of whom strode in front, the other behind, scowling at everyone who even glanced in our direction. I opened the door, but before Jenna and my sister could step in, another group stepped out. Four well-dressed women in a cloud of perfume slid past me, their stilettos tapping the sidewalk.

The last one out was Dianna. She never bothered to look at me, say thank you for holding the door—that was just her way. She expected such courtesies from others. Always had. But never gave the same niceties back.

Hell of a time to realize that. At least, I was wiser in the ways of the world and what to look for in a woman...if I ever did decide to settle into a long-term relationship.

Regan's lush mouth and dancing eyes slid into my mind, front and center. Regan couldn't be more opposite to Dianna, and not just in her coloring. But Regan was kind to her staff; I'd seen her thoughtful gestures to Darryl and Mindy.

Yeah, I'd definitely upgraded in the woman department.

As she stepped into her group, Dianna paused, having caught a glimpse of my sister's shiny red hair. My guts clenched as did my hand on the door handle.

"Kate Grace?" Dianna gasped. She smiled that one I hated—
the socialite smile that never did more than flex her lips upward
in the semblance of good humor. "I haven't seen you in ages.
How are you?"

Kate took a step closer to me, her anger at our current
dysfunction unimportant as the woman who'd broken my heart
stood nearby.

"This is bad," Jenna mumbled as she took in the shifting
dynamics. One of her guards ushered her into the building.
The other took up a position between Jenna and Kate, willing
to protect them both. While I appreciated the show of force, I
detested the audience for this unhappy reunion.

"I'm fine. I hope you are, too. Now, if you'll excuse us, we
have to eat before our next appointment," Kate said. Her tone
remained light and professional, but she rubbed her palm down
my back in a soothing gesture.

Dianna's eyes flicked up to mine and widened. "Carter," she
breathed.

I dipped my head but refused to say anything. Instead, I
ushered my sister into the air-conditioned space.

"Wait," Dianna cried out as I made to follow after the
dude in the suit. I paused, though I wasn't sure why. Maybe
curiosity got the better of me. She spoke briefly to the women
she'd exited with. They glanced at me with speculation before
moving off.

Dianna turned back and stepped in close, that same fake smile
drifting over her lips. "You look good."

I waited a beat, then once again turned to follow the ladies, who remained in the doorway, the guards, in turn, hovering over them. Dianna grabbed my wrist. My entire body tensed. I did not want this woman touching me. She gave up that right years before.

"Let go," I said.

"Carter, can't we talk? Please?"

"No."

"But that little misunderstanding was years ago."

"Misunderstanding? I caught you fucking my friend on my couch."

Dianna came closer, testing out a coy smile. "Don't be like that, Carter. You must remember the good times." She laid her palm on my chest. "How you adored me. Adored the life we were building together. And…" She bit her lip. "You know…it's a shame Sean doesn't know you."

"What?" I choked out the word. Sean was Dianna and Dean's son, born mere months after they married. Remy, always a cynic, said it was to solidify Dianna's position as first-in-line for Dean's bank account.

She batted her long eyelashes. "Well, there is always the chance Sean is actually your son."

My body seemed to freeze. I couldn't breathe or blink. Sean might be mine. No, that wasn't right. "You told me you'd been fucking Dean for months."

Her lips dropped into a flat line. "That's an ugly way to put my relationship with Dean. But that doesn't change the fact that you and I had a relationship then, too."

I couldn't catch my breath.

Dianna had lied. Again.

Sean might be my son.

The warm Austin air felt like it was stinging my skin.

She must be lying. *She must.*

But if she wasn't…

I had a ten-year-old son.

A child I didn't know. I'd never seen.

A son. *My son.*

Holy….

One of Jenna's guys moved toward us, no doubt at Jenna's urging.

"Miss, you're blocking the entrance," he said in a deep rumble.

Dianna, being Dianna, ignored him. I shook my head, wondering what I had ever seen in this woman. The harsh Texas sun was kind to her flawless skin and bottle-blonde hair, but not to the coldness in her eyes. How could I have missed her greed, her calculation?

Because I hadn't bothered to look for anything other than her soft skin and weekly blow jobs. In this case, ignorance had not led to any type of bliss. While my heart ached at losing her, my pride stung more that my supposed buddy lured her away with such ease. But, then, if she'd loved me even a little, she never would have treated me, our relationship, our future that we'd already plotted out, with such disregard.

Especially if we made a child together.

Hell of a number of epiphanies landing in my brain one after another, making me dizzy.

"I'll expect a paternity test. By a doctor of my choosing and without you there."

"None of that's necessary, Carter. Of course I want you

to know your child."

Now. After all these years, she wanted to make right. No way I was buying this.

"You're married to the man you claimed then was the father of your child. You said vows in a church. And we both know *I* loved a lie," I said, removing her hand from my body. I couldn't stand her touch, the smell of her perfume one second longer.

I knew from looking into her life periodically that Dianna had two kids: the boy, Sean, and a younger girl.

"Maybe it's Dean who needs to worry about which, if any, of your children are actually his," I said.

At my look, the guard stepped between us. I could have taken care of the situation myself, but I preferred to let him play bouncer and intimidator, especially with Dianna.

And with clarity, I saw the reason for this moment: Dianna knew Dean's company was in trouble. She knew that I wanted to buy him out. She was grasping for her next sugar daddy, and I was the best candidate, thanks to our shared past--and to the possibility of shared genes.

I did the math in my head a third time. From what I knew, I could have been the father of her first-born. If Sean were my son, could I take the boy from the life he knew? From his younger sister? Could I do that to the girl? I knew firsthand how messy and broken families could get and how much we needed the ones who loved us.

I stepped through the doorway. My sister eyed me with concern, a look I hadn't seen in much too long. But before she could open her mouth, the hostess called us forward. Instead of pressing the issue as I expected, Katie Rose followed Jenna toward our table.

I sighed in relief. Dianna had hurt me deeply, but I'd survived.

As soon as the waitress showed up, I ordered a drink. Shit. I needed it. No, I needed to talk to Regan…but how could I?

"Whiskey. Macallan," I clarified. "Neat."

I ignored both Jenna's rolled-in lips and Katie Rose's gasp. Damn Dianna.

"Carter…"

"I'm not going to talk about it, Katie Rose."

"I'm Kate. And I'm not going to ask…"

Jenna set down her phone—texting Cam, no doubt, to tattle on my drink of choice. Cam was the whiskey drinker. I maybe had a beer or two during the week, rarely more on the weekends. Just never really acquired the taste for any of the alcoholic beverages. I ran my hands over my face, wishing I had. Wishing I wanted to party more often. Maybe that would ease the tension ripping at my insides.

"I am," Jenna said. "Because that…that looked like some serious and painful history."

I met Jenna's knowing gaze. Yeah, she would understand. Didn't mean I wanted to hash it out. "It was. Now, we're nothing. Her choice."

Except I *might* have a child. A kid on the cusp of puberty. And I'd missed all those years because I hadn't insisted then that she prove the child wasn't mine. I'd simply accepted yet another one of her lies…

I needed to get a paternity test, stat. Sooner than that. Now.

My muscles tensed, telling me to get out, to find a lawyer, to get the answers I needed.

I sucked in a breath as I met Kate's concerned gaze. I blew it out slowly. I was older, wiser, than I'd been when I dated Dianna.

More than likely, what Dianna told me now outside the restaurant was a lie. I didn't know what to believe, but I vowed I would ferret out the truth.

No matter what it cost me.

Jenna tipped her head, no doubt watching the play of emotions as they ran across my face. "You're still hurting."

The waitress set the whiskey at my elbow and I downed it in one long gulp. I needed another, but I resisted the urge just as I ignored the three sets of wide eyes watching me.

"Know what you want, ladies?" I asked. Sooner they ate, the sooner I could contact Remy and get to the bottom of Dianna's newest bombshell.

Jenna and Kate ordered. I handed over my menu after ordering the fish I probably wouldn't touch. I wasn't hungry.

Jenna's phone vibrated.

"I'm not dropping this," Jenna said. She glanced down at her screen and nodded a little. "Cam's coming, by the way."

I wasn't surprised either that Cam would arrive soon or that Jenna wouldn't let the topic drop. That's why I hadn't left already. Jenna, Kate, Cam, even I deserved the truth.

I had poison in me—in the form of my ex. I covered my face with my clammy palms. My breath stuttered. *Shit*. I was doing better. After nearly eleven years, the edges of the grief, the anger were blunted.

Now, everything from that time with Dianna came back in sharp clarity.

"Carter?" Kate's voice rose in question.

"She told me she'd been screwing Dean and me for months. She said Dean knocked her up. She said she had to marry Dean," I said.

"But?" Jenna asked, her voice soft.

"She just said the boy…his name's Sean…" I stared down at the table, wishing the growing ache in my chest would dissipate. Wishing I could breathe.

"She said he's your son," Kate said.

"We heard her," Jenna said.

I heard Kate's chair drag closer and then her arms were around me, soft hair tickling my cheek. I dropped my hands from my burning eyes and hugged her back.

"If she kept him from you all this time, I'm so, so sorry," Kate said.

My swallow was thick, the emotion ripping at my throat. "Me, too." So goddamn much. I never even got to have a say in her decision.

"No wonder you got the hell out of Austin." Jenna's voice fell, quiet with sympathy.

"I'd just been too blind to see what was right in front of me. Dean was going to take over his father's business, earn six-figures straight out of college. That's what Dianna wanted. A rich man to let her lunch and shop. I didn't fit that bill."

Then. I smiled grimly. Now, I could buy and sell Dean many times over.

And I planned to. Soon. Because it was good business.

Jenna seemed to be on the same wavelength as my thoughts. "No wonder she's so interested in you now. You're on the cover of one of those techie magazines, and that article that came out about you and Regan a couple of days ago gave an estimated worth of your company."

"Yeah, I had no idea." Kate shook her head, seemingly dazed. "Don't I feel like the loser sibling."

"You're not a loser," I said, squeezing her fingers.

"And Dianna's not getting near you again," Kate said. "I won't allow her to sink those manicured fingernails into your savings account." Her face grimaced because we both knew Dianna would have access to my money and my life *if* Sean were my son.

"Not to worry," I said with the tiniest of grins. That I could find anything to smile about in this situation showed me I was finally able to face my history and my regrets. "I know well what she is. Today was an attempt to see if she could seduce me or hurt me or…whatever. Use me, I guess. She can't."

"Her betrayal all those years ago just made you stronger. Wiser," Jenna said. "Too bad it had to be such a painful lesson."

"Those are the ones we remember best," I said.

Jenna nodded, the golden highlights in her blonde hair glinting from the reflected light.

"I want to beat the tar out of her. I always hated her, near as much as I hated that…that bitch, Kim." Kate's face turned fierce, almost scary. "Now, though, it's pretty even which of the women were worse."

We had our share of problems, sure, but this gal would always look out for me, just as I would for her. My family was messed up, but I was lucky as hell to have each of them love me, and I knew it.

I cleared my throat, unable to trip further down the path of betrayals and bad memories. "What's with the curse words? Mama can still wrestle you to the ground and shove soap in your mouth," I said, trying for stern, but I was too busy enjoying the moment of closeness with my sister to care—that much.

Kate sniffed. "I'd like to see her try. It's her damn fault I'm angry enough to cuss in the first place."

I rolled my lips inward, refusing to condone our mother's choices. I hadn't wanted to go along with them then, and I could understand Kate's anger with our mother's choices now.

"Love you, Katie…Kate."

I felt her smile against my shoulder.

"Better." She hugged me harder. "Sorry I was grumpy. Jenna and Cam told me you wanted to clear the air and be honest." She patted my cheek. "Just so you know, I am serious. I plan to beat Dianna with my purse if I ever see her."

"You can borrow my bat," Jenna said. When I met her gaze, her gray eyes shining with ferocity. She looked like a Viking princess.

"No need," I said, my voice dry. "I've had years to get over her."

"Her, maybe," Jenna said. "But not the huge bomb she just dropped."

Right. She and Cam thought Jenna was pregnant a few months ago. They both mourned the loss of a child that had never been. With their kind of love, I could understand why. For me, if I had to raise a kid with Dianna…I just couldn't fathom what that would be like. We wouldn't agree on anything. That didn't mean I wasn't torn up over the choice of being involved taken from me.

"She sure does play dirty," Kate muttered as she pulled back, glancing toward the front door, no doubt expecting Dianna to materialize there. "I bet she read that article about you and Everly…*Regan*." Kate's smile was small and sly. "I bet she didn't like how into a famous singer you looked in that photo."

I shrugged.

"Why is money such a turn on for some women?" Jenna asked with a slight sneer.

"Or men," Kate said.

Jenna dipped her head. "True. I mean, so what if you're loaded? If anything, you're probably more of an asshole now than you were in college."

Kate patted my cheek. "I don't know. Carter's always been a good big brother."

"Thanks, chickadee," I said, falling back onto Kate's other childhood nickname. The familiarity soaked through me, giving me a moment of pleasure. But I had to focus on the issue at hand.

Jenna studied me with an intensity that made my skin prickle. Lucky for me, Cam showed up with his entourage, causing enough fuss with the patrons for the ladies' attention to be pulled off me.

Jenna's guys were at a nearby table and Cam's guys joined them as Cam slid into the seat next to Jenna's.

After kissing Jenna the way I'd kissed Regan just days before, Cam scanned our serious faces.

"What'd I miss?"

Jenna handed Cam her chopsticks. "I'll tell you later," she murmured.

I shook my head. "I'll tell him. I should have before now, anyway. But first I need another whiskey."

CHAPTER SEVENTEEN | Regan

Not gonna lie: My father stomped into my suite and blew into an irate tirade after he saw the picture of me with Carter. I mostly tuned him out. Thankfully, he received a call from the record label gushing about how good this relationship would be for my image.

Dad huffed into silence. That didn't mean the glares or the mean comments about Carter subsided. With each one, my anger and frustration with my father grew.

"If you'd just sign the papers for your next album, everything would get easier," he grumbled.

"I have to meet with multiple reporters—press *you* set up. And, I'd planned to look over the papers now…" I let the sentence die off. He didn't bother looking contrite. We both knew he didn't like Carter. More importantly, my father didn't like what Carter represented: me, having a life that was not run by my dad.

Oh, yeah, I was aware that's how the record label and even my staff saw the situation. Well, I was now that Mindy sat me down when the picture came through and told me that, Darryl nodding, arms crossed and scowl building, with each of Mindy's words.

That was a lot to take in.

"I'll sit with you," Dad said.

I shook my head. "They feel more comfortable with one-on-ones," I said.

"Maybe I'm not comfortable with what they ask."

I patted his hand. "I'm meeting with Susan Phipps for a piece in the *Times* and then with John Mitchell, the guy you embedded with us. It'll be fine."

But I worried the situation wouldn't be fine. John Mitchell wanted a scoop, a career-altering story.

I breezed through my interview with Susan, hitting it off with the forty-something woman. She was smart and insightful. Much as I wanted to tell her about my impending album to get her take on how the industry would react, I managed to keep that secret to myself. I did, however, enjoy the witty back-and-forth.

After watching Vannah implode, I understood anything and everything I uttered was fair game, and most of what celebrities said was taken out of context. Still, I was smiling when John Mitchell waltzed into the backstage room we were using.

It slid from my face as he continued to stalk toward me. Not likely we'd be friendly after the lies and nearly-nude photos he'd printed of me.

"Ms. Leroux."

I rose to shake his hand, tension building there and seeping up my arm and into my shoulders. Meeting him, here, now, was a strategic decision. One I hoped I didn't regret.

"Mr. Mitchell."

"John, please." His thin lips stretched in a smile. He had one of those narrow mustaches like Clark Gable used to wear. On John, the short, thin, graying hairs reminded me of a caterpillar. I forced my eyes up to his, trying to suppress a shudder.

"So, Everly," he said with that same narrow, tight-lipped grin. I tried hard not to be offended that he hadn't asked what I preferred to be called, but I was annoyed. I smoothed my face into that blank look I'd perfected over years of dealing with my father.

"Tell me a bit about your tour. Are you sad to see it end?"

"We put a lot into each performance. The fans deserve our absolute best, and I strive to exceed that expectation."

"So you're saying you do sing your own songs? That you are the talent as well as the…" He looked me over in a way that made my skin crawl. "Sex symbol?"

Oh, that was gross. I tried to keep the anger from my voice. "I sing all my own songs."

"That must be exhausting," John said, leaning forward. He was going somewhere.

"I've been on the road, constantly, for the last five months," I hedged.

John nodded, cocking his head in a way that might make me think he was sympathetic. It didn't.

"I can see how the late nights could wear on you. Is that why you take pills? To relax you? To focus your mind?"

I jolted upright, blinking at him multiple times. "Excuse me?"

"I wanted to talk about your drug habit—the one you started with James Peele."

"I most surely did not," I snapped.

"No need to get so defensive." That tone he used—could this man be any more patronizing? "James and I talk. Reminisce about his glory days."

I hoped those were in James' past, not out of pettiness but because the last time I saw James, he'd been so high he'd barely been able to put two words together, let alone stand upright for the photos on the red carpet. James hurt me, true, but watching him slowly destroy his mind and body made me ache. Not enough to help him—not after his role in Vannah's decision to end her life.

"James told me about your parties."

What parties?

Sure, we attended many and even threw a few at my house in Malibu. I'm sure there had been drugs there—no way to police everyone walking through the door. And God knew I'd been naïve about the hookups James had in the cabana and probably other rooms in *my* house as I played hostess to mostly *his* friends.

But I didn't own that house anymore. I'd sold that place not long after we broke up, needing a fresh start that had nothing to do with James.

John leaned forward like he was Oprah or Dr. Phil or something. "That's why I'm here—to hear the details about your struggles directly from you."

"You're going to have a long time to wait, then," I said.

"You don't have to hide it anymore. We can share your addiction with your fans, maybe get you the help you need. And, anyway, it's not like you really have any secrets."

And there it was. The offhand mention to the story he'd written about me. I glanced toward the door, wishing I hadn't sent Mindy out for a cup of tea. This interview was hostile and ridiculous.

"C'mon, Ev, your dad invited me. He wants you to get help."

My back stiffened and the blood thrummed through my veins in heavy pulses. This man…calling me Ev. James used to call me that. And to insinuate he knew the details about my relationship with my father…

John eyed me with a superior level of satisfaction, like he knew I was struggling to hold my emotions together.

"Most of my fans are still in high school, Mr. Mitchell," I said. My voice remained even, just as I willed it. Because it was my instrument. Something *I* controlled. This man did not nor would he ever see me undone.

"Those young ladies look up to me, and I take that role seriously. *Very* seriously." I had to, what with my mother's history of substance abuse. "For that reason, along with a myriad of others, I have not and do not ever plan to take illegal substances."

John sat back, his gaze flattening like a cobra's before a strike. "How about legal ones?"

"I don't know what you're talking about." I stood, my knees shaking with the stress. "And I don't appreciate you accusing me of activities I did not take part in."

I headed to the door.

"All I want is the exclusive from your own mouth as to why you're taking medication. Why you use in the first place." His gaze slithered over me in a way that had me wishing for extra layers. Darryl stepped in front of me and I wanted to sag with relief. But I couldn't—just as I forced my facial muscles to retain their neutral position.

John ignored Darryl and continued to talk around him.

"Or you can tell me about your relationship with the Grace

brothers. I mean, we've seen how close you are with Carter. Is that because Camden was already in a serious relationship?"

I opened the door to the room. "I thought we were going to discuss an ongoing, in-depth piece about my career," I said. My legs felt weak, like I'd run a marathon.

"That's what my editor wants to do," John said with a dip of his head.

"I'm more than happy to discuss the potential there, or my music and the evolving plans I have on that front. I'm happy to discuss my break from James, or the show, or even to focus on your dumb questions about this tour, but I will not have lies thrown in my face. And I will not discuss my relationship with Carter. Especially not with you."

His smile widened. "So you admit there is a relationship with Camden Grace's brother?"

My heart leaped against my ribs and I stood, facing off against a well-known reporter that could make my life much too challenging.

"We already made a statement that Carter and I are dating."

"So, you like to date rich men?" John asked.

Oh, my god, this dude was getting on my last nerve.

I wanted to tell him I had no idea about Carter's bank account. That Carter knew more Shakespeare quotes than I did. That he was sexy and well-spoken and everything I wanted in a man. But this reporter had already scented blood. I couldn't say another word. Not if I wanted to make it to the end of the tour without a huge blow up from my father.

"My private life is just that—private. Goodbye, Mr. Mitchell."

He stood as though he had all the time in the world. I bit off a growl of irritation.

"I'm here as long as it takes. And don't worry, I have more pieces to write already."

A thrill of apprehension bit into my stomach. Please, please not about my recording sessions in Austin. If my father heard my plans from a reporter, well…the chance of him leaving on that trip I'd bought for him shrank and so did the opportunity to record the album I wanted to create.

"I'd really like to tell my readers the truth." He glanced around. "Getting better access to you throughout the day would help with that. You know, so I can see what you do and how you do it."

"And if I decline?" I said through clenched teeth.

He shrugged. "Well, let's see…your father was here this morning, demanding specific water in your name. And then, there's the follow up with Camden Grace's camp. I'm still waiting for his brother, Carter, to return my call to give me his side of your relationship, though I think it's fairly obvious that you two share a physical connection."

The effort to keep my face neutral hurt. But I managed. At least, I hoped I did. "I'm really going to have to question the validity of your source," I said. "To your editor."

John's smile curved up more, giving him the impression of a vintage movie villain. "Oh, I'm sure you will. And that's why my editor sent me. Because I'm very careful with my sources."

A chill swept over me as the implication stabbed me in the heart. Someone close to me—someone I saw every day, that I trusted, had talked to this reporter. No. *Lied* to him about me.

I closed the door softly behind John, not willing to interact further. Nothing I said would change the trajectory of this story and what it would do to my life.

Because the person lying to John wanted to hurt me.

CHAPTER EIGHTEEN | Carter

As soon as I could extract myself from my family, I called Remy and explained the situation. He'd been there. He understood.

"It's your money," Remy said on a sigh. "Dianna sees the writing on the wall. I always said she was smart."

"Not if she lied to me about a child," I muttered.

My son.

If he was my son, I'd shower Sean with love and affection he'd most likely lost during those early years. I just hoped it would be enough for he and I to build a relationship. I needed to protect my heart, but already, I was planning a future with Sean.

I shook my head. This was Dianna. I needed to be cautious. Methodical. The next step was to prove my relationship to the boy.

"Get me the best family law lawyer, will ya?" I asked. "The very best. I want to get this paternity test done as soon as possible."

Dianna had been so adamant all those years ago that Dean got her pregnant. She'd seemed pleased when she informed me they were getting married in May, just days after the two of them graduated from UT.

Smug. That's how her face looked. Like she'd won.

I remembered asking her if she was sure.

"Positive," she'd responded. "It's not like I ever let you touch me without a condom."

That was true. She hadn't. At the time, I'd been so hurt I hadn't realized what she was saying—she and Dean had unprotected sex during the time she and I also had a sexual relationship. When that realization came, along with her blithe tossing over of my feelings, I'd been enraged. And scared about what she could have passed along to me. Thankfully, my tests came back clean.

"You sure you want to antagonize Dean with that right now?" Remy asked.

"I get where you're coming from," I said. "I do. But if he's my son… She didn't even care about Sean's feelings, Rem. He's just another pawn in her game. I can't let my kid be treated like that."

Remy had been there, in our shared living room, for moral support. He was the one who told Dianna to get out.

"You remember that conversation?" I asked.

"Yeah, that's not something I'll forget. God, I wish you'd never gotten tangled up with that woman," he growled.

"You and me both. But I can't regret a child."

"If he's yours."

Yes. *If.*

That's what I needed to find out.

———————— ★ ————————

I stared out into the dark night as I sipped more from my glass. I made a face. The whiskey was becoming too much for my esophagus and stomach.

I wondered what Regan was doing. I missed her. Badly.

I wanted to romance the hell out of Regan, in part because she deserved it but also to get us splashed many more times all over the big publications. Dianna loved those magazines, and she'd read each story they printed about Regan and me with growing dismay. I grinned drunkenly into my amber liquid in the pretty cut-crystal glass.

That would make Dianna realize I'd moved on. No, *up*. Up to a sexier, more talented lady.

I bowed my head and cupped my palms to my ears, wondering how my life had turned into such a cluster in the span of twenty-four hours.

My phone rang.

Regan was calling.

Huh.

I wasn't sure what to say to her. I stared at her name for a long moment, debating whether to answer.

I blew out a breath, trying to calm my nerves. Was she scared or hurt or…

"H'lo?"

CHAPTER NINETEEN | Regan

I closed the door to my dressing room and leaned against it, not worried about smashing my hair flat. My eyes slammed shut, hard, probably messing up the false eyelashes and eyeliner and whatever else I'd be in trouble for when the makeup and hair artists came to do their final check.

My head ached with deep tension. Even my father laid off his questions about the contract and badmouthing Carter when he noticed the strain during the last sound check. He'd brought me a pain pill that he said should stave off the potential migraine I couldn't afford to have. Not if I was going to perform. And I had to perform.

But my tension wasn't from my relationship issues Mindy and I had to smooth over earlier. The niggling that came from missing Carter turned into a full-blown ache. Unable to resist the need, I called him.

He answered the phone with a slurred greeting.

"Are you okay?" I asked.

"Sure." A pause. "I'm drunk."

That was obvious. I didn't know what to say so I settled for, "All right."

"Whatcha need, Regan? New pics of us show up? Damn, I hope I haven't failed you, too."

I nibbled at my lip. Something happened. Something bad if he was drinking heavily and worrying over my actions.

"Of course not. You tried to save me." I blinked back the tears that threatened as I realized just how kind that gesture had been. Getting backstage was never easy, yet Carter never hesitated to ask his brother for a favor to make sure I was safe.

He went out of this way for me. And I'd seriously considered ending any chance we had before we had that chance to begin with.

Even from that first night in the bar, before he propositioned me, I'd known this was a man I could fall for. Way harder than I had for James. Because Carter was a little broken, like me, but his heart was purely selfless. Once I realized that, he scared me. He scared me more now that John had people questioning my reasons for hanging out with him in the first place.

He sighed. "So, the article was right? You just wanted me to ease your meeting with Cam."

Maybe it was because he was drunk. Maybe I just needed to say these words. "That's the crux of the whole problem. I *do* want you. More than I've wanted any man. I wanted to see if we could have that next date."

"A date? Yes…I wanna be with you. You're the first woman since Dianna that's held my attention. You make me laugh. Being with you is…" He lapsed into a long silence. "It's nice. I'm gonna go now. Cam's sitting here on the porch, and he's glaring at me. Prolly cuz I'm saying stupid shit."

"I don't think anything you say is stupid. And while I do want to work with your brother, that has nothing to do with me spending time with you."

He hiccupped. "Huh."

"Carter?"

"Yep."

"Will you remember this? That I called and that I told you I…" I sucked in a deep breath and said the words that had wanted to burst forth since I saw him looking at me in that bar. "I really like you. From the moment I saw you in Denver…"

"I haven't ever wanted a woman like I want you," Carter mumbled.

He disconnected the phone call, leaving me gasping around the flutters in my chest.

Dianna. I didn't know who the woman was, but I understood that saying her name hurt him.

Someone knocked. I picked up my bottle of water and uncapped it as I called, "Come in!"

Mindy poked her head around the door. "How are you feeling?"

I'd closeted myself in my dressing room after my "talk" with John. I studied Mindy, wondering if I could confide my concerns in her. No, I wasn't ready to share the comments John made, not even with my closest confidante.

"Better," I said, which was true. I grinned at her. "A lot better, actually."

Talking to Carter, realizing he cared what I thought about him, eased my concerns. At least I knew *he* wasn't the mole in my crew. That all led me to realize that while the situation these next weeks was fraught, I could and would manage both John and my fans' expectations.

"How long until I go on?" I asked.

"About thirty minutes. Can I let hair and makeup in for final?"

"Sure."

She opened the door and I was swarmed by the crew. What I wouldn't give to go out on stage with just my guitar. Maybe the piano. To never again worry about how perky my cleavage was, how perfect my smoky eye shadow.

As I stared in the mirror, still, as the two men and two women fussed over my long hair and reapplied more bronzer, I made myself a promise: I was getting out of this life and building the one I really wanted.

Now I was old enough, and, hopefully, wise and strong enough, to survive the music industry and create a space of my own. One that my father did not share.

If not, meeting Camden Grace, one of my favorite singers, and picking his brain would help me get to where I needed to go.

I stood, and the chattering artists fell back.

"You look gorgeous," Sybilline gushed as she straightened a few hairs that trailed down my back.

"Thanks," I said. I headed toward the door. The sooner I went out there and did my set, the closer I was to the end of this tour and taking my life back.

CHAPTER TWENTY | Carter

"Real smooth with the ladies," Cam said with a faint chuckle from behind me.

I turned, bleary-eyed, but managed to make him out from the shadows. I clambered up the steps and collapsed into a chair with a grunt.

"Glad you laid off the sauce." Cam inclined his head toward the bottle still on the steps.

"I'm stupid when I drink." I stared down, at nothing as I sighed.

Oh, I would remember what I'd said to Regan. I winced. Alcohol didn't dim my memories, just my filter. I groaned. No way to pull myself out of this craptastic day.

"How come you never told me about a possible kid?" Cam lifted a cut-crystal snifter and took a sip of the same booze I'd been guzzling most of the afternoon.

"I'm an idiot." I dropped my head into my hands and groaned. "I believed Dianna when she told me the kid was Dean's. I am so damn stupid."

"That shady snake hurt you."

"Yeah, well, I guess I deserved it. For believing she ever loved me. And that she had any morals. And that she'd tell the truth about anything, ever."

Cam turned to face me, his face half in shadow. The other half seemed to vibrate with tension.

"That's kinda like me blaming myself for Kim's indiscretions."

I leaned back so that my head was propped against the wooden slats of the chair. "Don't you?" I murmured.

"I did." Cam gazed out into the darker shadows of the low, rolling hills beyond our property. "Now, after hearing the whole story, I'm not so sure I can shoulder that blame. There's a lot to go around."

I eased my head back, rolling it in an effort to relieve the tension in my shoulders. "Your situation was different than mine. And Laurence was a twatwaffle. So's Dean for that matter. Can't see him willingly raising another man's son."

Cam's lips twitched. Then, he threw his head back and laughed.

"You're right about that." Cam chuckled. "Twatwaffle. Never heard that one before but it suits our uncle."

"I'm laying off the curse words. Katie…I mean Kate's got a mouth on her now. I don't want Mama to think I'm complicit in those dirty words passing her lips."

Cam sobered up fast, as he did each time we discussed Kate. "Kate has a right to be angry. I'm angry with Mama, too." Cam held up his hands when I opened my mouth. "Doesn't mean I don't love her and respect her, but she made some poor decisions. Lots of hurt to go around because of it."

I went back to looking for answers in the sky and stars. None came.

"Back to Dianna," Cam said.

"Don't want to talk about her."

"Let's talk about how she's responsible for her actions, just as your ex-buddy, current twatwaffle Dean is responsible for his. Them hurting you, the cheating and the lies, taking away your choice to know your child, *if* that's what happened, that's all on them."

"I've got to find a way to get a clean test, Cam. Dianna'll cheat the situation, if for no other reason than to get at my money."

"Sounds like you dodged a bullet with her, no matter what happens with the paternity."

"Shit, man," I muttered. "I wouldn't have been in that situation if I'd paid more attention." If I'd handled our final confrontation better.

"Carter, you were twenty-three years old. Nobody sees the world clearly then."

I sure as hell didn't. Probably didn't now.

"I said some nasty things. To both of them."

Cam didn't miss a beat. "In the heat of the moment? That's to be expected. You were surprised. And hurt."

Damn, I loved my baby brother. He always, *always* had my back. Even when I quit talking to him for years and he thought I had sex with his scheming ex. I shuddered, detesting the mere idea of touching Kim.

In fact, now that I thought about it, Kim reminded me of Dianna, but at least I'd had the sense not to fuck her. And not just because she was my brother's wife, though that was more than reason enough.

I'd seen that calculating look in Dianna's eyes today; it was one Kim wore, too. I'd never understood why I found that so off-putting until I met Regan. She didn't have an agenda toward me. At least I hadn't thought so, but now that John Mitchell wrote those articles…

I slumped into the chair and drank the water Cam handed me. My life was complicated.

"I almost hit her, Cam."

There it was, my deepest shame.

He was silent for a long time. Finally, I looked over to find him waiting for me to face him.

"*Almost?*"

"I punched the wall near her. For a moment…" I swallowed down my whiskey-tinted bile. "For a moment, I really wanted it to be her."

Cam leaned back in his chair and stretched out his legs, crossing one ankle over the other. "And you think you did something wrong. *Almost* hitting her."

"Stop emphasizing the word." I set the glass down and tunneled my fingers through my hair. "I wanted to hit her."

"But you didn't."

I yanked at the strands of hair. "I wanted to," I said, my voice low, my guilt and disgust insidious, making my skin itch and my insides roil. "I really wanted to make her hurt like I did."

I heard Cam shift but didn't look up. I'd beat the shit out of the man we considered our father mere months before the situation with Dianna. That was why I started taking classes at the dojo once I moved to California. I had to make sure I had complete control over my emotions. I couldn't lose control like that—I couldn't take a swing at a woman. Or another man, for that matter. Not after seeing the damage I'd done to Laurence. Even if I did still think he deserved it.

If I'd unleashed that virulence on a woman... My stomach revolted, and I pressed a hand to my mouth.

"Look, Carter, I get you're hard on yourself because I pull the same shit. I destroyed an entire trailer and all the musical instruments in it when Laurence died." He paused, running his hand across his chin.

"You know, I hadn't really thought about it like this, but maybe that's how I let out all the pent-up rage I held against Kim and Laurence. The writeups about my 'temper tantrum' were ugly and deservedly so." Cam shut his eyes and shook his head. "I was out of control with my rage."

"You broke shit. You paid for it."

Cam met my gaze as he nodded. "I did. And I met Jenna because of my bad actions, so I can't be too upset about the whole mess. And neither should you because here's the bottom line: you were in a terrible situation and *you did not hurt anyone*."

"But—"

"But *nothing*," Cam growled. "I want to hit that woman for you now. I want to, but I won't. Just like I wanted to hit Kim for cheating on me with the man I considered..."

Cam blew out a breath.

"All I'm saying is I get it. I get why you wanted to lash out. And I'm proud of you for hitting that wall. In your situation, I don't know if I could have done any better."

I absorbed Cam's words and tried—I really tried—to see the

situation from his perspective. Could he be correct? Could I slough off the guilt and shame I'd held in for so many years?

My head pounded as some of my choices floated into focus.

"It's why I didn't want another girlfriend," I said.

"What?" Cam asked.

"I worried. I worried I'd hurt her. A girlfriend." The words tasted bitter, like rhubarb, on my tongue, coating my mouth and slicking down into my chest. *I might hurt a woman.*

"That right there's your answer, man," Cam said, his gaze filled with conviction.

"Thanks." The breath that left me seemed to take some of the anger and shame with it. Maybe holding the incident in, to myself, hadn't been the wisest choice. Maybe I needed to talk about my feelings, my anger, and my reactions.

Because right now? I felt…not good, but better. Like I could finally walk out from under the shadow Dianna and Dean cast over me all these years.

"I don't know what to do now," I said.

"About what?"

"My possible son. Dean. Dianna. My board wants me to buy the company," I said. "Dean's."

Cam sat for a long moment, then he leaned over and clasped his hand to my shoulder. I appreciated the affectionate gesture. "You've always been the sensitive one, Carter. I just hope you know what you're doing. And that it's for the right reasons."

Me, too.

"Buying his company makes sense on paper. I've had Remy involved from the start. But…" I blew out a breath. "If he isn't my kid, how can I take away Sean's security?"

"I don't know the right answer." Cam's face contorted into a strange combination of grief and anger. "If he's your son, Dianna has a lot to answer for, keeping him from you."

I exhaled some of the tension I'd carried since starting my conversation with Dianna. "I can't destroy the boy's sense of security."

"You said it's a good buy?" Cam asked after a long moment.

I nodded. "If I don't snap the company up, a competitor of mine will and they'll have better capabilities across the visual communication aspect of the apps than I will."

Cam settled back in his chair and stared out into the night. "Well, then. You've managed to land yourself in a right cluster."

CHAPTER TWENTY-ONE | Regan

Later that night, once I was showered and in a comfy pair of sweats, I picked up my phone and debated whether to text Carter or not. Before I could talk myself out of it, I opened the app and typed.

Regan: *I hope you're sleeping off your liquor. I liked talking to you earlier. I just hope you remember what I said and what you said.*

I set my phone aside and picked up my e-reader, hoping to get lost in someone else's drama for an hour or two. My phone pinged.

Carter: *Cam made me drink a gallon of water and a pot of coffee. Is your show over?*

Regan: *Yes.*

Carter: *How'd it go?*

I didn't want to talk about my show.

Regan: *Fine.*

Carter: *I'm sorry for what I said earlier.*

I squeezed my eyes shut. I didn't want him to be sorry.

Carter: *I ran into my ex earlier today.*

Regan: *Dianna?*

Before I could respond, my phone rang. I stared at his name. He knew I had my phone. With shaking fingers, I answered.

"Hello?" I whispered. I rolled my eyes. I was locked in my room on the bus. The air conditioning was on and we were heading down the interstate. No one was here to listen to my calls.

"I just wanted to hear your voice," Carter muttered. "Regan…"

I waited.

"I had a rough day."

"I kind of figured since you were smashed at nine."

"Hang on," he said. I heard a door open and close. "I came out on the porch so I wouldn't disturb Cam and Jen."

"You're staying with them?" I asked.

"Yeah. Cam and I…we had a rough patch for a few years in there. Didn't talk. Now, we're making up for lost time."

"Because of your ex?" I asked, holding my breath.

"Nope. That was because of his, actually. But…well, maybe. Dianna dumped me a few months after Cam's marriage imploded."

"Her loss," I said.

"Which one?" I heard the smile creep into his voice.

I grinned in response. How silly of me to get so giddy over Carter's amusement. But I was. "Both, I'd bet."

"Mmm. I am better looking."

"And that's all a woman looks for in her life partner," I said, my tone drier than an Arizona breeze.

"For a lot of women and probably men, too, yeah, that is."

Something in his tone told me I better tread carefully. I was famous enough to understand what he was saying.

"Not me," I said.

"Not you," he replied in a soft voice. "I haven't wanted to be anyone's partner of any sort for years."

I nibbled my lip as I looked up at the ceiling. The large bus hummed over the highway. I liked these moments. They were peaceful.

"I haven't either," I said. "James said some nasty things when he ended our relationship. They hurt me. And, well, I didn't take my mother's death well. I think…what you saw the other night with my father…"

I didn't know what to say. I wasn't sure how to express the growing certainty that I was making a mistake, letting my dad run my life. I just wasn't sure yet how to correct my error.

"His loss," Carter said, repeating back my phrase and causing my lips to tilt up in the first stirrings of a smile. After another beat, he said, "I'm sorry this James guy hurt you."

"Ditto for you, Carter. I don't want you to be sad or upset."

"Then let's talk about something else. It seems that our pasts are depressing."

"What do you want to talk about?" I asked.

"Not sure. Tell me about your show."

I hesitated. "I don't like performing," I said, the words tumbling out of my mouth.

"At all?" he asked.

"I like singing."

"Sing me something," he said.

My neck tensed. "You don't think I can?"

"Of course I know you can sing. I just want to hear you sing something that you love."

Oh. That was sweet. Though the butterflies pounded through my stomach, I started singing one of my new songs, keeping my voice soft, the longing for meaning and love pouring from my vocal cords.

When I finished, Carter whistled low.

"You need to sing that for Cam."

"We'll see."

"No, I'm serious, Regan. He's going to call you. I'll give him your number today. Sing him that song."

We were quiet.

"If you can sing like that, why do you do the pop music?" Carter asked.

"It's my brand," I said on a sigh. "Not that there is anything wrong with that music. But I don't want to have to dance or sing catchy lyrics all the time. I just want...I want..." I trailed off, finding telling the truth, even to Carter, even in the middle of the night, terrifying.

"To be you. To be real."

"Yeah."

We both waited, breathing softly into our respective phones.

"That's why you want to meet with Cam. I bet you like his music because it's raw. Just about as real as any out there."

"Yes, that's why."

Again, there was a lengthy pause.

"I...I think I need to make some changes in my life." Saying the words hurt, but relief coursed through me.

He made a soft humming sound in the back of his throat. "I stirred up some serious darkness in your father."

I squeezed my eyes shut. "It's been there, I think, for a long time."

I sucked on my bottom lip as I considered Dad's reaction to Carter. He'd done the same with James, but James had been so charming during those first few weeks of our relationship. Like he got me. Like he cared and was willing to fight for me—to help pull me out of my father's orbit.

Carter was speaking and I focused on him, though I continued to reel from my thoughts. "Part of that honesty I asked for? I want it to include telling me when you're sick of me."

I smiled. "I'm not sick of you."

"I'm glad." His voice seemed deeper, softer, when he said, "I think us meeting when we did… The timing's probably off for both of us, huh?"

My heart sank as my nose prickled with the beginnings of tears. "Probably."

"That doesn't change the fact I want to see you again."

And my emotions bounced back, my heart thudding in my chest. "Are you sure? I mean, you said earlier—"

"I'm sure," he said.

"All right." I snuggled deeper into my pillow. "I'd like that. You have no idea how much I'd like to be seen out with you."

"You understand people are going to put more expectations on this, probably sooner than we're ready for," he said.

"Yeah, I know. Are you okay with that?"

He didn't hesitate. "I am."

"Good," I murmured. "Tell me about you. About you and your brother."

"You just want details to help you win Cam over."

I giggled. "Nope. That thought hadn't crossed my mind, but now…"

He laughed. "All right. Let me think of a good story."

I fell asleep listening to Carter tell me about growing up on his ranch.

Those were the last peaceful moments I had the rest of the week.

CHAPTER TWENTY-TWO | Carter

Getting Dianna to agree to the paternity test proved as difficult as I expected. So was the conversation I had with my mama about Dianna's claim.

Mama, always a Texas lady with that core of solid steel most men couldn't match, simply nodded and then pulled me in for a hug. I rested my head against her shoulder and closed my eyes. I'd missed my family while I was away.

"Is this…situation why you left so suddenly?" Mama asked.

I took a deep breath. "Yes."

Mama pursed her lips in *that* way: the one that meant she had thoughts she wouldn't express about Dianna. Probably my actions, too.

"And she told you before the baby was her new boyfriend's?"

"Yes, Mama."

"Well, the first important detail is to find out what father is listed on the birth certificate," Mama said.

I raised an eyebrow.

She shrugged, patting her salt-and-pepper bob like she did when she was nervous. "I refused to have Laurence's named on you boys' certificates. Seems like this woman would have the biological father listed."

"I'll get my lawyer to get the documents. Thanks, Mama. For

the advice and for making sure we had something of our father to hold on to."

"You're welcome, son. I should have seen this earlier." She shook her head, distress stamped across her features. "If this boy is yours…"

"Sean." I liked saying his name.

She smiled. "If Sean is your son, I expect to meet him soon. I got lots of hugs to make up lost time."

My throat swelled with emotion so I simply nodded. Then, I hugged her. She smelled like she always did, and damn if I didn't hold on a little tighter and a little longer, just to soak up some comfort.

———————— ★ ————————

Much as I wanted to see Regan again, our timing didn't mesh for the next few days. I was frustrated to know she was within hours of me, but thanks John Mitchell's personal vendetta— now stating Regan was popping prescriptions pills and that her lip syncing was off in last night's show—she was too busy to talk.

She sounded depressed, which worried me. And, after hearing her sing, there was no doubt in my mind that Regan was one of the most talented performers in the industry. I told Cam as much, and he nodded.

"I'll call her," he promised.

"When?" I demanded.

"Soon," was his laconic reply.

I couldn't nag him because a bug in my newest release needed a fast, intricate fix that required me to fly out to my San Francisco offices and meet with my team of developers. Between us, it still took over thirty hours to complete the necessary update.

Even during my busiest moments, Regan and I texted back and forth. We'd both keep the Scrabble app open and add to our current game when we could. But with each day, I found myself looking forward to when we could connect in person. At least on the phone. I missed her laugh and her quick witticisms.

I missed smelling her shampoo and seeing her eyes light up with mischief and pleasure. I hoped she felt the same way but was too afraid to ask—too afraid to label us in case she didn't agree.

My new family law lawyer, Kelly Smith, told me her requests for further information and a testing time kept being stonewalled by Dianna's lawyer. Tomorrow, Kelly planned to file the eyewitness reports from Jenna, Kate, Jenna's bodyguards and some of the restaurant staff with a local family court to force the issue.

Dean was sure to go ballistic when he learned of the court filing, but what choice did I have?

I flew back to Austin just in time to run out to my new building and see the progress there. I needed sleep, but I tossed and turned all night, wondering if attempting a relationship with Regan was stupid. After all, my life took a turn into complicated and messy. Regan continued to struggle with that jerk-wad John and who knew what other issues.

By the time I woke the next morning, gritty-eyed and foul-tempered, Dean had sent a message back through the lawyers: if I added a few million dollars to my offer for his company, I could have access to the kid and the test.

The idea of paying huge sums of money to get in touch with

a child disgusted me, but part of me was desperate enough to write the check.

Kelly and Remy forbid me from responding.

"Then, what should I do?" I asked Kelly, as I pressed my fingers to my burning eyelids.

"Paying him would expedite the situation. But, like I said, I don't recommend doing so," she replied.

"What *do* you recommend? I need to break the stalemate, and it's not like I don't have the means. And it's not like I wouldn't probably have to dump the cash into Dean's faltering business at some point in the future anyway."

"Those are two separate issues, Carter. Let me work the legal angle. We'll get in front of the judge soon."

I left the meeting feeling more frustrated than I'd been before. The only positive to the entire Dean/Dianna/Sean situation came from my HR director.

I called Larissa from my car as I headed back toward my office.

"You have the magic touch with new hires," Larissa said with a laugh after we said hello. "All five of them accepted the offers. Only one negotiated, and they still ended up on the low side of the salary scale you listed."

"That's because you're an excellent negotiator," I said, trying not to let the flutters in my chest grow. Dean deserved to lose his staff. They couldn't be happy if they were all willing to jump ship for a nine percent increase in pay.

"I have them all slated to start in about three to four weeks, more or less. I've prepped a press release to go out tomorrow."

"Great," I said without any enthusiasm.

"Right." Larissa sounded less sure of herself. "Well, if there's nothing else…"

"No. You did a wonderful job. It went better than I expected."

"I can't take any of the credit, Carter," she said. I knew her gaze would be serious behind her thick, black-rimmed glasses. "Each of the candidates told me they were happy for this opportunity and to continue to work together. They said the CEO, Dean? He doesn't understand the business, and the company only has a few years at most before it's mismanaged into the ground. Or bought up and sold to bits, which is what they're expecting. They've all seen the writing on the balance sheets. Obviously, I didn't say anything about our takeover offer."

"Thanks. And, yes, that's why I went after them. Each of them has a proven track record of growth." That was true. And it had played into my decision. "I'll plan to meet with them once they've given notice. That'll happen today?"

"Any time now."

My phone beeped. I pulled it from my ear to check the number. I wasn't surprised to see it was from Austin, though the number wasn't one I recognized.

"I need to take this call," I said. Still, the timing was right. Dean must have received notice by now from at least a couple of his executives.

If it was Dean calling to yell at me about destroying his company, then I needed to catch him before he worked himself into a complete tizzy. Now that he'd lost his critical staffers, the company was more exposed to a hostile takeover, either by my company or another.

"Talk soon, Carter," Larissa said before hanging up.

I tightened my hand on the steering wheel, creeping forward in the bumper-to-bumper mess of Highway One. I scowled, wishing Austin's population hadn't exploded twenty years ago. Or the city developers had actually built enough highway lanes to accommodate the ever-growing number of cars on the road.

Texans liked their cars—they saw it as a personal right to drive wherever they wanted, whenever they wanted. Still, the amount of gas wasted and the emissions shooting out of each vehicle's tailpipe as we shuttled forward a car length at a time made a good case for mass transit.

I missed the BART. Get on, read a paper, get off and into an Uber to drive me to the office. Yeah, now I was waxing poetic about the shit traffic in San Francisco. I scowled as a Mercedes cut me off.

Damn right I wanted mass transit.

Still, the wait was normal and gave me time to think.

The largest issue was that I needed to let Regan know about my upcoming battle with Dianna. I didn't want Regan to walk into some interview situation with that reporter John unprepared.

How did I tell my current lover that a former lover might have had my child?

Not a choice. I'd just have to deal with the fallout. Which might well be losing Regan. And damn if that didn't cut deeply.

My phone rang once then went silent. I heaved a sigh and called Remy. "We got all of 'em," I said without preamble. "Each of Dean Russell's execs bailed. Larissa said like they were grabbing a lifeline."

"That's because they are," Remy said. "There's word swirling Dean's doctored last quarter's books."

"Send over our offer."

"Now, wait a minute," Remy said. "Did you hear me? You could be vastly overpaying for those assets."

"Then, Dean gets a great initial offer."

"You don't owe that guy squat," Remy snapped.

My phone beeped, telling me I had another call. Same number as before. Definitely Dean.

"And we both know he won't take it," I said.

Remy grumbled. "Fine. But let it be known I think you should cut the offer by fifteen percent."

"Duly noted," I said. "He's calling me now."

"And you are not going to answer," Remy said in a stern tone that I intended to ignore. "First, the guy needs to have the decency to go through your secretary. Second, he's going to be a dick. That's always his MO."

"Better he do it to me than Larissa."

"Carter…"

But I'd already hung up and accepted the call from Dean.

"You sack of shit," Dean spat as soon as the call connected.

"That's absolutely no way to greet another person. Hello, Dean. That's how you do it right."

"I should have known you'd push some seedy shit as soon as Dianna said she saw you. Just can't stand that I got your girl, huh?" His voice turned smug.

"I'm glad you married her," I said over his attack on my character.

He paused mid-tirade. "Why would you be happy I got the hottest girl at UT? I won, man. I beat you."

I considered his words. "That might well be true. But you also saved me from marrying her and, thus, me from years of misery and disappointment."

Dean sputtered.

"So, thanks for that. Now, I know you hate running this company. Your executives stated that you don't enjoy the work, possibly don't understand the intricacies."

In his industry, his currency was in the brain trust he'd surrounded himself with. Soon, his office would be a lonely place with some idle computers.

The thought brought me no joy.

"Are you calling me stupid?" Dean snarled.

"No." I bit my tongue. Talking to Dean was like trying to avoid getting punched. "I'm saying you aren't in the correct industry, one that fulfills you. I'm willing to make you an offer to buy you out."

"And let you win? No fucking way."

Well, I could say I'd tried.

"I'd make you more than a fair offer. It's the best you'll get."

"This is *not* over. No one takes from me. *No one.*"

CHAPTER TWENTY-THREE | Regan

Finally, I had a few minutes to myself, and I used them to text Carter as we traveled to Oklahoma City. He told me he was working on something, but he'd call me later. I tried not to be let down, but I was.

My disappointment disappeared when Carter's brother, Camden, texted me as I stepped into my dressing room at the venue that afternoon. I stared at his name, unable to believe the king of country reached out to me.

Camden Grace: *I'm looking forward to talking with you about your project. I have one of my own, and I may need your vocals to make it right. Let's find possible times to get together, though I heard you'll be in Arlington the night before I'm performing at AA. Maybe we can try to grab a quick chat then? I'd love to meet the gal who has my brother so happy in person.*

I responded with an affirmative, trying to ignore my shaking fingers. Much like his brother, he took my response as a green light to call me.

"Can you give me a sec?" I asked Darryl and Mindy. Darryl ambled out but Mindy shot me a narrow-eyed look.

I shooed her with frantic hands, then gulped before I answered.

"Hello?"

"Heya, Regan. Is it okay I call you Regan? Carter does, and I don't like him getting to do things I don't."

I laughed. The door thumped closed behind Mindy. "Sure. I prefer to be called my real name."

"Fantastic," Camden said in a lazy drawl that reminded me a bit of Matthew McConaughey. "And call me Cam, since that's what I prefer. Now, lay it on me. What do you want out of a collaboration?"

I tried to speak. Nothing came out. This man might be a relative newcomer—his career wasn't much longer than mine, but he was one of the big names in the music industry and he only got hotter with each subsequent month.

"You with me?" he asked.

"Y-yes," I stammered. "Um, I'm just not sure how to answer you. I mean…I want everything. A Grammy in the music of my choice."

Camden made a noise of approval. "Carter said you're a smart gal."

I giggled. I couldn't help it. I was talking to Camden freaking Grace. "Well, I'm not the straight-up country singer you are, though I love your songs."

"You worried about switching genres?" he asked.

"Yes, of course. But if I don't do this now, I'll get even more pigeon-holed."

"People connect with great music. You create something worth listening to, and people will. That's about emotion as well as technical expertise."

"I hope you're right."

"Tell me what you're thinking," he said.

Like Carter, this man put me at ease, making me spill more of myself than I intended. "I want to add a bit of bluegrass. I listened to a lot of that growing up in New Orleans. My mother loved it. We used to sing it together in some of the clubs."

Talking about my mother brought a warm feeling to my chest.

"And jazz. I grew up singing lots of that. I'm talking old school—Duke Ellington, that kind of thing."

"Oh? That could be interesting," Cam said. "You have that smoky Etta James quality that'd be excellent. No, not Etta—well, some of Etta. But Amy Winehouse. Carter said you have serious power pipes like her."

I grinned so hard at the compliment my eyes watered. Cam trusted his brother and didn't bother to ask if I could really sing.

"Got anything in mind?" Cam asked. "I mean, specifically for me?"

"Well…" I pressed a hand to my stomach. Carter told me to sing—not the tune I'd sung for Carter—that was so personal, and I still couldn't believe I'd shared it with anyone.

"C'mon, Regan. Carter loved the bit you sang him. He's been bugging me to call you."

A wave of warmth at Carter's insistence to his brother helped to override my worry. The worst Cam could do was tell me no. But I didn't think he would. Not if he wanted me to help him with a song or two for his album.

"Yeah, actually. I have this song I've been working on. It's called 'Perfect Weekend'." Before I could chicken out, I sang the opening stanza.

Cam hummed a nice harmony when I hit the chorus.

I stopped singing.

"Hell, yes!" he hooted. "I can totally hear this. And you're right. It's got a bluesy quality you mentioned. A bit old school but totally original. A modern take, I guess I'd say. Does it have another verse?"

"Yes."

"Sing it for me?" he coaxed.

I did, letting the power of the melody swim through my veins and pour out of my vocal cords.

Cam whistled. "Helluva song you got there all on your own. Can you send me the lyrics? I want to see what I can add."

"Yeah, sure. As soon as we hang up."

"Got any others?" he asked. He sounded much like Carter when he had a word to lay over a triple word score. I hoped that meant he was as excited about this project as I was.

"I've finished that one and eight others," I said.

"So a full album. Well, with one more song. Three would be ideal."

"Exactly," I said. I crossed my fingers and shoved them under my bottom. "I was hoping you could help me produce this. Maybe suggest someone to collaborate on the other tunes."

"Yeah," Cam said. "Me. I'm a selfish bastard and don't intend to let this megahit go anywhere without my name all over it."

My mouth fell open. His words caused my heart to pound. Everything I wanted fell into place with that conversation.

"When do you get to Austin?" he asked. "Carter said the end of the month? I'm going to be in the studio most of that time, so if you can get here sooner, that'd be better than meeting up in Dallas."

"Yes," I managed to gasp. "Yes, I can meet you, and yes, I have some studio time booked. But…" I squeezed my eyes shut, needing to be honest because this was Carter's brother. I couldn't lead them on or astray. "I'm not sure my record label will pick this up. It's such a departure from my current hits. My father was there, trying to negotiate a new album for me in the pop genre. But I don't want to do that. So, it's possible they'll pass…"

"If they do, you create an indie label either alone or with one of my buddies here. We'll get this out there with lots of fanfare, Regan. *Shit*. That song needs to be heard on every radio station in the world."

I laughed. "You're a charmer."

"Runs in the family," Cam said. "But I never bullshit."

I fanned my face. Camden Grace liked my song. Total fangirl moment.

"Now, here's what I was looking for," he said.

I sat forward and listened as he explained his single and sang a bit for me. I bounced in my chair with excitement as he finished. Collaborating with such talent was exciting. Contagious.

I asked him to sing it again and added a bit of high harmony.

"Just like that," he crowed. "Hit me with possible dates."

We finalized our plans to meet up in Austin for my only full free day over the next two weeks and said goodbye.

I hugged my phone to my chest for a long moment. I pursed my lips, wondering what I could do for Carter. He'd been so kind to me the past few days. I needed to send him something back—a token of my appreciation. I bit my thumbnail, considering. I smirked as the idea came to me. I organized the details, requesting a rush delivery to Carter's office building—the only address I had for him. Once I knew the gift was on its way, I dialed Carter's number.

"Regan," he said.

"I'm sorry," I replied, hearing the strain in his tone. "I can call you back later."

"No," he said, quickly. "Now's good. What's going on?"

"I just wanted to thank you. Well, and to tell you I'm going to be working with your brother." I practically squealed the last part.

"Yeah? Well, that's exciting."

"This is one of my biggest dreams, Carter. And you made it happen. Thank you. So much."

CHAPTER TWENTY-FOUR | Carter

Hearing the joy pouring through the speaker put the first smile of the day on my face.

"You're welcome, but it's not like I did much."

She was quiet for a long moment. "I feel like you did. And I want to do something for you. To celebrate."

Could this woman be any cuter?

"I like thinking about you smiling. You have a gorgeous smile."

She giggled. "I think yours is pretty great, too. What upset you?"

I settled back in my chair. "A deal I'm working to close." No need to tell her it involved a child with my ex. Not yet, anyway.

"Oh. I hope the negotiations go well."

"They aren't right now." I sighed. "But they will." I glanced at the clock again. I had another call scheduled with Kelly in twenty minutes. Hopefully, she was going to tell me we could move forward with the paternity test.

Impatience licked at me, making me want to run or yell or…I wasn't sure. Just not continue business as usual.

Not that my current week was typical.

I needed this deal closed and soon. Not because I wasn't patient, but because I wanted to be the one to close it. On my terms. Dean was going to fight me, maybe even sell to another company just to spite me.

A knock sounded on my office door. "Hang on, Regan."

"You need to go. I'll talk to you later," she said as if she wasn't at least as busy as me.

"I'll call you back. I want to hear more about your day and what you and Cam talked about."

"Okay," she said. "I'll look forward to it."

"Me, too, gorgeous." Huh, apparently, I'd given her a nickname without conscious thought. Not that a pet name meant anything more than familiarity. Except that I knew it did.

I was falling for this woman. Hard and fast.

And I was man enough to admit that scared me. Especially because I didn't know how to bring up Sean or my past…or how Regan would handle any of that.

I set my phone onto the gleaming surface of my desk and called for the person to enter. Janice, my secretary, stuck her graying head in the room. "You have a delivery, Mr. Grace."

I waved her in.

I was thrilled she'd been willing to relocate from San Francisco to Austin. Granted, I made it worth her while financially, but nice as Austin was, we didn't have the Pacific Ocean, Napa and Sonoma valleys within an hour's drive, let alone skiing and beaches within a few hours' drive of the city.

But, lucky for me, Janice's daughter and son-in-law had moved to Austin a few years earlier to enjoy the cheaper cost of living and the hill country. Janice herself was going through a bluebonnet phase.

I'd have to get Regan to take a picture with me in the sea of small blue heather-like flowers that grew in such abundance on the side of the road, thanks to Lady Bird Johnson's beautification initiative decades ago.

Janice opened the door, allowing a young delivery man carrying a wooden crate into the room.

The college-aged man in a cycling helmet settled the crate on my desk as I thanked him.

"We've never had a delivery like this before," he said with a smile.

I raised an eyebrow.

"From such a big star," he said, flushing. "Um. I'm the owner, not the usual delivery guy, but I wanted to make sure you received this as quickly as possible."

"You own the delivery service?"

He nodded.

"Good for you. I did something similar in college."

A huge smile spread across his face. "And look at you now. Huge office and gifts from a hot singer."

He seemed to realize he'd once again crossed a boundary because he cleared his throat before telling me goodbye. Janice ushered him out. Sure, I knew Regan was beautiful, but the bite of protectiveness that reared its head at his words was annoying.

I wasn't used to feeling this way. Much as I'd cared about Dianna, I hadn't worried about her looking at other men. I hadn't worried much about men coveting her, either.

And look where that got you, whispered an insidious voice.

"Are you all right if I take off?" Janice asked. "I'd like to get home and prepare for the sleepover with Kinzie."

Janice's granddaughter was spending the weekend with her so Kinzie's parents could have a weekend in the Hill Country for their anniversary.

"I thought you'd already left," I said. "Make sure you grab those passes."

Janice hugged me. "You're a good man, Carter. Kinzie is going to freak out when I tell her you got her tickets to Schlitterbahn."

That was a water park in nearby New Braunfels. Kinzie had wanted to go since her family moved here. I patted Janice's back once, desperate to know what Regan sent me.

"Not a problem."

"All right. I'm out of here so you can enjoy opening your present from your lovely girlfriend." Janice's smile bloomed across her face. "She's a keeper, young man."

"I'm figuring that out," I said.

Janice patted my cheek just as my mother would. "This is why I still work for you. You're smart and caring. All my previous bosses were one or the other. I'd begun to wonder if it was possible to be both. Your young lady's lucky to have you."

With Janice's words, a heavy weight settled in my stomach. I tried to ignore the voice whispering I was making a mistake by not talking to Regan about Dianna and my potential relation-ship to Sean and instead focused on the gift. I pulled out a large burlap sack. Inside was fifty-year-old single-batch whiskey. Not a brand I knew well but a quick internet search proved it was exclusive and pricey. I shook my head. That alone would have been a nice gift because when Regan called the other night, I mentioned I'd been drinking whiskey, and she remembered. The next item I pulled out was four six-packs of Austin Works beer.

Regan and I still had much to learn about each other, but this gift box showed her interest in what I said to her.

The last two items in the box were also wrapped in burlap. I picked up one, surprised by the heaviness. I unwrapped it slowly and then shook my head, shocked by the lump of emotion in my throat.

Scrabble. A collector's edition with a swivel base. I set it on the edge of my desk, unable to resist one more stroke of the gleaming wooden box. Was this how women felt when men sent them flowers?

I liked this feeling, very much. Not because she'd clearly spent a lot of money on me but because she'd thought of me—of things that would make me happy.

I pulled out the last item.

This one was a chess set. Not just any chess set—the letter on heavy card stock said this was custom-carved from sustainable woods. I had to chuckle. That was so Regan. Thoughtful. And the sustainable woods, focusing on the environment, was Austin-centric, a place Regan couldn't wait to move to.

I loved that about her.

Liked. I liked that about her. Very much. No way I could love the woman.

Except…

No. Not going there. Too soon. *Too soon.*

I picked up my phone and dialed her number, forgetting for the moment about anything but thanking her and hearing her voice as she told me about her day.

The worry about Dean and Sean and the whole mess slid off my shoulders as she sang me the song she wanted Cam to help her make into a hit.

Not the one she'd sang me. "That's really personal," she whispered when I asked why she hadn't shared it with Cam.

"I'm glad you sang it to me, then."

"You're the only person who's heard it," she replied.

With those soft words, I placed a hand to my heart and admitted this woman already owned a piece of it. She'd own more if I weren't careful. Very, very careful.

Instead, I chartered a flight to Oklahoma City so I could thank her in person.

CHAPTER TWENTY-FIVE | Regan

John Mitchell's newest story about me taking calls from a drug dealer in my dressing room hit the front page of all magazines even as I spoke with Carter about my dreams for this new record with his brother.

I didn't know how that was possible. My father and the rest of my crew were in the larger room, attacking the catered lunch the venue provided—at my father's insistence.

I hadn't been able to eat a bite, too upset by the newest lies dished about me. Weary from thinking about who was John's source, I collapsed on the hotel sofa as soon as I made it into my suite.

The knock on the door inflamed my pounding head. I moaned softly as I glared at the white wood, wishing the person would go away. No one ever left me alone for long, so I hauled myself off the plush couch. Each step caused my temples to throb. It was late, after midnight. I wanted to sleep, but I needed my headache to go away. And I needed to develop a plan to refute these newest accusations. Another knock.

I opened the door, then gasped softly.

"Carter?"

"What's wrong?" he asked, his gaze intent.

No use avoiding the truth. My head hurt too much. I tapped my temple and winced.

He edged past me and shut the door, turning the lock. He faced me, a faint scowl building between his eyebrows.

"Change in plans," he said.

"We don't have plans. Not until Dallas."

"Well…I'd hoped to take you out. I wanted to say thank you for my gifts in person."

"You're welcome."

He cupped my cheeks and placed his thumbs on my forehead, rubbing gently. "Let me help you."

I let my head fall to his chest as I moaned with pleasure. He continued the gentle pressure until I could blink without wincing. Then, without me asking, he led me to the couch and lowered me to the cushions.

"Lie down on your stomach."

I did without questioning him. He brushed my hair aside and began to massage my neck and shoulders. This time, my moan was louder.

"You are so good with those hands," I whispered.

"Sh. Just relax. Once some of the tension is gone, I'll draw you a bath."

"I planned to do that. Once the headache wore off a bit."

"You know what causes them?"

"Stress," I said.

Carter grunted. "And is there anyone specifically who has you stressed?"

I bit my lower lip. "It might be a shorter list to name who hasn't."

Another knock sounded on the door. I sighed as Carter quit rubbing my shoulders.

"Want me to get it?" he asked.

I didn't. Not at all.

The knocking continued. Within a moment, it was more like pounding. The frame rattled.

"I better see who it is," I said. I didn't really care. In fact, based on the force of the blows to the door, I didn't *want* to know.

I wanted to be left alone, especially now that I had Carter's magical fingers easing the tension in my aching muscles and the pounding in my head.

Carter patted my shoulder blade. "Stay there. I'll get it."

He padded over to the door and opened it. For a moment, nothing happened. The silence was unnerving enough for me to raise my head and squint at Carter who stared at my father, who all but foamed at the mouth.

"What are you doing here?" My father snarled as he shoved the door from Carter's hand and stalked into the room.

CHAPTER TWENTY-SIX | Carter

I inhaled sharply. I didn't know how Regan would want me to handle this.

"I'm here to see Regan."

Olin lunged forward and gripped my shirt. My heartbeat ratcheted up as his face came within inches of mine.

"Dad!" Regan cried. She stood, her face pale. "Let Carter go. Now."

"Don't think I will just yet," Olin growled. "Not until this… young man and I have some words."

Laurence, my stepfather, used to use that same tone of superiority. I hated it when Laurence used it, and I hated it just as much when Olin applied it toward me. I didn't need this shit. I had more than enough drama in my own life.

"I really don't see that you and I have much to discuss, sir," I said, my tone impatient.

"You're taking my daughter's focus from her music." He pulled me closer so that our noses touched.

Regan sobbed.

More doors opened up and down the hallway.

Shit.

This was about to turn into one hell of a scene.

I broke Olin's hold—a move I'd used for years on Cam, much

to his irritation. He might be Army-Ranger trained, but I'm the one who'd taken years of martial arts. I stepped back, once again ensuring a decent distance between us.

Darryl hurried down the hall, a dark scowl building across his face. I wasn't sure if he was upset with me or Olin.

I didn't have time to worry about it because Olin lunged at me again. I grabbed his arm and pulled him into an armbar. He grunted and squirmed but he didn't have the same level of training as I did and he sure as shit wasn't making the situation better for himself.

"Will you stop it?" Darryl asked. "This is upsetting Regan."

"You're an idiot," OIin snarled.

"No, that would be you for giving her prescription drugs and causing her all kinds of issues with the media," Darryl snapped. He shoved his way into the room and positioned himself in front of Regan.

For a moment, no one moved.

"He did *what*?" Regan gasped.

Darryl shot her a sorrowful glance. "The pills he gives you. I know you thought they were like extra strength ibuprofen, but they're not. They're some kind of opioid."

Silence fell. Olin stopped struggling.

As I feared, John stood in the hall, taking in the scene. No way I could turn back time, but I could at least try to make this better for Regan since more people were walking into the hall, some rubbing sleep from their eyes while others looked irritated or shocked.

"Darryl, you're saying Olin gave Regan drugs without her knowledge?"

"He did," Mindy said, elbowing past John and moving to stand next to Darryl. "More than once."

"Without Regan knowing it was opioids?" I asked again.

"Yes," they both said.

I turned to look at John. "I expect you to write that up and to see it all over the news first thing tomorrow morning."

"You wouldn't," Olin whined.

That's what I feared. Olin was a weak man who blustered and threatened, and probably even hurt others to make himself seem and feel more important. Not unlike my Uncle Laurence. I hated that d-hole.

Olin strained, trying, no doubt, to reach around and nail me with his fist. He groaned instead when his shoulder began to ache from the pressure.

"Ow!"

"Carter," Regan said. Her eyes filled with tears. "Please let him go."

I did, stepping back as Olin took a swing at me.

"Stop it," Regan shrieked.

Olin didn't. He swung again and I blocked him. Before I had to make the decision of what to do next, Darryl and John stepped in, each grabbing one of Olin's arms. They dragged him from the room. John seemed torn as to whether to follow Olin down the hall or stick around for the juicy business here in the suite.

"Are you okay?" I asked Regan.

She wrapped shaking arms around her middle and shook her head. I went to her but didn't touch, not sure how to comfort her. She flung herself into my arms and trembled against me.

"He didn't hurt you?" she asked into my shirt.

I pressed a kiss to the top of her head, shocked by how much comforting her comforted me. "I'm fine."

Regan turned to Mindy. "Can we get some privacy?"

Mindy nodded, her face tight with an emotion I couldn't read. She shut the door to the suite, leaving Regan and me in silence.

We stared at each other for a long moment. "Want to get out of here?" I asked.

"Yes," she practically moaned.

"We can go down to Austin for the night."

"Maybe," she said. "I just…I need to get away from all this." She waved her hand. Yeah, I got it. There was a lot of drama.

"You need to be in Tulsa when?"

"For sound check tomorrow night."

"Go pack a bag," I said.

She rolled her eyes. "I live with a packed bag."

I smiled as she went into the bedroom and grabbed it.

"Easy peasy," she said. "I hadn't unpacked anything."

I grabbed the handle from her, but she laid her hand over my arm.

"I want to keep this quiet. I mean, I have to take Darryl with me, at least. But I don't want my whole crew there."

I smiled. "I'm happy for it to be just us, if you can manage it. Cam has security at the ranch, and his guys'll be there with us everywhere but when I transport you there and back. I already arranged for a private charter to get here, and I can get another for you tomorrow, so you don't have to worry about being mobbed by fans."

Her face took a dreamy expression. "Just us? No Darryl or Mindy or…"

"Would you like that?" I asked.

She smiled, but it was a bit wan. Not that I could blame her after that showdown with her father.

"Yes. Let's go," she said

———————— ★ ————————

We crashed at Cam's place since that's where I was staying. Neither my brother nor Jenna batted an eye when we stumbled out of my bedroom on too few hours of sleep.

"I let Mindy know where I am," Regan said. "They're transporting to Tulsa now."

"Wanna come to the studio with me today?" Cam asked. "No pressure, but it'd be fun. We can post bits of video of us working on the music to tantalize the fans."

Jenna bumped him with her hip. "You mean *your* fans who are already chomping for this album."

Cam's grin was unrepentant. He snagged an arm around her waist and brought her against his side. "That's exactly what I mean."

He turned toward Regan, who sidled closer to me.

"It'll help get people interested in your new project, too," he said.

"And put to rest those absolutely ridiculous rumors that you can't sing," Jenna said.

She slammed her mug down, her jaw tilted at a pugnacious angle that meant she was not happy.

"*Please*. Like it's possible to get to your level of success without a whole lot of talent and hard work."

I looked down at Regan. She seemed to be measuring something inside, going over a difficult problem. She nodded once, slowly.

She glanced up at me and then beamed out that big smile that made my breath catch and my heart stutter. "Can you get me back in time for my concert tonight?"

"Of course," I replied.

Regan smiled at me, then turned the full force of her good mood on to Cam and Jenna, who both looked entranced. "That sounds like a really good idea. A great one, actually."

"You know it," Cam crowed. Then he winked at Jenna, who smiled up at him.

"I just don't get why people seem to enjoy ripping each other down," Jenna grumbled.

Cam focused on us. "Grab a shower. We're going to see Ronnie."

————— ★ —————

Ronnie was Cam's producer. He reminded me of Willie Nelson but with anger issues. Cam swore he was the best in the business and Regan seemed impressed to meet the man.

Sure, I should have gone into my office, tried to work through my problems—the ones with Dean and the fact I still hadn't told Regan about Sean. Instead, I let my people know I was out of the office for the day. What good was being the boss-man if I couldn't take advantage every once in a while?

And, I assuaged my guilt by reminding myself that Regan had too much on her plate, especially with the bomb Darryl dropped last night. By tacit agreement, neither of us looked at the news, and I asked Cam not to share anything with Regan either. He nodded. But I could tell there was trouble brewing by the tightness around his eyes.

I hoped this time for Regan proved healing. She needed it. And, I found myself fascinated by the creative process.

Watching Cam and Regan work proved jaw-dropping and awe-inspiring. Regan's nerves faded within the first hour of their studio time when Cam managed to lose his thread for a melody as Regan held a note before ending with a pounding bluesy flourish.

"Do that again," Cam said as he strummed his guitar.

Regan followed him through the song, holding that last note.

"Fantastic," Cam whooped, hopping up off his stool.

"Holy tamales," Jenna murmured. "She's got some lungs. I've never seen Cam so excited about working with another performer."

I nodded, my smile stamped on my face. Cam relished the challenge of working with Regan and she was throwing out some spell-binding harmonies. Cam's eyes widened when she hit an F nearly as low as his before spiraling up to high C before coming back to a middle range tone that totally worked.

"Please tell me you got that one?" Cam said into the microphone.

Ronnie nodded, his smile seeming permanent, too.

Four more takes and the song came together.

The hair on my arms stood up as my brother and my girl threaded their voices together, building something so much richer than either of them could produce individually. For a brief moment we all sat, spell-bound, then Ronnie spoke through his mic into the sound booth where Cam and Regan stood.

"That was, without a doubt, the best tune I have ever recorded."

"Aw, Ronnie. Don't go making me blush," Cam said with a grin.

Ronnie, his grizzled goatee quivering, cleared his throat. "That, right there, is pure platinum. I stake my forty years in the business on that."

I sucked in a breath and Jenna did the same. Ronnie rode Cam hard. That's why Cam liked working with the old goat. He refused to lay down anything less than the very best. And if he was already seeing sales at that level…

Regan's eyes found mine and I bounded to the door. She met me there, throwing herself into my arms.

"Oh, my gosh! This has been the best day," she said against my lips.

Ronnie cackled with delight before he turned to me. "Where you been keeping this one?" he asked.

"Pop-ville," Jenna said.

Ronnie scowled. "Good thing we found her and pulled her from that synthetic garbage. Damn, she can sing! Cam is gonna own the Grammys this year thanks to Regan's talent."

"That was the best studio time I've ever had," she said, smiling up at me as we headed toward the studio's inner door.

I kissed her pretty lips. "It doesn't always go this smoothly."

A frown puckered Regan's brow as we all pushed out toward the small lobby. "No. My producer doesn't like my natural voice. He likes to put it through all those filters and stuff."

I kissed her again before she was mobbed by Ronnie and his

team and the studio musicians who all wanted to congratulate Regan on a job well done.

"We got skads of great bits to add to my YouTube channel," Cam sang as he poured over footage on a phone. "This is sweet, Chuck."

Chuck shot his boss a thumbs up. "I'll get it posted while you work on your next tune this afternoon."

Regan's hand trembled as she sought to hold mine. I squeezed her fingers since she seemed to need the reassurance.

By the time we left the small, nondescript building, we were all starving, but Regan needed to get back to Tulsa for her show. I palmed my keys as we said our goodbyes to my brother and Jenna.

Regan remained quiet as we drove toward the airport.

"You sure I can't get you something to eat?" I asked. I should tell her about Sean, about Dianna, about buying Dean's company.

She shook her head. "I'm too nervous." She glanced off, and I knew she was thinking about Darryl's pronouncement last night.

Nope, not time to drop my shit on her now.

"What? Why?"

She nibbled at her lip. "I haven't told my father about this new project yet. He...um..." She sighed. "I mentioned my mom performed this kind of music. Well, memories of her are hard. For both of us."

Her voice cracked.

"Cam won't do anything you don't want him to," I said.

Regan sat up straighter and squared her shoulders. "No. It's time. I need to do what's right for me." She turned to look out the window and added softly, "Even if that means facing the inevitable battle."

CHAPTER TWENTY-SEVEN | Regan

Carter didn't want to leave me at the airport.

"We need to talk," he said. "That's part of why I flew up to Oklahoma City." He fidgeted. "Mainly to see you."

I loved that he seemed a bit insecure. Carter appeared to be successful, powerful, in control. If I was honest, that turned me on. But him having a little vulnerability? That heightened the appeal. Big time.

I wanted to request a reprieve from whatever had Carter nervous; I couldn't handle more overload at the moment.

We settled into the airplane cabin. Before I could think of a way to ask him to hold off on his deep conversation, Carter leaned forward and took my hand between both of his.

"I take it that reporter is always around?"

"I assume so. You know I didn't read what he wrote this morning," I said. "But Mindy didn't send me anything terrible, so I guess that's something."

"Hang on." Carter pulled up the internet on his phone. He pursed his lips and narrowed his eyes. "Just a recap of last night. There's talk about you popping pills," he muttered, his brows pulling together. "But it looks like most people are mad at your father for not telling you what he was giving you."

I slid my hands under my thighs, which bounced up and

down. The plane lifted into the sky and I released the breath I'd been holding. I wasn't afraid to fly.

No, I was frightened of my father's reaction to Cam's video and my continual rebuff of the label's newest contract. While we'd ridden to the studio this morning, I'd sent a message to my direct contact at the record company, letting them know that while I appreciated the offer, I'd chosen to move in another direction musically. Now that Cam had posted his snippets to his channel, I pulled out my phone and directed the label there.

I held my breath when I noticed an email from my father. Instead of reading it, I put my phone back in my purse. Yes, that was avoidance. I just…couldn't right now.

"John will stick around because he wants a juicy story and doesn't like me telling him I don't have a drug problem," I said, continuing my conversation with Carter. "Or an alcohol problem. Or a sex fetish. So he's writing that his source says I do—to all of the above, apparently."

"We could work on the sex fetish." Carter caught my right hand and pressed his thumbs gently into the space between my thumb and forefinger.

"But the most hurtful comments are that I can't sing."

"Like hell," Carter said, truly offended. "I *just* heard you drop one of the best performances even Ronnie's ever heard. I'm so sorry this is happening to you," he murmured.

"Me, too." He hit a spot that caused my muscles to go lax. "That feels good," I said. How did he know I was getting a headache?

He chuckled. "I can do better."

"Right now, this is perfect."

Carter waited, let the silence grow between us. It was companionable. Nice.

"Tell me about your relationship with your father."

And just like that, the tension doubled and I squeezed my eyes shut.

"It's okay, Regan. You need to talk this out. Maybe I can help."

I wanted to shake my head, but settled for gritting my teeth. "I have to deal with that. And I will."

"Can you?" he asked. "I'm asking you seriously if it's possible for you to handle everything you have going on."

I pulled out of his hold. Carter let me go.

"I'm working on it," I said.

"And I don't want to ask. Or push you," he said, shifting in his seat.

"Then why are you?"

He pulled me close to his side, almost as if he needed me there. I let him. Fool that I was, I wanted to be able to lean on him.

"Because I'm really worried about what happens if I don't ask these questions." He hesitated before meeting my eyes.

"Your father gave you a controlled substance." He inhaled sharply, then exhaled slowly. "Does that happen often? Him giving you drugs?"

I hesitated, nibbling at my lip. "It's not the first time," I said. Wow. Look at how interesting my feet were.

Carter touched my chin and raised my face, waiting patiently until I once again looked at him.

"Did you know?"

I shook my head. "I just knew they worked." Tears welled in my eyes and I blinked them back. "I told you my mother died. That's a sore subject with my father." I clamped my jaw shut to stop the trembling. "What I didn't tell you was she was high when she rammed that freeway exit."

I bit my lip, wondering if I should tell Carter why she was out that night, about her lover. I wasn't ready to go there.

"No one knows if it was intentional." A few tears spilled over. I bent down and retrieved a tissue from my purse. I dabbed at my cheeks.

"I miss her. I don't want to do something stupid like that. I mean, it's not like I have a kid who'd miss me."

"I'd miss you," Carter said.

I managed a tremulous smile. "You know what I mean."

"I do. And I appreciate your honesty now. So, what can we do about this situation?" He settled back against on the plane's couch cushions and rolled up his sleeves. What was it about men's forearms that just…I shivered. This man, sitting there, ready to work on my problems, to help me, melted my heart and made my stomach quiver with desire.

"I don't need you to fix my problems for me, Carter."

We began our descent into Tulsa. Both Carter and I buckled back into our seats.

He reached over and grabbed my hand. I settled against his shoulder, shutting my eyes against the ache once again taking up residence in my temples. He pressed a kiss to the top of my head.

"I get that. But I'm a man. And a CEO. I've been told

executives like to solve problems. I even like to think I'm good at it."

"But if I let you solve this one, then what happens when I have another? And another?"

He pressed his fingers into the tight, knotted muscles in my shoulders. I sucked in a breath as the tension slowly ebbed. Goodness, the relief was intense.

"How about we talk potential scenarios and then you pick the one that suits you best?"

He found another sore spot. Damn his magical fingers. They made fighting with him difficult. "Okay."

"Right. So, what do *you* want to do first?"

Nothing. I wanted to hide in my bed and pull the covers over me. "I need to set up a press conference. Tell the whole press corps what's going on."

We taxied to the terminal. A dark SUV sat near the hangar, Darryl leaning against the gleaming side. I wondered if he'd missed me. I wondered if he saw me as more than a paycheck.

And I had to wonder if he was the person selling me out to the media. That, more than any other reason, was why I was so happy to leave my entourage behind. I pressed my shaking hand to my chest, wondering when trusting people became so hard.

"All right. Sounds smart."

We walked down the stairs and toward Darryl. He opened the door to the vehicle, censure rolling off his every movement. Carter laid his hand on Darryl's arm.

"Thanks for your help with Olin," Carter said. "And before you get angry with Regan, I took her straight to my brother's house. Two of Cam's guys followed us there, and we had Cam's full entourage with us this morning. Another two followed us back to the airport."

Darryl's scowl eased a little.

"I wouldn't do anything to jeopardize her safety, man," Carter said. "I know you take that seriously."

Darryl tossed me a relieved look, no doubt thinking I'd finally chosen a decent human to spend my time with. He wasn't wrong. Carter was more than decent. He was a good man, one I cared about, deeply.

The ride to the venue was short. When we arrived, I brought Carter into my bus. As soon as he ascertained we were alone, he leaned closer and took my lips in a soft kiss. I sighed against his mouth, appreciating his acceptance.

He kissed me again, keeping it light and easy until he slipped his tongue along the seam of my lips. I parted them and welcomed him into my mouth as I raised my hands to cup his cheeks.

He tested and tasted, learning me. I liked how he took his time, and I also liked when he clutched my hip when I sucked on his tongue.

He eased back and brushed my hair off my forehead.

"You're worried about something."

I hesitated. Carter didn't like my father. If I mentioned my concerns about my team or even my desire to send my father away, Carter would ask more questions.

Questions I'd prefer to avoid.

"It's not important," I said as I eased my mouth closer to his. "Kiss me again."

"Regan…"

My heart fluttered.

No, I didn't want to go there.

I stepped back and ran my hands down my sides, smirking when Carter's eyes flared. I lifted my hair from my neck and began to unknot the bow of my halter top.

CHAPTER TWENTY-EIGHT | Carter

Was it my imagination or was her top looser?

"Are you taking off your dress?"

This time she smiled as she nodded. The dress slid off her hips and pooled at her feet. "Now, I'd like you to kiss me, touch me…"

She clasped my hand in hers and placed my palm on her lace-clad breast. I moaned at the feel of her nipple pebbled against my flesh. "I want you," I breathed.

With tiny steps, she once again plastered herself against my body. "I want you, too. Please, Carter."

Like I could say no to her. But…

"I need to tell you something."

"All we've done is talk about hard things. Can't it wait?" she asked as she kissed along my jaw.

I groaned when she ran her tongue down my neck toward the open collar of my button-down shirt.

I wanted to grab her, kiss her. Love her.

Regan collapsed back into the narrow bed in her small sleeping chamber, her eyes closed as she groaned. She looked so sexy in her lacy lingerie yet so fragile with her palms up and open and her lips slightly parted. I wanted to hug her close and comfort her even more than I wanted to get inside her.

That was new.

For years, I'd run on autopilot. Sex felt good, so I assumed I should do more of it. But this, with Regan, wasn't just about sex. Obviously.

I wanted to love her. For more than this afternoon. Maybe forever.

We continued to stare at each other, the moment spiraling out into something bigger, deeper than I'd anticipated.

"Are you one of the good guys?" she asked, her voice loud in the silence.

"Yes." I didn't hesitate even though I knew I wasn't good. Hell, I might just be barely passable when it came to my ethics. I'd nearly fought with Regan's father, I planned to destroy a man's company, his livelihood.

No, I wasn't good. But I would be for Regan. I'd be a fucking knight in hot, clunky armor for her.

"You aren't going to hurt me?" she asked in a small voice.

I couldn't stand it. I gathered her body to mine, tucked her in close to my chest and smoothed my hand through her long hair.

"I don't think I can. Not without hurting myself."

She nodded.

The silence built again, but I didn't mind.

"Whatever this is happening between us, it's big," I mumbled.

She leaned back to meet my gaze. "You know enough to really hurt me. And that's scary."

"Scary as all hell," I said. I leaned in again, needing to touch her more. My thumbs swept across her cheekbones. "Because of how much I want you to be happy."

I hesitated, knowing I needed to tell her about Sean. If I did, now, would it be too much? She'd just asked me not to hurt her.

I leaned in and pressed a soft, sweet kiss to her lips, liking the way her mouth parted under mine.

"Just..." She gripped my wrist. "Just don't let me fall."

CHAPTER TWENTY-NINE | Regan

Carter seemed to glow with his conviction when he said, "Never."

I turned myself over to him, even knowing then I was stupid to do it. That I'd have to pay my pound of flesh to the media, to my father… No, I wasn't thinking about him or the outside world. I was focused on Carter's lips, his tongue in my mouth, his large, callused hands on my body.

His touch left trails of heat so great I was sure smoke must fill the space, but my eyelids were too heavy to open. When he tweaked my nipple, my hips lurched up against his.

I'd never—ever—felt this strong a reaction. My stomach quivered with a need that poured out of my mouth in a low keen as Carter kissed his way down my throat. He pulled away my bra cup and latched onto my nipple with the same intensity I felt as my hips cradled his thickening erection. I licked my lips in anticipation of touching, tasting him. All of him.

I yanked his shirt from the waistband of his pants and slid my hands underneath, reveling at the thick slabs of muscles there. He worked his way to my other breast, molding them to his pleasure. My nails scraped his skin and he grunted but didn't stop.

He worked his way down to my navel and slid his tongue into the narrow indent. His hands settled on my waist, his thumbs stroking upward against my ribs. Then, all of a sudden, he was gone.

I moaned out a rejection. I wanted him on me, in me. But, then, he was there, settling me further up the bed, taking in my streaming hair with hot eyes.

"You are the most beautiful woman I've ever seen. Damn, Regan…"

He unbuttoned his shirt with hurried movements and then yanked it down his arms. The man had *gorgeous* biceps. His shoulders were broad and his chest rippled down into those spectacular abs. I sat up and ran my lips over all that warm skin.

His hands settled on his belt. "Are you ready for this?" he rasped.

I nodded. I lay back so I could slither out of my damp panties. Carter's pants dropped to the floor, his belt buckle clanging as it hit. He slid next to me, his chest flush to my side, his large hand once again covering my breast. I arched into his warmth. He chuckled.

"I've wanted you naked since the moment I saw you," he said.

"But it's more?" I asked. Sure, I was desperate to have him touch me again, but I had to know he felt as I did. That he wanted me.

He dipped his head, his mouth an inch from mine.

"So much more," he whispered, his breath a warm puff over my sensitized skin.

I took his mouth this time. My hand slid into his hair as I rolled so we were chest to chest. Carter reached behind and unclasped my bra. He pulled it down my arms before he trailed his fingertips back up, and I shivered. And all the while he kissed me.

More, he drugged me with those kisses. Some were soft, light, a mere brush. Others were deep, soul-stroking. This one now was a nibble at my lower lip with a swipe of tongue across my upper before he tasted my mouth. I clung to him, unable to do more than feel.

And did I feel good.

So good.

I let my hands wander across his skin. I trailed my fingertips over his back and he grunted when I found a place he especially liked. Me, grabbing his amazing butt for one. Trailing my fingers down the slope of his spine for another.

We tangled our limbs as much as we tangled our tongues, touching, learning. All the while, heat seared through my veins and my desire ratcheted to unknown heights.

When I couldn't stand it any longer, I sat up and slid his maroon boxer briefs from his narrow hips. His erection jutted out, bobbing a little. He was thick and the tip bulbous. I leaned forward to taste him. His hands tangled in my hair as his hips lifted at the first swipe.

"Regan," he groaned.

I smiled at the warning in his tone just before I slid my lips around him. He tasted good. His broad head hit my tongue and I moaned. His hips snapped upward as he cursed.

"You feel so good," he whispered. "But you have to stop. I don't want to come in your mouth. Not this time."

I considered ignoring him but I wanted to orgasm together the first time tonight, too, so I let him slide from my mouth.

He tugged me by my arms until I was sprawled across his chest. He cupped the back of my head and kissed me deeply. My toes curled at the heat of his mouth. His free hand smoothed down my back and over my butt cheek. And then his fingers found my center and it was my turn to moan as he touched me.

I shifted, trying to take more of him inside me, but Carter took his time. He teased and flirted with my core, causing me to clench tightly on the tips of his fingers. His thumb found my clit and I reared back, gasping my pleasure.

"Don't stop," I managed to say. "Don't ever stop."

He grinned as he shoved a finger into my wet channel. The sounds of my readiness should have embarrassed me, but I was too far gone with need to care.

"You ready for me, gorgeous?"

"Yes."

He reached to the floor and snagged a condom from the pocket of his jeans. I took the latex ring from his hand and slid it over his thick head and down the shaft. I shimmied forward so that my knees were at his hips and slid down onto his waiting cock.

He gripped my hips, hard, and pressed up into me, spearing me open. I'd never been stretched like this—never knew how good it would feel.

We both waited, breath baited.

Carter began to move and my lungs leaked out what little air was left. Pleasure rippled from my core, up through my belly and breasts, to my very fingertips and down my legs to my toes. Each thrust brought greater tingles.

Carter slid his hand between our joined bodies and touched me. Right there.

I screamed.

His hips snapped up, slamming into my pelvis. I needed to writhe, to twist, to limit the pleasure, but Carter held me securely, able only to take his thrusts. And I did and the pleasure grew and I gasped as the sensations built beyond anything I'd ever known. He pulled out almost all the way and I made an inarticulate sound of need. He slammed back into me as I exploded.

Each wave grew stronger as I shuddered through the release. Carter thrust once, twice more, then shouted my name as his cock jerked inside me.

I fell against this chest in a daze.

After a long moment, his hand came up and combed through my hair. He seemed to like doing that.

I managed to lift my head and settled my chin on his chest. He met my gaze, his eyes wary.

"That was…" I bit my lip, unsure how to continue.

"Amazing," he said, his voice reverent. "So fucking amazing, I'm almost afraid to go again."

He rolled me over, his fingers entwining with mine, our bodies still joined. "But I will go again because there's no way to stop myself from wanting you, and I've already loved you enough to know each time is better."

"You've ruined me," I said as he pressed against my pelvic bone. With one swivel of his hips, my blood ignited again.

"No, gorgeous," he said as he leaned down to kiss me. "No. I helped you find your pleasure."

He took my mouth and began the process of taking my body, and I understood why he said he was scared.

Sensuality this intense would come with a high cost.

I feared the payment would be my soul.

CHAPTER THIRTY | Regan

We slept like the dead, which we both needed, but not for long enough. Mindy roused Regan much too soon. She yawned but nodded, needing to get ready for her show, and I needed to head back to Austin.

"So, down to Dallas tomorrow?" I asked over a quick bite in the traveling coach's small kitchen table.

She nodded, swallowing her sip of water. She dipped her spoon into her cup of yogurt.

I liked this moment. Just us, sitting across from each other at a table, enjoying a meal. I bit my tongue to keep from asking if that's all she planned to eat.

"Cam's called a couple of times. He's hoping you can come back down to Ronnie's studio after your Dallas concert. I can make sure to get you back in time."

She fiddled with her spoon again, before blurting out, "I'm nervous."

"Of Cam?" I asked. "I thought you got along well."

She nodded. Her eyes wide and fearful. "Yes, and maybe that's silly. I mean, I like him. He reminds me of you."

I smiled as I shook my head. This gal was a charmer.

"What if I don't measure up to his expectations?"

I took her hand in mine. "One thing neither Cam nor I does

well is bullshit. So, if he says he's excited to work with you, he is."

After a long minute where I had no idea what was going through her head, Regan nodded.

"All right. If we can get to Austin after my Dallas show."

I kissed her goodbye, already wishing I didn't have to leave. From the way she clung to me, at least she seemed to feel the same way.

Only after I left did I realized I hadn't told her about Sean.

I sent her a text. *I really do need to talk to you about an issue that came up.*

The dread in my belly said I might not get the chance.

CHAPTER THIRTY-ONE | Regan

Boarding the bus after the show that night was a relief. I continued to avoid my father, though I remained on edge until my driver took off, half expecting him to hop on board and glower down at me.

These moments were a break from performing, from the mess my father created. No, I allowed him to make the mess my life had become. I tossed my e-reader onto the empty seat next to me with a groan and covered my eyes with my palms. Would I ever learn?

Apparently not. I stood, ignoring Mindy's gaze and headed to my sleeping bunk.

"You're on Camden Grace's YouTube channel," Mindy said first thing the next morning. "You did a studio session?" she asked, incredulous. Then she gasped. "It's already got a few hundred thousand views."

"Yeah, I'm working on a song with him," I said, trying to keep the nervousness from my voice.

"Vannah was obsessed with his first album," Mindy said.

"I was, too, because of her. She would love this opportunity. I miss her." We both chuckled.

"She was so much fun until…" Mindy didn't say the words, but, then, she didn't need to. *James*. He somehow talked Savannah into an affair, and between the guilt eating at her from sleeping with my boyfriend, and her declining music venue sizes and sales, she believed her best option was to take her own life.

Part of me was angry with her for that. Mostly, I missed her.

James really messed me up, not just because of how casually he hurt me with his words, but because he'd needed to have sex with my best friend. Unfortunately, that wasn't what hurt me most.

"I lost Vannah before I could tell her I would have chosen her over James a million times," I murmured, looking out.

"What?" Mindy asked.

I glanced up, surprised by the sharpness of the question. "When he told me he'd had an affair with Vannah…" I sighed. "If I'd known that, then, before she died, I would have ended my relationship with him."

"You think you would have," Mindy said, an edge to her tone. "But you were pretty wrapped up in him yourself."

I shook my head. "Vannah meant too much to me," I said. In some ways, losing her hurt as much as losing my mother. We'd grown up together on that TV series. Savannah had shielded me from the worst of the drugs and abuse between the producers and other actors.

"I would have let her have him," I said. "In a heartbeat." I knew that, at least, to be true. "Because losing him never would have hurt as much as losing her."

While true, that didn't mean I wasn't still upset and scarred by Vannah's betrayal. I was. But Vannah *alive* I could hate. I could refuse to take her calls and make her grovel. The finality of her death, especially because she cheated with my boyfriend, ripped at me.

I missed her. So much. Like my mother, who also hurt me, though in different ways. Only now was I coming to understand that the pain of losing those two women would never fully dissipate. Just as I couldn't completely forgive them for their duplicity.

Mindy made a strangled noise.

"What?"

She shook her head, her face set in a grimace. "I miss her, too," Mindy croaked. "Every day."

"How'd you meet?" I asked. "I mean, I don't think you ever told me."

Mindy smiled, but it was bittersweet. "Van was my best friend from kindergarten onward."

I reached over and gripped her hand, which was cool in mine. It trembled as she worked to keep from crying. We sat together, looking out the window.

"She loved you," Mindy said, her voice high and thin. "She knew what she was doing with James was wrong, but he…he was another one of her drugs."

I sniffled. Even as Savannah shielded me from those substances, she'd slid down into addiction, flitting from one form to the next, always trying to mask the pain caused by her demons.

"Do you know why?" I asked.

Mindy shook her head. She pulled her hand from mine and wiped her eyes. "It doesn't matter. She's still dead."

Mindy straightened, patting her hair, signaling the share time was over. She turned to face me, all business once more.

"I'm glad your father's on another bus, but you do realize he's with John Mitchell, right?"

I hadn't. I'd been too busy escaping a possible confrontation I wasn't prepared for to worry about where my father ended up. I cursed under my breath. Too late to do anything about it now.

I slipped from my seat and grabbed my guitar case. I pulled out my trusty acoustic and bent over the strings. For the rest of the drive, I lost myself in the melody of the song I wanted to create with Cam. Once I was sure I had that one down, I played my songs, but I spent more time focused on covers of bands I loved, belting out the lyrics and enjoying the ability to create good music.

Once we pulled into the venue parking lot where we'd leave the buses, my exhaustion overcame me. I trailed Mindy and Darryl to the SUV that took us to our newest hotel for the night, studiously ignoring my father.

I texted Carter: *I think I need to fire my father.*

I didn't think I did; I needed to. I just wasn't sure I had the emotional strength to do it.

CHAPTER THIRTY-TWO | Carter

The knock on my office door took me by surprise. I opened the door and stared down into the face of a young boy with dark hair and wide, scared, hazel eyes. He had an abundance of freckles across his nose.

"Carter Grace?" he asked. His voice cracked. He shoved his hands into his jeans pockets. I noted his skinny arms and the freckles at his elbows.

"Sean?" I said.

He nodded.

I opened the door wider.

He eased into my office, his eyes wary.

"Do your parents know you're here?" I asked. "It's the middle of the day. Don't you have school?"

"I…uh…I left."

My stomach iced over.

"You can't just skip out on class," I said, trying not to let my concern steal into my tone.

"I didn't," the boy said. "We…uh…had a field trip near here, and I just…"

I closed my eyes as I swallowed down the rising concern for this young boy caught in a tangled legal web he couldn't possibly understand. "You saw the articles that you might be my son and decided to walk on over here."

He shook his head, still stuck to the floor in the middle of my office. "My friends told me about it. Bobby's parents talked about it at dinner last night."

"How'd you know where to find me?" I asked.

"Google," Sean said.

I guess that should have been obvious.

"I have to call your mother. Once the teacher realizes you're gone, someone will call your mom. She'll be worried."

"Don't," he said in a frantic voice. "I don't want to go back there. I mean, even if they are my parents. They fight all the time and no one listens to what I want and—" His eyes welled with tears and he sniffled. "Can't we just pretend I'm your son? I mean, then you could take me to see your girlfriend's concerts or your brother's. I could quit school and travel with them."

I came over and rested my hands on his shoulders. The bones there were fragile. I kept my touch light, frightened I'd hurt him somehow.

"I can't, because right now, I have no legal claim to you. I want to change that. If you are my son, I'll fight for that time tooth and nail and with all the resources I have."

His shoulders slumped. "But you don't think I am," he muttered.

"I don't know what to think right now, Sean." How could I tell this boy that his mother lied to me—either back then or now?

"Can you just do it?" Sean asked. "The test I mean. Before you send me back there?"

I pursed my lips and considered his request. "Let me call my lawyer. I need legal advice before I call your parents."

Sean's eyes lit up and he nodded eagerly.

I dialed Kelly's number and explained the situation.

"Call a doctor, Carter. This is your best chance to get the DNA you need."

"But I need to let Dianna know—"

"I texted my friend who works at the hospital, Dell Seton," Kelly said, overriding my response. "He's going to have someone come by. After you get the requisite DNA, you call his mother."

"Doesn't she need to sign something to allow the test?"

Kelly made a growly noise in her throat. "Yes, she has to agree, but we can make that happen by suing. Look, I'm on my way to your office now, too. Let's worry about the rest as it comes. I'll call Remy and let him know what's going on."

I hung up, not liking the scenario, but I didn't have a better plan.

All I knew was this might come back to bite me in the ass, no matter the outcome.

———————— ★ ————————

Sean proved to be a funny kid. Unsure what to do with him, I suggested we play Scrabble since I had a brand-new box sitting next to my desk, courtesy of Regan. Apparently that was my new go-to ice breaker for awkward situations. Sean sat across from me, intent on his pieces.

"I guess you must have known my mom a while ago," he mumbled.

His ears and cheeks were bright red. Well, shit. He was asking if I'd had sex with Dianna.

"Yeah. We were together for a couple of years."

"The article said she married my dad—I mean Dean—just after they graduated." The boy kept his head ducked down, avoiding any whiff of eye contact.

"That's true."

He lifted his head. "Were you mad?" he asked in a rush.

I settled back in my chair. "At the time, yes. Mad and hurt."

Sean's face fell but he nodded. "My mom's having an affair. With one of my dad's friends. She doesn't know that I know," he added.

I bit the inside of my cheek to keep the scathing response in my mouth. Christ. How could Dianna continue to think only of herself? This boy was obviously sensitive and observant.

"It's okay though. My dad's banging his secretary."

I closed my eyes and groaned.

"Too much information?" The boy shifted around like he had to pee, and his face flamed. "I'm sorry. I just thought maybe you'd like to know they don't love each other."

"I wish they did," I said. Shock detonated in my chest as I realized I meant that. After meeting Sean, I wanted him to have the best possible childhood, whether he ended up being my son or not.

But living in a toxic environment like the one he described couldn't be good for the boy's potential future relationships.

"Why?" Sean asked. "I mean, from what I read, it sounds like my mom at least screwed you over."

"Language," I said, sounding just like my mother. I rolled my eyes. "Sorry. My mama has a rule about words coming out of younger people's mouths."

Sean dropped his gaze back to the table, and I wondered at his hesitancy.

"I'm not mad at you. Just an ingrained habit of good manners not to cuss to older people."

He nodded.

"And to answer your question, your mother and…" I wavered. "Dean hurt me. I thought I was going to marry your mama back then."

I shook my head as a lightness spread in my chest. If I had, I wouldn't have been in that Denver bar, and I never would have met Regan. She made me happy and crazy in ways I'd never felt before—much more than Dianna ever had.

For months—no, years—after my breakup with Dianna, I cursed fate and whatever deity existed for taking my love from me. In these past few weeks, I'd learned how lucky I was *not* to be tied to someone as manipulative as Dianna.

A knock sounded at my door. I rose even as I noted the panicked look in Sean's eyes.

"It's okay," I said. The words were reflexive, and I cringed as soon as they were out of my mouth. I wasn't sure it was okay.

"That should be my lawyer," I added.

"My mom's going to be really mad at me," Sean said, a shiver running over his skin.

I tried not to delve too deeply into his reaction. Maybe Dianna yelled—how would I know what type of parent she was? I'd never seen her in action.

Remy, Kelly, a social worker and the doctor stood in the doorway. Clearly, Kelly or Remy had waited to collect the whole team.

As everyone shuffled into my office, I had Sean call Dianna. Remy insisted Sean use Kelly's cell phone so that Dianna wouldn't have my number. I thought that silly since Dean had called me on my cell.

I cut my gaze away from Sean's face as he dialed the phone.

"I'm okay," he said.

After a long moment where I held my breath, Sean said, "I'm at Carter Grace's office—"

I couldn't hear the words, just the angry, loud tone. I winced in sympathy at the pained look on Sean's face.

"I came here all by myself. No, Mom, he didn't…he opened the door when I knocked."

After another bout of yelling, Sean held out the phone, his face contrite. "She wants to talk to you."

I smiled at him, trying to reassure the boy. "Hel—"

"What are you playing at, Carter?" Dianna screamed.

I pulled the phone from my ear and pressed speaker.

"Kidnapping my son to force my hand," she shrilled.

"Dianna," I said, keeping my voice neutral. "You're on speaker phone. Sean is in the room as are my attorneys, a social worker, and a doctor."

"I'm not agreeing to anything you want, you underhanded sack of shit," she yelled. "I want my son."

"And I assure you he'll be home soon."

"But first, there's the little issue of a buccal swab," Kelly said, leaning over my chair to speak into the phone.

"Dean said no. Sean's his son. It says so on his birth certificate."

Which I knew, thanks to Kelly's public records request.

"But you dragged me into a paternity test the other day at the restaurant when you said Sean was my son."

"I never said that, you lying, cheating, son-of-a-bitch."

"So, you now deny that Sean could be my son even though he was born within the nine months from the last time we were…" I glanced at Sean and cleared my throat. "Together," I finished weakly.

"Yes! You lied to the media and everyone in some strange need to get even for our breakup. What else can this be?"

"Well…considering three sources standing outside the restaurant are quoted in the story stating you specifically said Sean is my—"

"He's not!" she shrieked. "Bring my son home now."

I glanced over at Kelly, unsure how to continue.

"Mrs. Russell, this is Kelly Smith, Mr. Grace's family law counsel. As there are witnesses to the conversation, my legal advice to Mr. Grace is to request the paternity test through the courts. I've already drawn up the documents—"

"Fine," Dianna snapped. "Do the damn DNA test. At least we can put this whole ridiculous situation behind us."

"I'll need that in writing, Mrs. Russell," Kelly said.

Dianna growled. We all stared at the phone as if it would grow teeth and launch itself at our faces. Instead, she said, "I'll bring it over when I pick up my son."

Then she hung up.

I glanced over at Sean, hating how his head hung low and his shoulders slumped. I laid a hand on his shoulder, unsure how to comfort him or what to say. Lucy, the social worker, scooted in on the couch next to Sean and touched his elbow.

"Hey, now, that anger can also come out of fear," she said.

Sean shook his head. "She yells. A lot."

Lucy met my gaze, her lips pursed. She riffled through her large tote and pulled out a legal notepad.

"Why don't we talk about your parents a bit," she said.

Sean raised his face, and my heart constricted at the fear there. I'd seen that same look, many times, on Cam's face when he had to deal with Laurence.

"She scares you," I muttered.

Sean dropped his gaze.

"I grew up with a…" What to call him? "A stepfather." Close enough. "My younger brother and he butted heads often. From your age on up. It was bad at our house. If it's bad at yours, Lucy might be able to help."

I hoped I'd said the right thing. Based on Lucy's smile, I did okay.

"Carter's right. I'm here to make sure you're safe and healthy, Sean. These adults in your life are supposed to ensure that for you."

The boy took a shuddering breath. "He hits her sometimes. My dad hits my mom."

The words burned over my skin and flayed my heart.

I squeezed my hand into a fist. "Has he hit you?"

Sean's face was stamped with misery. "Not often," he said quickly. Too quickly.

Lucy picked up on that, too.

"He's never hit my little sister, even when she cries." Sean paused. "She cries a lot."

I placed my arm around Sean's shoulder, my heart aching when the boy leaned into my chest as if he needed the reassurance of my body heat.

Lucy continued to question him, but for my part, I simply kept my hand around the boy's shoulder, wishing I could do more.

★

Dianna's arrival went about as well as the phone call. Lucy had called the police by this point, so that my office, spacious though it was, seemed full of people by the time Dianna strode in.

Her steps faltered and her face whitened when she took in Lucy sitting with Sean and me and the police officers standing behind Sean, arms crossed.

Lucy smiled at Sean in that way that did nothing to reassure the boy. She rose, but before she could speak, Dianna rushed forward and slapped a piece of paper on my desk.

"Here. Sean, we're leaving."

Kelly swiped the paper, reading it quickly. Her lips pursed, but she nodded and handed it to the doctor. He put on his gloves and readied his kit.

Lucy stepped forward and interceded between Sean and Dianna, the police officers stepping in to close ranks behind the social worker.

My heart raced because I knew how Dianna would react... poorly.

As soon as Lucy began to speak, Dianna's face flushed red and then turned an alarming shade of purple. The one plus was the doctor had Sean's mouth open and was swiping his cheek, so the child wasn't aware of his mother's consternation.

"He isn't abused. Neither am I," Dianna sputtered. "Where did you get this ridiculous…" Her gaze landed on me. "You," she gritted.

Remy stepped forward with Kelly, both of whom had told me not to speak. Kelly adjusted her glasses.

"No, Mrs. Russell, Mr. Grace hasn't spoken one ill word against you. These accusations came from another source."

Dianna looked ready to blow up, but she managed to swallow down her indignation and once again tell Sean to come with her. The boy sent me one last pleading look before he followed his mother out of the room, followed by the social worker and the police, who, Kelly explained, would visit the family's house.

CHAPTER THIRTY-THREE | Regan

I missed talking to Carter. I wanted to discuss my plan for dealing with my father with him, but Carter hadn't responded last night or this morning.

He'd mentioned he needed to talk to me about something and I'd put him off. What if he needed to break up with me?

I kind of wanted to be done with me. Well, the professional me.

With a grunt of frustration, I leaned back against the couch in my dressing room, and closed my eyes. I started, hard enough to drop my guitar that I'd been strumming, when someone cleared their throat.

I pried my eyes open and glared at Mindy.

"You scared me."

"Well, I wasn't sure you were awake. You didn't notice me walk in and order you dinner," she responded. "You need to eat something. We don't want you collapsing on the stage." She crossed her arms over her suit-clad chest.

"You did?" I glanced around, noticing the deep shadows. "Whoa. What time is it?"

"Almost six. We'll have to get makeup in here soon."

I grunted. Another show. At least there were only three left after tonight.

"Have you heard from your father?" Mindy asked.

I shook my head. "That's weird. Normally, he'd be wheedling or yelling at me to try to get me to do what he wants."

Mindy fidgeted with a cover plate before removing the lid with a flourish. I whimpered as the garlic and fresh parmesan slapped my nostrils.

"I can't eat that." But as I stared at the plate, tears built in my eyes. Pasta, especially creamy pasta, was my weakness.

"You have to. Otherwise the venue chef will want to know what wasn't to your liking."

My fork hovered over the long strands of buttery linguine. "My diet," I whimpered. Damn being a performer. I had to be thin and fit and sexy—as soon as I failed one of those "beauty" markers, the pop world would run me over and find a newer, younger, shinier version to promote.

"You haven't eaten much the last few days. You can eat some pasta now."

I scooped up a bite and shoved it into my mouth, moaning as the delicious flavors burst across my tongue. Yes! Who needed sex when I had food made by angels from heaven?

I snorted. I needed sex. With Carter. It was better than any meal I'd ever eaten. I took another bite just to make sure. Yes, Carter-delivered orgasms were better.

"So good," I mumbled.

I took the piece of bread Mindy handed me and practically stabbed it into the sauce. Just before I took a bite, I paused. I set the bread on the plate as I peered at her.

"You feel guilty. What did you do?"

"Me?" Mindy asked. But her voice squeaked. "Erm…"

I started to shove the plate away just as Mindy's Google alert pinged. She glanced down and tapped her screen so I couldn't study her face, but I thought I saw relief flare in her eyes at the interruption.

"Eat while I pull up the article," she directed.

I shoved another bite of pasta in my mouth so I wouldn't ask what the media had dug up on me.

She waited until I'd managed to stuff my face with two more bites before handing me the phone with a long-suffering sigh. I was glad I'd swallowed, otherwise I might well have choked on the food.

The article had a prominent picture of Carter. Below his portrait was a picture of him with a gorgeous woman. My stomach plummeted as I looked for the name I knew I'd find in the caption: Dianna.

She had to be my complete opposite, all blonde and petite. One of those cheerleader girls to my mixed-race heritage. Not that I wasn't proud of my family; my mother's family line in Niger dated back about fifteen generations that I knew about, and one of her uncles a few times removed had even held a high place in the country's government.

My mother's beauty was in her bone structure but the richness of her skin and hair remained arresting and exotic until the day she died. And her voice...I'd been so lucky to inherit more than her bone structure.

Media and my fans found me attractive and reported on my success. I stood proud, thankful for my mother's African heritage, but I wasn't a sparkly white girl who might well have fathered

Carter's son. That's what the article said: the fight over Sean
Russell's parentage had heated up and court dates were imminent.
But that wasn't the bombshell.

The article went on to make some shocking claims of
abuse by Dianna's husband Dean. Social services planned to
investigate further.

That poor child.

Carter. If the mother of his child—or his son—had been
abused, wouldn't Carter wish to offer her his support?

My stomach twisted. He hadn't told me.

Maybe he hadn't known.

Another alert popped up.

I collapsed into the chair, almost missing it. Mindy grabbed
my arm as I sagged.

"What? What is it? Regan! You're scaring me."

Feet running. Darryl's voice, questioning Mindy.

I didn't look up. I devoured the words even as my mouth
formed the negation. Dean Russell stood outside a building—I
couldn't tell where. The picture showed a successful man in a
well-fitting suit. His words were ugly, so damn ugly.

He said that Carter was out to destroy his company because he,
Dean, fell in love with the same woman Carter had been dating.
Dianna chose him, Dean, because Carter was the abusive one.

I sucked in a breath, trying to blink past the black dots
popping in front of my eyes.

Mindy's device pinged. More hits piled up, one after another,
in a discordant chime.

She wrangled the device from my hand and cursed. I tried to

steady myself, tried to prepare myself for what was coming next.

"Reporters, especially John, are clamoring for a statement," Mindy said, her voice quiet. "If you plan to step back and let Carter heal his family."

I met her eyes, unable to blink, unable to breathe. "I can't…"

Mindy's mouth tightened until the skin pulled taut and white. Darryl hovered over me. My heart thrummed in a painful rhythm in my chest. My stomach ached from the richness of the food I'd just ingested. I was going to be sick.

I staggered toward the restroom. Mindy's words followed me.

"You better figure out if he matters and how much because this…this kind of attention might well destroy your career."

CHAPTER THIRTY-FOUR | Carter

I drove up to the huge stadium in Dallas, and Darryl met me at the doors to the backstage area. He scowled as he led me through the maze of corridors. Not a warm welcome, but then, why had I expected one?

He turned to face me when we were alone in one hall.

"Did you hit that woman? Your ex?"

The feeling of dread that weighted my guts grew heavier. "No. I never hit her."

"Then why is this coming out and why is that part of the story gaining momentum?" His face turned fierce, his words clipped with anger.

"If I had to guess? The guy's mad about losing his business. I'm in the process of dismantling everything he's built and worked for. And it's salacious. That's what sells." I ran a hand through my mussed hair. "And I totally screwed up, because I should have told Regan as soon as Dianna said something."

I considered telling Darryl about my conversation with Sean—about his claims of violence by Dean. But the horror of that was too fresh, and I didn't understand the legal ramifications enough to blurt it out to Regan's favorite security guard.

Darryl's eyes narrowed. "Yeah. You should have. She's worried. She's hurt."

My heart slammed against my ribs.

"You need to promise me something," Darryl rumbled.

I nodded.

"Promise me you won't hurt her."

I straightened and stared straight into the big guy's eyes. "I will never do anything intentionally to hurt her."

The standoff lasted a moment, but then Darryl turned and began to walk again.

"Better than her father," he muttered.

———— ★ ————

Seeing Regan again, especially after my conversation with Darryl, touched something deep inside me. Something I should have paid more attention to.

As she had in her previous concerts I'd attended, Regan spent these last moments on stage bowing down to touch fingers and thank her fans.

Regan cared what these girls thought of her, sure, but more of themselves. Of keeping them self-confident and healthy. And, damn, if pride didn't puff out my chest as she spoke to them.

"This is my last concert here in Dallas for a while."

She waited for the screaming to stop. A loud voice called out, "I love you!"

"And I love all of you," Regan said. She gave them that megawatt grin that made me want to smile back. "I love you for coming to my concert, sure, and for buying my music." She leaned in closer to the crowd. "But I have another reason to love you. Each of you. I love you because you're unique, and interesting, and fun, and special. Just as you are. Right now."

The audience seemed to stop fidgeting, talking, joking, hell, even breathing. They hung in rapt silence on Regan's every word.

"I love you because tomorrow you're going to go to school tired and hopefully satisfied with tonight's show. You're going to focus in English class on that book you can barely stand to pick up because you know that your education is your ticket to being the best you possibly can be. You're going to ignore the fools who say girls aren't good at algebra and physics and perform better than you have before. Maybe better than the boy sitting next to you, no matter how cute, because you *can* and *should*."

She paused. This speech was longer than any I'd heard before. Introspective as if Regan were actually talking to her fifteen-year-old self. I shifted my weight even as I waited for her to speak again.

"I love you because you know, deep in your hearts, that no one else can tell that story, from that moment in the lunchroom, quite as well as you can," Regan said, her voice catching. "And I love you because you're here, soaking in something that we made together."

She got down on her knee and clasped about fifty young hands, making sure to linger for each as they squealed and danced.

"So, here's my task to each of you. Let me know on Instagram what your success is this week. I'll keep it going for as many weeks as you respond. I want to know what you mastered, conquered, overcame, learned, and mostly, how you became a better you."

She stood in one lithe motion. "Bye, now. We'll meet up again soon."

As she walked off the stage, she blinked back tears. Mindy met her at the edge of the curtain and handed over a small towel.

Regan pressed it to her face. I watched her shoulders rise, then fall. Unable to stand alone a moment longer, I strode over and wrapped her in my arms. For a moment, she melted in against me, clearly in need of comfort. Tears slid down her nose as she rested her cheek against my left pec, her arms encircling my waist.

"I'm going to miss each of those young ladies. They're so bright-eyed and full of this amazing mix of innocence and fire."

I pressed a kiss to the top of her sweaty head, inhaling the unique scent of Regan's shampoo intermixed with the intoxicating aroma of fresh, warm, perspiring female. I shifted so she wouldn't notice the growing bulge behind my zipper.

Then, she stiffened. Darryl's words swirled through my head. Regan was angry. I knew that before she tilted her head back, eyes blazing blue fire.

I braced myself for her words.

"You lied to me." She stepped out of my embrace as she hardened her stance.

So, Regan had read about the situation with Dean and Dianna. Not that I should have hoped she wouldn't see it. Though, I had hoped that. A fist seemed to slam behind my ribs and I winced. She had every right to be upset with me.

"I've been trying to tell you." Sort of. Not very hard. Because I didn't want to have this conversation. "That's why I came up to Oklahoma City. Why I texted you about needing to talk…"

"You were going to tell me *then*?" She paused, seeming to gather her composure. "Why didn't you?"

I ignored the people moving around us, needing to set the record straight *now* before she built new walls I'd have to scale.

"The night I was drunk? Dianna cornered me outside a restaurant earlier that day. And she said the boy…Sean…could be mine."

Regan stepped back, color draining from her face. "I read that. In a gossip magazine, Carter."

I wanted to look away, to let my guilt overwhelm me, but I forced myself to hold her gaze, which blazed with righteous indignation but also…aw, hell. She was hurt. Deeply.

"I read the story about *my* boyfriend, a story everyone else seems to already know, in a stupid tabloid."

"Look, I'm sorry. I did try to tell you." When her gaze slashed at me, I held up my hands. "I…it's been a long time since I've had to consider someone else's feelings, and I guess I just missed the mark there."

That sounded pathetic even to my own ears. We both knew I hadn't wanted to tell her. And I was pretty sure I'd just made the situation worse with my lackluster apology.

She closed her eyes as emotions flitted across her face. She blew out a breath and steadied herself, clearly needing some space. I didn't want to give her any. She didn't let me decide. She hugged her arms over her chest and stepped further back.

"You lied to me," she said again.

"I didn't," I said, adamant.

"You never mentioned you might have a child. With your ex. That's a big, big deal."

"I might," I said, my voice tight. "Though…" Again I trailed off, unsure what to say.

Disappointment flared through me. I wanted her to tell me she'd continue to stick by me, but how could I ask her to do that?

"Can you give me a minute?" she asked. Her eyes were dazed and she didn't seem steady on her feet. Then she said, "I want you to leave."

"What?" I asked. I felt supercharged, like I'd been hit by a bolt of lightning. No way Regan was kicking me out.

She squared her shoulders, her jaw set. "I thought about this earlier, and I can't be with someone who lies to me."

"Regan…"

She made a chopping motion with her hand as she blinked back tears with the same ruthlessness I'd seen her do the first night I met her. "I can't be with a man I can't trust. I've done that already. With James. With…with my mother. With Vannah." She drew herself up, much as she'd done when she prepared to face her father.

And then the words, those terrible words fell from her lips, landing between us.

"I can't trust you."

I recoiled even as I shut down. I was the one who'd been wronged. By Dianna and Dean. How dare Regan try to paint me as the bad guy.

I clenched my teeth, the anger fueling my ability to keep the hurt from Regan's rejection at bay. "Fine."

I spun on my heel, stalking toward the door. In the reflection of the glass offset in the stage door, I saw her crumple to the floor, almost as if she'd used up all her reserves to get through these last, emotionally-charged moments with me.

Mindy rushed to her side. Darryl scowled as I strode past him.

Her choked sob ripped at my heart, but I kept going, my vision focused on the space between me, a buzzing building in my ears.

Regan broke up with me.

As I exited the venue, I leaned against the wall, taking a halting breath.

My chest ached and my eyes stung. I'd just lost something in that room, something with Regan, that I'd never had before.

My heart, definitely. But I feared, in my unwillingness to trust her with my deepest secrets, I'd lost the only woman who could ever love me with the ferocity and strength I felt for her.

CHAPTER THIRTY-FIVE | Regan

Mindy was at my side. She cleared her throat, her gaze apologetic when I finally met it. "Your fans are going to start coming back now."

I nodded, numb. "I'll be right there."

She grabbed my hand and pulled me through the backstage corridor. She led me into the large room we used for the meet-and-greet and shut the door. I struggled to keep my lip from trembling. Tears threatened to fall.

I'd done what I set out to do: I broke it off with Carter. I'd been smart this time, not like I was with James.

"Get it together," Mindy said. "These girls are going to want to see the fun woman who was out there tonight. Personal drama cannot interfere."

"Carter's more than drama." Rather, he had been. Until I told him to leave.

I tried to control my shaking hands. Forcing Carter from my life might hurt now, but, in the long run, I'd saved myself more hurt.

"Because he would have hurt me like James did, wouldn't he?" I asked Mindy.

Mindy shrugged. "You seemed to like Carter. And he clearly liked spending time with you. I mean, he came to another one of your shows tonight…"

We froze when a noise from the far side of the room echoed off the walls. We turned to see John Mitchell sitting on a couch, his recorder on his knee, a smug smile firmly planted on his lips.

"Don't stop on my account." John tipped his head toward the door. "Ah. This ought to be interesting."

Footsteps sounded just outside the door, and then, Olin stood, poised in the doorway. His face was darker than a rainy Austin night.

"Dad." I reeled around to face my father. "What are you doing here?"

"I heard you threw Carter out tonight." He smiled, genuine warmth radiating from his lips. In fact, he beamed with joy. "That was so smart, sweetie. He's a lowlife. Knocking up women and then manhandling them."

Hearing the words from my father's mouth, and in front of a rabid reporter, made my spine stiffen.

"You sure about that?" I asked.

Dad spread his arms, fingers splayed. "That—man—just wants in your pants and your bank account."

Mindy grimaced as she turned away, her distaste at my father's account obvious.

"No, he doesn't," I said. Carter didn't want or need my money. That, at least, I was sure of. "If he did, he could have already been there. And the only one in this room that's focused on my money is you."

I sucked in a ragged breath. Why had it taken me so long to see that my father didn't care about me? He cared about the money I made. The wealth he seemed to consider his own.

"No, Everly…" he began.

"My name is Regan. That's the one on my birth certificate."

Carter called me Regan. Carter saw me, not the stage persona. Maybe he wasn't like James. Maybe he wasn't like my father.

I'd asked him to leave. Told him we were done. Because he lied to me. Like my father had.

John Mitchell shifted in his seat, clearly enjoying the drama unfolding in front of him. I wanted to run. I wanted to cry. I wanted to rage.

John would write up every little detail and I'd have to relive tonight again, in stories and through another round of questions from other reporters.

"Your mother named you Regan," Dad said on a long sigh. "I always wanted a sweet little Everly. A pop princess. And you are, which is why you can forget that silly little side experiment with Camden Grace."

I'd known my father must have heard about that, and he assumed that since Carter and I broke it off, I wouldn't want to pursue any more songs with Cam. My dad looked so smug, like he'd won an important game. He wasn't concerned about how I felt, what I wanted.

And, as I looked at him, I could admit the painful truth: Olin Leroux wanted a famous kid under his thumb. One he could manipulate and control. And I'd let him do that to me for years because I feared he'd stop loving me if I stood up to him.

Trying to avoid that truth didn't make it any less valid or real. I wasn't sure if Cam would want to work with me now that I'd cut my relationship off with his brother, but that didn't negate the direction I wanted to take my career.

I sucked my lower lip into my mouth, appraising my father. Darryl stood behind Dad, his face contorted with concern. I glanced over at Mindy, who wore an identical expression to Darryl's.

My dancers poured through the door, all of them veering away from Olin. They always did that, I realized. They went out of their way to avoid my father.

Because he was toxic. He pushed and prodded me into doing what *he* wanted for my career.

Never mind that I had my own opinions and aspirations.

Tonight was a night of painful decisions. Ones that might not all be correct, but they'd allow me to focus on my career, on becoming a woman I could face in the mirror each day.

"It's time for you to go," I whispered.

"What?" Olin snapped.

I'd forced Carter out of my life for lying to me. Now, it was time to force my father out of my professional life for using my talent for his gain.

I drew myself up as my gaze flicked to Darryl. The big man and two others stepped forward, barely leaving enough space between our bodies for me to peek through toward my dad, almost like it was a prepared and choreographed response. It wasn't, at least on my end. But Darryl took protecting me seriously.

I drew a shaky breath and said the words I'd forced down so many times in the past. "You're fired."

Utter silence filled the room. Olin tore his gaze from mine, then dropped his head to his chest.

"You'd do that?" he rumbled. "To me?"

I trembled, but I faced him full-on. "I should have done this months ago. Maybe years. I have to take control of my career, and I've been too afraid to do so because of *you*."

John edged closer, no doubt recording this entire interaction. Yet, even knowing this would more than likely be tomorrow's juicy news, I stood tall and firm. Because severing this part of my relationship with my father was the right choice.

"I've always wanted to make music like my mom. You've known that and yet you pushed and pushed me in another direction. That has to stop." I sucked in both my lips in an attempt to stop them from trembling. My entire chin wobbled.

I swiped at my tear-filled eyes. "I'm not happy, Daddy. And I'm not my mother."

Instead of arguing as I expected, Olin studied me. Then, he seemed to pull into himself further. "You're right. I didn't want to see it, but you're right." He pressed his hands to his face and his shoulders began to shake.

My fingers turned icy and my whole body trembled.

"After James hurt you so badly. But I worried after your friend..." He cleared his throat.

Mindy stood, tense, arms crossed, near the door.

"What do you mean?" I blinked, trying to keep more tears from falling.

Olin swallowed, a thick, heavy sound. He wiped his cheeks. "That girl, Savannah. Your friend. She propositioned James. I saw her."

"What?" Mindy and I spoke in unison.

"She was killing herself. James was, too, and all I could think is I pushed you into that show, into that lion's den. You told me you didn't want that, but how could I let you track your career like your mother?"

He cleared his throat, his eyes red. "I didn't want you to end up like her. That Savannah girl. Or your mother."

Whatever else my dad was, he'd loved his wife. Even I could see he cared for me, too. But the way he went about showing that left much to be desired.

"I thought going out on your own might solve the drug issue. That's why I pushed so hard for that initial record deal. I've seen how unhappy you've become, and I know you've been putting me off during this tour."

"I kept thinking it would get better. You'd see how I was making the best choices to ensure your future. But you just kept getting sadder." My father glanced over at Darryl before dropping his gaze, his face filled with contrition. "I don't want you miserable, so I got you pills. Darryl was right about that."

"Why?" I could barely choke the word past the lump in my throat. My father just admitted to intentionally drugging me. I'd heard Darryl before, but until this moment the enormity of what he did hadn't hit me.

My father gave me drugs without my knowledge. Without my consent.

That betrayal rippled through me. Another level of pain I didn't know how to handle. I managed to stay standing, keenly aware of John's bright gaze and his recorder.

My entire life was going to be splashed all over tomorrow's papers and the Internet.

Savannah propositioned James. My eyes flashed over to Mindy, asking if she'd known. Her face was pinched as she shook her head, her eyes drifting toward John before dropping to her white knuckles where they clutched her clipboard.

My father sucked in a deep breath. "I don't know what I was thinking. I know what drugs do. I saw what they did to your mother, to your friend. Savannah wasn't the same person. She laughed about hurting you. They both did."

A new slash of pain cut into my heart. "I didn't know…and you didn't tell me…"

"I didn't want you to suffer more. James made you miserable. You wouldn't talk to me, but I could see it. I was so glad when you broke up with that boy."

Olin turned toward John, as I tried to process these newest revelations. "My daughter means the world to me. I can only hope that you'll tell the world the truth about her. I…"

He cleared his throat again. And I had to swallow hard to battle down the ache building in mine.

"I apologize for the way I behaved. I should never have forced you to do things you didn't want to do."

Darryl kept me from launching myself at him. My mind buzzed with the information he'd tossed at me, so casually. Details of my life I hadn't known but that hurt, terribly.

"Daddy, I love you. I will always love you. But you hurt me by not listening to what I need. You can't make these decisions for me anymore. I have to stand on my own. I have to live *my* life."

He nodded once. "I'm just…I'm going to go back to the hotel to pack."

He dipped his head, his face having aged, thanks to the ravages of grief. He shuffled toward the door as though the weight of the world had settled on his shoulders. While I felt for the man, concern weighted my chest and limbs as I worried over the hurt he'd so willingly caused me over the years.

He'd drugged me.

That story hadn't been a lie.

And now all the world would know it, thanks to John Mitchell.

———— ★ ————

I'd fired my father.

Late as it was, I insisted on driving down to Austin just in case Cam still wanted me there at the studio tomorrow. I couldn't give up that hope as well.

Not as everything else in my life imploded.

I ignored Darryl's grumbling as I sat in the passenger seat of the fancy SUV Mindy had rented for me. I'd showered and changed into a soft tee and cotton capri pants. My suitcase was in the back. But for the second time in a week, I'd left Mindy, and the rest of my staff. This time, they would head out of Dallas toward Houston without me. I needed space from them, space to figure out what I wanted. What I needed.

We sat in silence for a while, me absorbing what I'd said and the enormity of what I'd just done, and Darryl glancing at me much too often for a driver. He finally reached over and covered my hand with his.

I jolted at the contact. He wasn't a touchy-feeling man, and I had never encouraged that level of closeness. I didn't want it now.

"I…" No further words formed.

"You were really brave, Regan. What you did tonight. That was hard."

"My father probably hates me now," I said. My nose stung but I blinked back the building tears.

"I doubt it," Darryl said, his tone thoughtful. "I mean… he's maybe embarrassed. But tell me this…does he love being your manager? I mean, truly look forward to getting up each day talking to the record people and the concert venues?"

I shook my head. My father enjoyed power but he didn't like this work.

"Then, in the long run, he'll be relieved."

"What if he won't talk to me again?" I asked.

Darryl's big hand squeezed mine. "That's his loss."

Silence filled the luxury cabin of the Land Rover. Just like Carter's vehicle. Had Mindy gotten it on purpose, to make me feel even worse? I extricated my hand from Darryl's and once again looked out the window.

"But I don't think it'll come to that," Darryl said.

"And Carter? Do you think he's like James?" I asked.

We drove by trees and buildings. The desolation of the road surprised me. But, then, I normally stayed in the back of the bus, not paying attention to the scenery.

Darryl was quiet so long, I started to nod off. When he spoke, it was so softly that I suspected he didn't want me to hear. "No. I don't think Carter's like James. But it doesn't matter what I think."

Darryl drove to my house, the one I'd bought a few weeks ago, sight unseen. Online, I'd liked the mid-century feel of the place, but mostly, I loved the view of the lake.

The house was better than the pictures. I loved the fifties décor and the smooth wooden floors. The beds were all made, courtesy of the decorator I'd hired. So far, she'd managed to complete two of the bedrooms and the dining room. I still needed furniture for the living room and the rest of the house, but it was functional enough. I showed Darryl to the made-up guest room.

Sleep proved difficult. Maybe it was the newness of the house, but my brain refused to turn off. I was fearful of what the world would say. Eventually, I fell into a fitful sleep, wishing even in my dreams Carter lived anywhere but this city I planned to make my own.

I woke to the scent of coffee. After a quick shower, I dressed and headed out to the main room of my new home.

Darryl handed me a to-go cup of coffee.

I took a sip of the coffee and let the rich brew trickle down my throat. "That's good." My phone chimed from its spot in my purse. I pulled it out and felt the first flutters of relief mixed with panic.

"Cam asked if I can be there in the next thirty minutes."

Darryl nodded, snagging the car keys. "Let's go."

Cam smiled when I walked into the space, Darryl in tow. My nerves jangled up my spine. Today was important to me—to my career, especially since I'd put forth the first public hint that my next album would be a departure from the previous ones and I'd fired my father as my manager, but also because I wasn't sure how to handle the situation with Camden.

I pressed my hand to my fluttering stomach. I could do this. I had to do this. Time to knock my first single out of the park.

"Carter let me know he couldn't make it," Cam said.

I studied him, looking for censure. Finding none, I nodded.

"You wanna do the same thing with the video?" Cam asked.

He gestured to Chuck who was filming us. "I know your big following is on Instagram, so I asked Chuck to break videos down into fifteen to twenty seconds. Should give your folks a little sampling without giving away too much of the song."

"Sure," I said. I straightened my spine and tossed my hair back. "Absolutely. And…I'm in the market for a new manager in case you know anyone."

Cam winked. "I'll put some feelers out for you. Seeing as how you're finishing up your tour this week and then have some time in the studio, we can find you the perfect person."

"Thanks," I said, trying to ignore the flush creeping up my cheeks.

Cam tugged at his lip. "Y'all have had your share of drama. Good news is Jenna has adopted you, so now you're family. We'll take care of you."

He said that now. But would he feel the same way when he knew that I'd blown Carter off last night?

That had been the smart decision. Carter had lied to me. By omission, sure, but the worst of the betrayal came from his refusal to be honest when given the opportunity, and he'd had many. In fact, he hadn't said anything until I pushed him.

That couldn't bode well for a long term relationship.

My breath fluttered in my chest. Is that what I wanted?

I'd seen my life moving in that direction with Carter. Now...

Darryl settled into the booth with Ronnie and Cam leaned in closer. "How's he doing?"

I realized he meant with Dianna and the child situation. "He seemed okay," I hedged. "I mean, I only learned about it last night, so..."

"He didn't tell you?"

I shook my head. "Just so you know, I...um...I told him to leave."

I held my breath, waiting for Cam to tell me to get out of the studio. Instead, Cam considered me before he turned away muttering, "Damn idiot."

"Let's get going," Ronnie called through the speaker. "Our girl here has a concert in Houston to prep."

I settled onto the stool and strummed out the opening chords to my song. Ronnie asked me to sing it once through. Afterward, Cam made some suggestions, grabbing his guitar to show what he meant. I riffed off his addition to the melody.

Oh, that sounded fabulous. I began to sing and Cam's smile burst across his face. As we hit the third verse, I dropped my voice into a low, smoky range I rarely used.

I faltered when Cam gasped.

"Don't you dare stop," Ronnie howled. "That was amazing as hell. But this time hold off until the last couplet."

I sang about wanting my partner in bed. When I'd written this song, it had been all about longing, but now that I'd spent time with Carter, no way I couldn't think of him when I sang those lines.

I missed him.

Our connection had been instantaneous but our relationships so tumultuous that I wasn't sure if we could survive my touring and his crazy coding hours. I worried from the get-go if I took us too fast, if I let us keep going at this breakneck speed, we'd flame bright and flame out.

"Again," Ronnie said. "I want to hear the whole song with that same low, needy note. Think about that band I was telling you about, Cam."

He turned to face me. "The Sweeplings. Ronnie's obsessed with 'Hold Me.'"

"Can I hear that?" I asked.

Ronnie fumbled with a few buttons and then this haunting melody with breathy vocals and rich harmonies filled the space. I locked my jaw as the soprano lilt through her song of longing. A lump filled my throat.

"Got it," I said after the second verse. I couldn't listen to the rest and sing. Now, I just needed to channel those emotions into my own song.

I could sing my song. The career I'd always wanted depended on it.

We tried again, but Ronnie stopped us again. His comments had me focusing on him, not the situation with Carter. I tried to pull my mind from Cam's brother, but the version felt off—stilted.

Undeterred, Cam began to play the song from the stop. He

sang the beginning, a lament of missing his love. I met him for
the chorus, my fingers plucking extra notes from my strings
as the worry over my relationship with Carter caused nervous
energy to build. The second verse was mine, and I thought of
James, and my father, and all the loss and worry those relationships caused me. That led to my fears of Carter and his possible
child. My voice quavered but I pushed through.

"Stop!" Ronnie yelled, causing me to jump.

"What's up?" Cam asked, unperturbed.

"Camden, will you quit trying to compete with her vocals?
Play background. She's shining, it's her song, and I want to hear
her. So will the rest of the world."

Cam whistled into the microphone. "First time I've played
second fiddle, but I'll try."

"Not on your verse. It was perfect, but let Regan hold court
on these next few stanzas, then, Regan, drop back some of the
power and let Cam own this second chorus. For the final verse,
I want you to trade off lines, starting with Cam since you're
coming in hard. Build this tune up, y'all. I want to get slammed
in the gut. Like with the song I played you."

He switched off his mic and signaled to me to begin playing
my guitar. Cam joined me and then the drummer matched the
beat on a slow, steady roll, the kick drum a powerful throb that
hit me in the solar plexus.

I closed my eyes and channeled the emotion from hearing The
Sweeplings, from my heartache over Carter's lies and my decision
to kick him out of my life.

We hit the final verse as Cam pulled out certain words to hold in a single note while I sang the rest of the words. I opened my eyes as my voice tumbled low with the pain, making it huskier than usual.

"Better take a break while I listen to it and see what we need," Ronnie said, his tone dark.

——————— ★ ———————

After playing it over a few times, Ronnie decided he liked that version, but said it was missing something. He took bits and pieces of multiple more takes and mixed them for us to hear the rough cut. I was blown away by his ear for melody and emotional smackdowns.

"That's mighty fine," Cam muttered.

I nodded as I lifted a water bottle to my mouth, unable to speak around the lump in my throat.

Cam and I managed to work through another of my songs before my phone alarm chimed, signaling my need to wrap up and head down to Houston, which was only a couple of hours south.

Ronnie pulled me in for a hug after I stored my guitar. I inhaled the faint scent of cigarettes and…was that patchouli? I wasn't sure. My nose twitched but I hung on to the sinewy man for another long moment, basking in his approval.

"I'm thrilled Camden brought you into my place. We're going to make this album soar."

Darryl grasped the handle of my guitar case and tilted his head toward the door.

"I hope so," I said.

"And you got yourself a good family to fall back on," Ronnie whispered in my ear. "Camden and his brother are good people."

Unfortunately, his words caused my heart to stutter. I couldn't look at Cam without seeing Carter, remembering the worry in his eyes morphing into hurt when I told him to leave.

Ronnie stepped out of my embrace and patted my cheek. "I'll expect you back here in a week. We still have songs to work on."

"Yes, sir."

Ronnie cracked a smile, which made his scraggly goatee tremble.

"So, I'll see you Saturday night," Cam said.

I shifted my weight back and forth between my feet in an effort to stifle the nerves bubbling through me. "Um…are you sure?" I let Carter hang between us for a moment. Then, unable to leave it there, willing my flushed cheeks and damp eyes away, I continued, speaking fast to cover my faux pas. "I mean, is the song ready?"

Cam grinned his megawatt smile. "Darlin', the only thing I'm more sure about is Jenna. We'll get your fans worked up with the debut of your song, then you can sing it with me to my fans next week. We'll add my song to that rotation and I'll put out some stuff on my website."

I nibbled at my lip. Cam tugged at a piece of my hair, much as a boy would do to a sibling.

"Trust me. This is our home turf. Our *best* crowd. They'll be on board, so only good things are on the horizon."

Darryl stored my guitar in the back of my rental as I stood in the doorway, unwilling to pull away from Cam. I hesitated for another moment, and Cam seemed to understand.

Cam leaned in closer so that we had a modicum of privacy.

"He called me earlier, and I talked to him while we were on that break. His lawyer Kelly called. He's meeting with his team now. I told him I was working with you and he said he was glad."

I licked my lips, staring at Darryl. He motioned me out and I said goodbye to Cam, resisting the urge to ask what the lawyer said about the child and Carter's likelihood to get custody. Those details were no longer my business.

———— ★ ————

The next day was filled with sound and costume checks that seemed to go on for hours. But that was the price of such a large-scale tour. The audience didn't want just a concert—they paid for an experience. Mine was a bit darker than some of the current pop divas—as were my songs—but these young ladies paid to be entertained, and I wanted to make sure they got what they were anticipating.

I did my typical press junket before the concert that night, and the questions flew fast and furious. I did my best to answer honestly. The questions about Carter hurt the most.

"Why did you break up with Carter Grace?"

"Is it true you were just using him to get an in with his brother, Camden?"

"We knew from the beginning neither of us really had time for a relationship," I said.

We'd both been willing to make time for each other, though. Carter created that Scrabble app, just for me, which sat open on my phone, my turn to fill in a word.

I stared at it just before I went on stage, wishing I could answer, missing Carter's voice and knowing that he'd be here, smiling at me when I walked off the stage.

I thought back to the final question of the night: "Do you have a comment on James Peele's bankruptcy filing?"

I hadn't then, and I didn't now. Except that I knew James was not just a terrible businessman, he was a user of people as well as substances.

Carter was not. He'd tried to help me. He'd held me when I hurt and when I cried. Yes, he'd also lied to me about a huge revelation in his life. And, if I was being honest, that's what hurt: his not wanting to bear his soul to me as I felt I'd done with him.

Yet, instead of saying that, I clammed up and kicked him out.

And I didn't feel any better for it. In fact, I felt worse.

The show blew the previous few out of the water. Cam's teasers of us spending time together in the studio, the hints of the melody, Ronnie's responses, all drew great interest. And when Cam's crew started dropping bits from our most recent time in the studio on Instagram, my current fans wrote millions of comments of support.

I found myself looking for Carter, or pulling out my phone to call him, only have to remind myself I'd ended our relationship.

Missing him hurt more each day.

Since I'd fired my father, sympathy shifted and most of the press corps seemed more inclined to write about my music and my future. Except for John Mitchell, who continued to malign my character.

Carter had been asked about us outside his temporary offices earlier. I knew because one of my backup dancers showed me the video, cooing over how sweet Carter was.

"Re...Everly Leroux is a beautiful woman, inside and out," Carter said, his eyes focused on the reporter. He looked tired, his skin wan. He smiled but it never reached his eyes, which remained clouded. "Getting to spend time with her, getting to know her...that's been the highlight of my life."

I re-watched the video in the privacy of my bunk until I ran the battery out of my iPad.

Mindy ran around, so much, her phone a permanent fixture to her ear, I wondered if she was avoiding me so that we couldn't talk about my father's accusations about Savannah. Whatever her reason, I decided to handle the issue myself. After considering my choices, I pulled up Susan Phipps number.

Carter had suggested it before—me talking one-on-one to a reporter I could trust. One to refute the partial truths or flat-out lies that John reported.

I made sure the door to my narrow bedroom was locked and called Susan.

When she picked up, stating her name in that clipped tone, I nearly lost my courage. Instead, I gripped the phone tighter as I stared out toward the Galleria area's gleaming glass high rises. A second downtown, the locals called it. After so many cities, I'd noted a skyscraper looked like most others.

I was tired. Of traveling. Of this tour. Of the drama with my family and stirred up by John. But, mostly, I was disappointed in myself for not realizing that I was allowing my fears that Carter would behave like James or my father to cloud my judgment.

"Susan, this is Everly Leroux. I wanted to offer you an exclusive into both my and Carter Grace's lives."

"Oh, my God," she breathed. "Yes. Please start talking."

I did.

CHAPTER THIRTY-SIX | Carter

I was still reeling from Regan's dismissal three days later. Dammit, I missed her. The scent of her skin, the soft curls that tickled my chin, and her intent gaze.

And once the test came back stating I wasn't Sean's father, the first person I wanted to call was Regan. I knew she'd understand how devastated I was. But I'd lost that right when I failed to be honest.

I'd lost the woman I loved and a son who was never mine.

Both hurt, deeply. But my need for contact with Regan grew with each passing minute into a painful misery I wasn't sure I could overcome.

As soon as Sean walked into my office, I'd known, deep down, he wasn't my child. The tilt of his chin and the way his nose sat on his face reminded me strongly of Dean. But when the child began to open up about his home life, I couldn't just walk away.

I'd been him, more or less, dealing with a disinterested stepfather who cared more about his own pleasure than his dissolving marriage or the kids he shared with his wife. Thankfully, both Cam and Remy understood my need to do something for the boy and his little sister.

I missed Regan's Houston concert, and wished I had the right to be there for the San Antonio one. I told Cam and the press I wasn't there because of the potential forward momentum in my court dates. Cam simply snorted at me, disgust causing his lip to curl.

"She told me y'all broke up."

"Oh." I shoved my hands into the pockets of my jeans and stared down at my bare feet. I needed to get my own place. I just didn't have the energy right now, mainly because I wanted some place Regan would like.

I was an idiot.

"That's all you got to say?" Cam asked.

"No." I met his disappointed gaze. "I chose not to tell her what a cluster my life was. I didn't want her to know I was caught up in a ten-year revenge plan."

"How's that working out for you?" Cam asked.

"Terribly."

Worry clouded Cam's features.

"Look, I'd drop the whole buyout if I could. Believe me. But…" I sighed. "New video games and new apps that can benefit from the illustrations and video graphics the company produces are popping up in the marketplace. It'd be a shift in focus for the group but a better long-term strategy that might continue to grow for a decade or more."

"And if you did that—incorporated this company into yours—you'd still want to get rid of your ex-friend because you don't work well together."

I snorted. "No one works well with Dean. That's the problem. And he'll make it *my* problem."

"All right. So that's it?" Cam asked.

"Of course not. But he thought I was horning in on his family, and that's why he came out with the next salvo." I shook my head. "I should have expected that. I knew what Dean was like, what Dianna was, too."

I slumped back into the sofa where I'd spent most of the past few hours. "I haven't let myself spend time with a woman like Regan—one I could care for—because I feared she would be like Dianna. That she would never see or care about me, just my fat bank account."

"Seems to me that's all Dianna does want from you," Cam muttered. He settled into the chair next to the couch. At least he didn't seem as angry with me.

"You're right. And I have to live with the fact there was a time in my life I fell for a woman like her. But seeing her the other day after meeting Regan, after loving her…"

I blew out a long, slow breath. I'd loved more than Regan's body. I loved her fighting spirit, her care toward her staff. Her willingness to make time for me in an endlessly hectic schedule.

"That was the past slamming into my future. I told Dianna not to touch me, not to have anything to do with me again. Because all I wanted was to hold *Regan*."

Before Cam could respond, Kelly called to let me know we needed to be at the courthouse in an hour.

———— ★ ————

Dianna tried to corner me as soon as I walked into the courthouse, but Kelly, Remy, and three other people who were part of Kelly's legal team surrounded me. While I didn't need the physical protection from Dianna, I probably needed the legal one.

"Mrs. Russell, I'm going to have to insist you leave my client alone," Kelly said.

Remy stood next to Kelly, his arms folded across his chest, his face neutral. Dianna flashed me a puppy-dog look that caused my shoulders to tense but she turned on her heel and headed down the hall.

Once the judge read the paternity results, Dean stood, clearly planning to take the offensive as soon as he walked out the door, smirking at me as he passed.

Prick. The judge must have thought so, too, because he banged his gavel hard.

"Mr. Russell, we are not finished here," he barked. "Sit down."

Dean took his sweet time, which incited greater fury in the judge's expression, turning his complexion from ruddy to tomato-red.

"I'd like to hear the testimony from Lucy Maher," the judge said. "She's detailed information from interviews she conducted with the children."

Dean leaned over and began to whisper in his lawyer's ear. Dianna sat next to him, her back straight and her fingers white as she clutched her Hermès handbag. I wouldn't know the design if my sister hadn't been drooling over it the last time I saw her. On her other side, sat another person who looked an awful lot like a lawyer. I frowned, wondering who that guy was.

"We object to pursuing this line of information, seeing as how Mr. Grace has no bearing on Mr. Russell's son," Dean's lawyer said as he smoothed down his expensive wool suit coat.

I managed to squash the need to roll my eyes. Yes, yes, we all noticed the precise cut of the jacket. Who cared? Kids' lives were at stake here.

The judge's head swiveled toward the gleaming table where Dean sat next to his standing lawyer. Because of the angle, I couldn't tell who the judge scowled at, but I assumed he hated Dean as much as I did. That guy cultivated the emotion in pretty much everyone he met.

"Overruled. Now…"

"This is ridiculous," Dean exclaimed, standing and buttoning his suit coat. He slicked back his already-slicked-back hair. "Why do we need to hear from a social worker who obviously is being paid by Carter?" Dean flung his arm in my direction.

Before the judge could speak, Dianna spoke. "Because her statements are true." Dianna's chin tilted up. "You do abuse both Sean and me, which is why I've asked the judge to hear this testimony and speed up the divorce proceedings."

She nodded to the suited man behind her, who rose and handed Dean a sheaf of papers. "You've been served. Since we fear for my client and her children's physical well-being, we've asked the judge to expedite a restraining order and request you return the keys to your shared residence until a time when the house may be debated between your counsel and me."

Dean sputtered, his face mottling. When he turned toward Dianna, she scuttled back, nearly falling over another chair. I rose, as did Remy and the rest of my team, though Kelly laid a hand on my arm.

"Don't get involved," she said.

Dean's chest heaved as he struggled to gain control of his

temper. Dianna's lawyer and the bailiff interceded between the couple. Dianna's face remained pale, her lips set in a tight, harsh line.

"I will have order in this courtroom," the judge snapped. "Mr. Grace, you and your counsel are free to leave. The rest of this discovery no longer concerns you."

I leaned over to Kelly. "I want to make sure Sean's okay. Whatever the legal way to do that is."

Kelly nodded. To the judge, she said, "Sir? If I may approach the bench?"

The judge, clearly exasperated by the irregular events, gestured her forward. Dean and Dianna's lawyers moved forward, too, but the bailiff cut them off after a look passed between him and the judge.

Kelly leaned forward and spoke quickly. The judge shot me a look, and for the first time I saw a flash of something in the softening of his expression. He dipped his head at me.

"I'll take it into consideration," he said, directly to me.

Kelly, Remy, and my other lawyers walked toward the doors. Dean's glare burned into my skin, but I refused to look his way. Within an hour of us walking out, a series of stories hit the major news outlets. Each one refuted Dean's version that I hit Dianna. Each story had multiple eyewitnesses to the event.

I called Remy to thank him for setting those up.

"You would have done the same for me, man."

"Yeah, but you haven't done anything to need eyewitness rebuttals."

"I'm a lawyer," he said. "I just think them deep in my head at night."

I shook my head. "You're a good friend. Thanks."

"I'd say any time, but I don't want to go through this again."

"Me either."

I drove back to the ranch and up to Cam's cottage. I wanted to call Regan and tell her about my day. I missed her. Worse, I was certain I always would. I climbed out of my car and headed into the house, grabbing my computer and a glass of sweet tea. I'd start house hunting.

Sometime later, Regan's number popped up on my phone. My mouth dried as I stared at the tiny picture of her blazing from the screen. Scenarios streamed through my head. None good.

I scrambled outside onto the porch before I answered her call. I needed the beauty of the family ranch to ease the pain in my heart and the fear boiling through my veins.

Thankfully, Jenna and Cam were out, visiting Jenna's mother. They went over at least once a week while Jenna's father was at a grief counseling group. I wasn't sure what, exactly, went down with her dad, but from the little Cam said, it was bad.

Right now, I was thankful for the solitude. This conversation would prove hard at best and blow up the world I wanted to build at worst.

"Regan. How was your show?" I asked.

She heaved a deep sigh.

My breath caught. "What's wrong?"

"I read so much news today, Carter. I wanted to make sure you're okay."

If I told her, that would make the situation more real. Regan was concerned, and I didn't want her to worry. But it was now or never. Either I told her everything or I lost her for good, forever. I might have already.

I could hear the finality of this call in her voice. "Preliminary results are in for the paternity test," I said, starting with my greatest pain, the worst of the truth.

"Okay. Not where I expected you to go. And?" her voice was soft.

"There's over a ninety-nine percent chance I'm not biologically related to Sean."

Damn, those words ripped me up, leaving me bleeding inside. "Oh, Carter. Oh."

She knew that already, but her words washed over me, a balm in this horrible night. The bleeding slowed and I breathed deeper past the pain in my heart.

"All right," she said. "Hang on."

I heard Regan talking to someone and then the chiming of a car door. I wondered where she was and wished she were here with me. San Antonio and Austin weren't that far apart. Maybe I could drive down there, see her.

"I just..." I trailed off. "I like the kid. I don't think I can leave him in a household where he's not safe."

"I hope you don't think you need to defend those feelings to me," Regan said, her voice filled with regret.

Something warmed in my chest, melting the angry knot of ice that had grown since Regan pushed me away. She'd called to hear the truth from me.

"I'm so sorry I didn't talk to you about Sean, about Dianna and Dean, when we started. I'd like to think I was too focused on getting to know you, but that's only part of it. I mean, I was tied up in knots about you, but I didn't want to give you another reason to think I was rotten. Like I did that first night, when I tried to seduce you."

I winced, wondering if I could be a bigger idiot. Bringing that up, now, was not going to endear me more to Regan.

"I've spent a lot of time thinking about your reasoning these past few days. I think I understand why you didn't want to talk about your past. I mean, I'm not proud of large swaths of mine. And…" she blew out a breath. "I was afraid that you'd want to get back together with Dianna."

I snorted. "Not ever going to happen." *Dianna can't hold a candle to you.* Much as I wanted to say those words, I wasn't sure Regan wanted to hear them.

I hesitated, but before I could mention Dianna's impending divorce, Regan said, "If Sean had been your son, I would have been so happy for you."

"I would have, too." I stared up at the small blots of light interspersed between the thick black cloak of the night sky. Because she deserved my thoughts, I said, "It hurts, Regan, because part of me wanted him to be mine."

"I get that. From the other side, though. I wanted my mom to stick around longer. To care more about me than the drugs and everything else spiraling out of control."

Cicadas hummed and a whippoorwill called. "Want to tell me about that?" I asked. Hopefully, I handled that correctly. So many years had passed since I'd tried to share with another person. I didn't know if I was doing this right or well, but I did know I cared, deeply, about Regan's well-being and her happiness.

"I hate talking about it," she muttered. "But it's why I kept my dad around so long…why he was upset with you and was relieved when I broke up with you."

As I waited for Regan to talk, I went inside and grabbed another glass of sweet tea. Coming back outside, I leaned against the white pillar. The air was warm. I sipped my drink, thankful to be talking to this woman. No more whiskey for me—not even the good stuff Regan bought. I needed to feel this pain I'd caused her and myself. I needed to own it.

"I told you my mother had an affair," she said. "She planned to leave my father. This all happened right around the time scouts became interested in me. For the television series."

"How old were you?" I asked.

"When I found out about the affair? Twelve."

"And the show?"

"Fourteen. My mom wanted me to do it so that she'd have a comfortable cushion to leave my father. No one asked what *I* wanted. Originally, my dad said no. He…um…he became verbally abusive. To my mom."

I pressed my thumb knuckles to my eyes. "And you saw it. Lived it."

"Yeah."

"Did he abuse you that same way?"

"No," Regan said. "He's not a bad man, Carter. You have to understand. My dad's world imploded. Like, big time. He lost his business. He was in the process of losing his wife, who planned to take me away. He knew he'd lose me because my mother was smart. She taped him. But…here's the kicker. My dad loved her. So much."

She inhaled hard. "Give me a minute."

I waited, staring out into the night.

"She killed herself," Regan murmured. "That night…she and her boyfriend broke up. I heard her begging him not to leave her. He was married, too, and decided he couldn't do that to his wife and kids. My mom…my mom took a bunch of pills and got in her car. We're lucky she didn't hurt anyone else. She was going so fast when she hit that pylon."

"Regan." What to say. *I'm sorry* seemed inadequate. "What you've been through."

"I loved her. She was a good mother to me, but she wasn't a good wife. She was selfish, thinking about herself. What she gained from her relationships."

"So you kept your father on your payroll to try and help him."

"And I hurt to think he was John's source. He told me…the other night when I fired him? He said he loves me. But I know he resents that I look like my mother. Well, minus the eyes. Mom's eyes were dark. She was an incredibly beautiful woman."

"So are you."

Headlights cut down the driveway. I sighed. Cam must be home. I didn't want to interact with my brother tonight. I wanted to keep talking to Regan.

"I asked you before if you were one of the good guys," Regan said. Her nerves vibrated through the phone line.

And there was the question.

"I've tried to be one of the decent ones. I haven't always lived up to that. Look what I did to us." Those words hurt to push past my lips, but they were the truth.

The headlights blinded me for a minute as I squinted. Not Cam's truck. The lights went out and I saw the outline of a woman with long, curly hair sitting in the driver seat.

"Regan?"

"James hurt me. He broke my confidence, my self-esteem, and even my faith in the people I allowed close to me. I let him do that because I wanted someone to love me for *me*. He was supposed to be that person."

She swallowed, a thick sound followed by a sniffle. I gripped the phone tighter, trying to stop my shaking. After she'd seen those awful news reports, she'd driven here, to see me.

"I lived in a world of beautiful people and easy sex, but I didn't know how to *be* those things. I just wanted to be loved. James… He never did. He never *could*."

Shit. Regan and I were more alike than I'd realized. Her mom, my stepfather. Her first love betrayed her just as mine had. Yet, she kept going, trying to help her father and me.

"I'd never hurt you, Regan. Not on purpose and never with my fist." I stood so that I could make eye contact, but I made no effort to step toward her SUV. I didn't want her to feel threatened or coerced. If she wanted to come to me, she would.

I had to hope that she wanted to. I swallowed, trying to get some moisture back into my dry mouth.

"I didn't hit Dianna. I know you're wondering. I would, too. Even with all those articles."

"Remy's name was in all of them. He spearheaded the effort to clear your name, didn't he?" Regan asked.

"Yes. And just so you know, I didn't ask him to do that."

"But you were worried something like this would come out," she said.

I nodded. "I've never been more ashamed of anything I've done more." Just saying the words burned up my throat.

"I swear to you that I didn't hurt her," I said. "I started taking martial arts and meditation classes—when I moved to San Francisco, after college—to make sure I could control my emotions. I can't promise you I'll never get that angry again. But I can swear on my life, on my mama's, on my future children's, I'll never hurt you."

She stepped out of the vehicle, all that long leg still encased in her silver-sequined high heeled-boot. She'd come straight to me, not bothering to change.

"I saw you with my dad. Darryl said I can trust you." She paused as if gathering her courage. "More importantly…I know I can."

My heart thudded hard in my chest, and I nodded as it thrummed out her name: Re-gan, Re-gan.

Losing the chance at fatherhood with Sean ached. But this… what I had the chance to build with Regan was real; I knew enough about the entertainment business from my brother to know we'd have to work hard to keep our relationship our main focus, but we could do it.

Because we needed each other.

And she'd come here, to see me.

She let her phone drop from her ear as she closed the door.

"I believe you. That you didn't hit her, that you don't want her now, that you want to love me."

"God, Regan." I moved toward her, not stopping until she was in my arms, my face buried in her thick mane of hair.

"This week's been terrible. I've missed you. I thought earlier that today's been the worst day of my life. But now, it's the best. Because you're here. You're with me. You gave me the chance I probably didn't deserve, but you need to know that I love you."

She smiled as she wrapped her arms around my neck. "I love you, too, Carter."

"That doesn't mean all this media drama is going to disappear."

This time Regan's smile turned sly. "I have a plan there."

"Do I want to know?" I asked.

She shrugged. "I offered Susan Phipps an exclusive. It was supposed to come out today but then the story about the Russell divorce and Sean's paternity came out. And that was followed by those articles from your friends, refuting everything Dean's said."

I winced. She speared her fingers into my hair and began massaging my scalp. "None of that, now. By the way, Susan called me just before I went on stage. She spoke to what she says were multiple 'credible' sources that discredited Dean, not just his comments about you, but in business. She's turning my interview into a series. The first one releases tomorrow morning." She cleared her throat. "It's about us. Our relationship. I hope that's okay."

"More than okay. I want the world to know I love you. That I'm with you."

She smiled, that little dimple popping out in her cheek. Her bright eyes gleamed in the starlight, and I wanted to remember this moment forever.

"That you're mine," she said.

"I am," I whispered, my lips a hair's breadth from hers. Happiness bubbled through my chest.

I kissed her. Her lips tasted like cherries and her mouth tasted like home.

———— ★ ————

Kelly called me just after I exited the shower the next morning to tell me Dianna's lawyers reached out to Remy and Kelly, letting them know she was interested in selling her shares in Dean's company.

"She wants the market rate for those shares, but the market rate from last week, before the world knew the company was in turmoil."

"Done," I said. "I'll have Remy draft the purchase order."

"You don't need to be generous to the woman," Kelly pointed out. My lawyer was steel over supple leather—a strong Texan who didn't like to be pushed around or taken advantage of. I got it because we shared those qualities.

"Before you lecture me on being too softhearted, I'm doing this because, yes, I want the company and think it'll be a good long-term investment, but also because I plan to have Remy set up some of the money in trusts for the kids. I want to make sure they're as protected as possible from Dean."

He was the common threat, the one who could continue to

disappoint and hurt Sean, his sister, and Dianna. I didn't want that to happen.

Based on Sean's and his little sister's testimony, Dean was going to have to handle child protective services for a significant amount of time.

Funny how taking over Dean's company fell so far back on my list of priorities now. Part of me thought I should let the man keep the company just to assuage his pride, but doing so wouldn't ensure his kids' future. Not the way buying him out would.

Regan stepped into her bedroom where I sat on the bed. She looked gorgeous in a pair of white linen pants and a pale blue lacy halter top. She nibbled at her lower lip, showing her nerves. I walked toward her and took her hand. Of course she could hear this; she needed to know what was going on, to be a part of my decision-making.

Regan squeezed my fingers and smiled at me. I took that to mean she approved of my thinking. She leaned down and kissed my cheek. Much as I wanted to kiss her again, more fully, she pulled back and pointed toward the door.

Right. She needed to get to the stadium to go through her sound checks and interviews. I dipped my head in understanding.

"Hang on, Kelly." I put the phone down.

I stood as I pulled Regan in close. "I'm going to miss you today but I can't wait to be there, cheering for you tonight."

She patted my chest, her eyes still holding some anxiousness. "Susan's article came out. I need to get to the venue and answer questions."

I pressed one more kiss to her lips, thankful when she kissed

me back. Then, I had to let her go to face her demons as I went
back to the phone to fight my own.

———————— ★ ————————

Tonight was important for so many reasons. Cam and Regan
planned to debut their duet for the world to the Austin crowd.
No way I could miss that.

Regan fought for me, for us. I would do the same. We
could—we would—have a future. A beautiful one, together.

I kept up the silent litany all the way to the venue. I road with
Cam, Jenna, and Kate in the back of Cam's big SUV, letting Kate
take shotgun. She and Cam's head of security, Chuck, chatted the
whole way while I worried over Regan's day. We hadn't had the
chance to talk much.

Most of the security detail at the venue knew Cam by sight
and ushered us into the bowels of the huge space. I'd texted
Regan of our arrival from the parking lot and she padded out of a
dressing room in a short blue skirt and a men's shirt, bare feet and
full makeup and waterfall-smooth hair. Her toenails were painted
a sparkly blue a few shades lighter than the slinky skirt. Seeing
her like this, vulnerable, with cute toenail designs, caused my
chest to ache. She was so unbelievably lovely.

Kate stood next to me and made a sighing whimper as Regan
welcomed her.

"I love your music," Kate stammered.

Regan smiled but it turned guarded. "Thanks. That means a
lot coming from a woman with so much talent in the family."

Kate apprised Cam and then shrugged. "He didn't get me
through my last breakup. You did."

This time Regan offered a full-blown grin. "We ladies must stick together."

"Amen," Jenna said, reaching out a fist that Regan and Kate both bumped.

I glanced over at Cam, who raised his eyebrows back. Yeah, we'd managed to get ourselves outnumbered. But his smile matched my own because he loved that his gal got on so well with our sister and my girl.

"You still sure about this?" Regan asked Cam.

"Double sure and triple ready. My album's ready to drop early—my fans love when I can pull tricks like that—thanks to you doing the vocals."

"He was waiting for the right singer for that song," Jenna said, practically bouncing on her toes. "I told him you were it."

Cam smiled down at her, his good humor as indulgent as his affection. "True. Regan rocked that tune. I have this feeling it'll be the most popular on the album." He turned to Regan. "I'm going to make some vinyl available after the show tonight."

Regan's eyes widened and she whistled. "You do know how to work your marketing machine."

Cam winked at her. "Keeps me on top of the heap."

"Like Yertle the Turtle," Kate muttered.

We all laughed at that. Cam always had to be king of the mountain. I might be competitive, but my brother took it to levels previously unseen. Probably how he made it back from his multiple army tours alive.

I slapped his back. "Glad to be here tonight with you, baby brother."

"Glad you came to your senses and decided to keep this gal close," he returned, smiling at Regan, who blushed. "She's pretty fantastic, and I'm not just talking about those pipes."

I shook my head. Cam might lay it on thick, but he was right. I was lucky Regan gave me another shot. These next days wouldn't be easy as the press attempted to shred my reputation. Maybe I'd sue Dean for slander. I'd have to see what my legal team thought the best course of action to clear my name.

"I'll call you out for my first encore," Regan said. "I have a feeling we'll be there a while."

"You got it." Cam rubbed his hands together, his mouth stretching wide with glee. "I want to check out your refreshments table. I've heard good things."

CHAPTER THIRTY-SEVEN | Regan

Maybe it was knowing Camden Grace stood off to the side—my knees were jelly and my hands shook. I channeled every bit of my inner diva and not only danced my heart out but sang with an abandon my father had always frowned upon.

Until my conversation with Carter, I hadn't realized that it wasn't so much me singing that upset Olin—it was the fact I reminded him of my mother.

At least now I could see the parts of my relationship with my father that needed work. And we would once Dad returned from his trip. Though I missed him, I was glad he'd chosen to go. We both needed to get used to me as a competent adult.

After an hour and a half of performing, I walked off stage, out of breath, and grabbed the bottle of water Mindy held out. My chest heaved as I drank, and I used the bottle as cover to study her.

Mindy had been off since our last conversation about Vannah, drawing in more when my father told us our friend was the one to instigate the affair with James. Thanks to the drama with Carter, I hadn't had a chance to talk to her, but I would. Soon.

I ignored John Mitchell who scowled at me from behind Carter and his family. Kate jumped up and down, clapping.

"You are so freaking awesome," she gushed.

I smiled, happy Carter's sister was happy. With greater

trepidation, I turned toward Cam and Jenna. They were the professionals, and their opinions mattered to me.

Jenna grabbed my hand. "Carter just told me you wanted me to make you a guitar. Yes with sugar on top!" Her face shone with sincerity.

I smiled, still trying to catch my breath. "I'd love to talk to you about that. Soon."

Jenna continued to hold my hand, her eyes intense. "I *have* to add you to my roster now as you begin your new direction. While you were singing, I had one of the guards run to the shop and collect a couple that might work for now." She turned and scowled at Carter. "If I'd known about this sooner, I would have been better prepared."

"Don't blame Carter," I said. "I hadn't gotten up the courage to ask you."

Jenna scoffed. "Please. Like I'd let anyone else make you an instrument, Miss Superstar."

She bent down and opened the clasps on the cases, opening the lids to reveal two gleaming works of art. She lifted out the right one, which was made from a lighter wood. Ash, I decided. The narrow, almost feminine body was awash in an intricate pattern of sunburst.

"I thought maybe this one was right for the edgy bluegrass sound you're going for," Jenna said as she strummed out a chord. The resonance was deep, gorgeous.

I stared at her, dumbfounded, unsure how to answer.

Carter hugged me to his side. "Jen's serious about outfitting all the best acts. It's great press for her, too."

"Okay," I managed to stammer. "You're sure it's okay for me to play it?" I asked.

Jenna and Cam smiled, probably amused by my awestruck tone. But…a Jenna Olsen original? Nope. I had not expected that possibility. At least not tonight.

Jenna nodded. I unhooked my older model and handed it to Mindy.

Everyone ooohed as I secured it to the strap. I strummed, finding it in perfect tune. My eyes flashed up to Jenna's, who smiled wide.

"Welcome to the family," she said. "But I'm still making you a custom instrument."

I shook my head, unable to speak.

Mindy touched my elbow. "You need to go back out."

I nodded, trying to breathe past the emotion in my throat. I was standing on the precipice. This was the change, taking charge of my life and my career, just as I'd wanted to for years.

I one-arm-hugged Jenna, leaning in to whisper a thank you. She patted me with a gentle hand as if she understood how big a deal these next few moments were to me.

Carter pressed a soft kiss to my temple. I still felt the lingering sweetness of the kiss as I stepped out onto the stage, blinded, as always, by the lights. But my smile was genuine as I waved.

I walked to my mic, trying to ignore the butterflies in my stomach.

"Like my new guitar?" I asked.

The crowd screamed. I chuckled, calming. Most people were uncomfortable in front of crowds, but I'd lived my life on the stage. This was one of my homes. And these people were here because they loved my music. Hopefully, they'd still love my new direction.

"Jenna Olsen made it. She's letting me test it out tonight. Know why?"

I waited for the screaming to die down. "I worked on a new song with her fiancé, Camden Grace."

More cheering. Still, my nerves grew, my neck chilled. I fought back the urge to shiver. "I guess you heard those snippets of the song," I said, chuckling. "Guess what? Cam's here tonight."

Gasps and screams littered the air. I leaned in closer, making this moment more intimate.

"In case you didn't know, I'm dating Cam's brother. Carter's smart, funny, and just about the most perfect boyfriend a girl could ask for. I told all that to the *Times*. You can read Susan's story if you want."

There, that kind of public statement would quiet any speculation about our relationship. That was the best I could do for now.

"So, like I said, Cam and I worked on a song for his album." I winked. "I'm telling you, it was a blast to be in the studio with him. It's not often I get to work with a musician of Camden Grace's caliber."

I held my hand out to the open second microphone, next to mine.

"Cam suggested we play it for you. Our home crowd. If you want to hear it."

The screaming made me wish I'd worn two earplugs. I'd taken to wearing one in my left ear, and it took all my will power not to wince at the noise level. Cam strode out in his worn jeans and motorcycle boots. I'd never thought of it before, but he didn't wear a cowboy hat either. Sometimes a ball cap. But tonight, his dark hair—so like Carter's, yet shorter—was combed back. He waved to the audience, who had to be getting hoarse.

"Y'all ready to rock, Austin-style?" he called into the mic.

This time, I winced even as I laughed. This crowd just blew the lid off the stadium and I was pretty sure they could be heard all the way out in California.

Cam started strumming his guitar. He looked over at me, shimmying his shoulder a little in that signature move that made women everywhere faint with lust.

"Once you try a Jenna Olsen, nothing else measures up," he said.

He winked and I shook my head. His love for Jenna made me giddy because I loved Carter like that. And, it seemed Carter loved me with the same devotion. A girl couldn't get much luckier.

He began the melody to his tune. I joined in, just as I had during the studio session. Cam's grin widened to Cheshire-cat scope.

"Did y'all know she could play like that?"

The spotlight fixed on me and I worked my way through the chords, loving how the notes reverberated through my fingers and chest.

Cam began to hum. The entire stadium fell silent. I could actually feel their concentration.

He hit the opening note and held it. The audience leaned

in as he continued singing the first verse. I hit my mark at the beginning of the chorus, and we harmonized. Cam turned toward me, holding my gaze. We'd practiced together a few times, but I appreciated his cues.

Our voices blended and rose into the chorus, slamming into the second verse. I sank deeper into my range, my eyes staying fixed on Cam. His eyes were burning with pleasure as we climbed back up the octaves. He hit his top note, then he pulled back into his rich bass as I sang higher into soprano.

Our chords remained in perfect synchronicity. Each note sounded pure and perfect. Cam wasn't kidding—now that I'd played one of Jenna's guitars, I didn't want to go back to my other one.

We barreled into the last chorus, catching our notes with that perfect precision that left a tiny pause between—that magic so tricky to achieve.

My heart pounded because this was the best I'd ever sung. *Ever*. Not even with my mother had I managed such a beautiful melody.

Cam raised his guitar's neck high and finished his last chord with a flourish. I blinked out into the audience. The faces staring up at me appeared to be in a stupor.

Then, the applause began. And if I'd thought it was loud earlier, I was proven wrong. So wrong.

Cam bowed. He held out his arm to me and I bowed. Then I rushed over, careful of our guitars, to hug him. He rocked me back and forth before stepping back to his microphone. He mentioned this single was on his new album that was on sale in limited vinyl copies at one of the local music shops. The digital album would drop next week.

For the first time in my concert-career, people made a mad dash to the exits, clearly excited to get their hands on the vinyl version. I walked off stage and straight into Carter's arms. After a long and perfect kiss, he set me back on my feet.

John Mitchell touched my arm. For the first time since meeting him, his expression had lost that smug look I resented. His face held a combination of consternation and regret.

"I wanted to talk to you earlier because I owe you a deep apology. I wanted you to know I plan to write a full retraction tomorrow for that article."

I knew which one he meant—the article that still burned me so badly because it said I had little to no musical talent and relied heavily on auto-tuning and other technologies to get my "signature" throaty sound in my music.

"Thank you," I said, my tone stiff. I couldn't help it. This man had written multiple critical editorials about me. Carter wrapped an arm around me, his fingers warm against the exposed skin at my waist.

John turned to Carter. "I wanted to let you know that Dianna Russell reached me earlier. Actually, she called me on the urging from Susan Phipps."

I nibbled at the corner of my lip. Yes, I'd given the interview John wanted. But I'd given it to the reporter of my choosing, and she'd handled the history with my father and even that love triangle with Vannah and James with a sensitivity John never attempted.

"Susie called me afterward. I take it Mr. Russell is not pleased with your takeover of his company. Since the business aspect isn't our normal story, I contacted one of my friends at *Wired*. They'll be running the piece about Mr. Russell's lies and his attempts to extort funds from you, Mr. Grace, tomorrow morning."

Carter raised his eyebrows in surprise.

"Thanks for letting me know," Carter said. He held out his hand and John shook it.

The reporter turned back to me, hands shoved deep in his pockets. "It's likely I've lost my job over this set of pieces I reported on the past few weeks."

For the first time, John looked unsure, maybe even disappointed.

"I just wanted you to know, I did believe everything I was told," he said.

A cold chill slithered down my spine, ruining the high of moments before. "Not my father," I said.

I paused, unable to get out the next words for a moment, thanks to the giant knot of emotion tearing into my throat. "He's not your source."

John shook his head, his mouth turning down. "I spoke to my editor this afternoon about how to handle this situation because your father brought a couple of pertinent facts to light after the Dallas concert. Ones I needed to research before I went to my editor." John swallowed as if trying to swallow a too-large pill.

Dallas, the night I fired my father. In that moment, I moved from a massive high of a perfectly-performed song to tears. I missed my dad. Carter hugged me tighter.

"I've been working to verify—triple verify—facts to make sure we have eyewitnesses for everything we're going to report. I have to since I wrote those first articles. And this new exposé contradicts most of my previous ones."

I took off the guitar and handed it back to Jenna, who settled it into its case.

I glanced around at Carter, Cam, Jenna, and Kate, trying to process what John was saying. So…who could have told him those lies about me?

"I'm not sure I understand," I said.

"That's part of what's going in my article tomorrow." John looked at something over my shoulder. His eyes burned with anger. "It's not typical to reveal a source, but my editor and I agreed it's necessary so that the readers understand why we printed what we did before. Hopefully, the readers will continue to trust the magazine once they understand who was providing us with the 'facts'."

"You're revealing your original source?" Carter asked. By his wide eyes and tone of voice I could tell he was as shocked as I was.

That little mustache on John's upper lip twitched. I had to resist the urge to step back. I was not a fan of caterpillars, real or imagined. He dragged his gaze back to mine, his face finally filled with something other than that smug expression I'd come to expect.

"I wanted to give you, Everly, the professional courtesy I should have shown you from the beginning. My editor asked why I didn't take your negations as seriously as she says I should have." He swallowed hard, clearly finding this crow-pie a difficult one to ingest.

"I think you'll understand once you hear my original audio recordings. I emailed them to your record label so they can forward them to you. My editor chose to make those available tomorrow for our subscribers as well."

Wow. Wow. I'd never heard of such a step. John's boss must be really worried about the fallout from the retraction. Or…dread pooled in my stomach. My eyes sought out Darryl. His lips were mashed into a flat, angry line. He shook his head, telling me he wasn't the source. I wanted that reassurance to calm me. It didn't.

"Who is it?" I whispered.

John's face filled with pity. "Mindy Evans."

CHAPTER THIRTY-EIGHT | Carter

I felt helpless when Regan darted past us down the hall. She locked her dressing room door, and I understood her desire to hide. This betrayal slashed her deeply. I needed to be there, to help her through the first tidal wave of grief and pain. I hugged my brother, Jenna, and Kate goodbye, noting their shell-shocked expressions.

Yeah, finding out her friend, her personal assistant was trading in lies? Regan's world just capsized. I could only assume the emotional ride was about to get really bumpy.

"Regan?" I asked, rattling the door handle.

Nothing.

I stood there, worry licking through my guts. Was Regan okay? Darryl stepped to my side, looking as blown away as I felt.

"I can open the lock," he said.

"Did you know?" I asked. "About Mindy?"

Darryl shook his head, tension radiating off him. "No. But now that I think about it, I'm not surprised. I just don't see how she could do that to Regan."

No wonder Mindy seemed to disappear as soon as possible these past few days. I hoped she felt guilty for the pain she'd caused Regan.

I tapped on the door again. What if Regan had fallen or passed out? "Pick the lock," I said.

Darryl went to work. After a minute, he grunted and eased the door open. Regan stood clutching her middle, head bowed, shoulders shaking.

My heart ached for her obvious grief. From the brief glance I shared with Darryl, I sensed he understood how deep Mindy's actions cut Regan. He swallowed hard and dipped his head toward me in a good luck, brother gesture. He drew the door closed, giving Regan and me privacy.

"Regan," I began. I had no further words.

Regan shook her head, tears streaming from her eyes.

"*I should have known.*"

"How could you?" My heart clenched in my chest as I watched her struggle to contain her emotions.

"Stupid! I'm so stupid!" She screamed the words, the full power of her lungs and voice behind it.

I flinched, my ears ringing. I turned my head at a movement in the doorway.

"Who else had access to my personal information? To John's contact information? To John himself?"

Mindy had opened the door. She clutched the white molding surrounding the frame. Her shoulders sagged, her face was ravaged by fatigue—and, I hoped, pain.

She deserved to feel a sliver of what Regan felt now.

"I'm sorry," she whispered.

Regan's head whipped toward her. Her chest heaved, then again. Her breath stuttered from her lips.

"You saw me *every day*, saw how much those articles hurt me."

Mindy's hand raised in supplication but she dropped it at

Regan's caustic tone. She lowered her eyes. Mascara streaked down her cheeks.

"Why," she whispered, so softly, I almost missed it. "How could you?"

Mindy dipped her head. Her tears splashed onto her top, darkening the material.

I'd never understand this world where people lied and broke each other with a casual acceptance that it would happen again to the next unlucky victim. First Dean and Dianna, and now Mindy, all trying to seize fame or money or glory, hurt so many people. But my main concern was for Regan. Would *always* be for Regan.

Hell of a time to realize she wasn't just my lover, my love. She was my missing pieces and my other half and all that romance-y bullshit I'd never believed in—even with Dianna. Because Dianna could never be the *right* woman for me. The right woman, the woman who had fought for an us, for a future from the minute I met her, stood in front of me, her heart bleeding.

That revelation rocked me to my core. My knees turned liquid and I staggered, catching the arm cushion.

As I tried to catch my breath, Regan faced her former confidant. Her eyes flashed and her face turned regal, cold. More beautiful than I'd ever seen it.

"You are not part of my life," Regan said. "Turn in your badge and other credentials right now. Drop them on that table and get out."

"Regan." Mindy's voice held supplication. "It doesn't matter that I thought I was avenging Vannah, does it?"

Mindy slowly shook her head, her eyes bleak as the tears poured from her lashes. "I thought you were the one who talked her into suicide. James said—"

"James!" Regan snarled. Her hands balled into fists and she shook with emotion. "You thought I'd convinced my best friend to kill herself? You *listened* to him? You let him own you all these years."

Regan had offered Mindy family, love. A person to mourn their lost friend with. But Mindy couldn't let go of her need to find justice for Savannah, and in so doing, she pushed away the one person who cared as much as she did.

I straightened. My own hurt from the revelations I'd made throbbed through my chest, but right now I needed to protect Regan.

"Go," I said to Mindy. "Respect her wishes."

Mindy's eyes flashed up to mine. This time Regan gripped my hand, clearly asking for support. My heart stuttered as I realized she was also showing me she trusted me to help her through this situation.

"You made your choice," I said, my voice calmer than I expected. Who knew handing over one's heart, one's happiness, could both rock me to my core and make me feel more stable than I had in years? I pulled Regan into my arms, knowing I'd do anything in my power to protect this woman.

"You chose to believe James, a known liar, over the woman who paid your salary, who treated you as a friend."

Mindy's tears poured out of her eyes faster. "I was wrong," she whispered.

"Susan Phipps's article proved that," Regan murmured against my chest.

I wasn't sure if Mindy could hear her, but it really didn't matter. I was so proud of Regan, for fighting for her career and her reputation through this personal attack. She'd even fought for us to have a chance.

"When you love someone, you stand by them, you share, and you try to see their point of view. Even when it's hard." I held Regan tighter, finally understanding why I'd devastated her by not sharing my own problems. I hadn't shown my trust, but, as importantly, I hadn't opened up to her about the parts of me that I didn't like.

"I—" Mindy began again.

Darryl cleared his throat from behind. Mindy looked back to see him and a few members of the stadium's security staff.

Mindy gulped as she opened her purse. She pulled out the passes that gave her access to all of Regan's holdings and backstage. She dropped them on the small side table with a thud.

Regan shuddered. I held her more tightly.

Mindy walked to the door, looking, I thought, much as a person walking to their execution. She stopped and turned back. She met my gaze, held it for one long moment. "For what it's worth, once I realized I was wrong, there wasn't any good way for me to back out."

"You could have told the truth," I said into the growing silence.

I glanced down and met Regan's watery eyes, letting her know I understood. Regan rested her cheek against my chest and began to sob.

CHAPTER THIRTY-NINE | Regan

"She's gone," Carter said, dropping his cheek against the top of my head. I shuddered, squeezing my eyes even more tightly shut. My first hire, a woman I considered a sister, betrayed me. And because I trusted her, she might well have destroyed Carter's business—definitely his plans for the next few years. Mine, too, but that seemed secondary to the trouble I'd caused Carter.

"I'm so sorry," I managed to gasp.

"I am, too, sweetheart." His words were laced with regret.

I pulled back, needing to see his eyes. He cupped my cheeks, his thumbs running under my eyes to clear away the few tears I couldn't stop from falling.

"Let's sit down," he said. His chest heaved as if he, too, were trying hard to hold his emotions together. He'd gone so pale there for a moment.

"I realized something today. With all this going down."

Carter stopped. He met my eyes with his. So beautiful. Everything about him was breathtaking—even the wounded, broken bits I knew he wanted to hide even from himself.

He smiled as he pressed a soft kiss to my lips. "You turning me down was the best possible wakeup call. You made me realize I wasn't living. You made me realize what I wanted."

His thumbs caressed my cheekbones, his eyes and voice steady and sure.

"I love you. I've said that before, but I need you to hear me. I love you so very much, more deeply than I ever thought possible."

He stroked his thumb over my cheek, his expression both serious and sad. "I get how deeply Mindy's hurt you. I want to take that pain away from you, though I can't. So I have to settle for working through it with you."

"She could have ruined your reputation. Your business—"

"But she didn't. You heard John," Carter said. "I'm going to be fine, not just on a personal level but on a professional one, too."

"But—"

"Regan, you have to let what might have been go. I, of all people, understand just how much that can ruin your life."

I threw myself back into his arms. He fell back against the far cushion with a grunt. His arm tightened around my waist. "You're my future, Regan. I want a lifetime of singing and fighting and loving with you. Mostly loving. And while I hope we don't argue, it'll be okay as long as I get makeup sex."

He winked. I shook my head, but I appreciated his attempt to raise my spirits.

"I promise to listen to you sing, even if it's country music. Forever."

I lifted my face to his, eager to kiss those beautiful lips. My heart still ached from Mindy's betrayal—her nasty lies to John hurt me, though, ironically, the constant drip of juicy, and false, gossip probably kept me in the forefront of fans' minds. Not that

I wanted negative press—unlike James, I didn't appreciate the ugly, frenetic emotions that came from reporters clamoring for the next big scoop about my life.

But Carter…his words were a boon to my heartache. Meeting him when I did proved tumultuous, sure, but also the best thing that had happened to me in years. He'd stood by me through the defamation, through the doubt. He would have continued to until I pushed him away.

What more could I ask for in a partner? I met his eyes. "I want that, too."

He smiled and his eyes lit up with joy, and my whole body flexed into his, so thrilled by his beauty.

"We've had a crazy few weeks," I said on a sigh. "But I just…I knew from the beginning you were special."

He shot me a cocky smirk and a wink that had an answering smile form on my lips. "I am."

I laughed. "I love you, Carter."

He brushed my long bangs off my forehead, his eyes tender. "I know, gorgeous. Now, kiss me."

I placed my lips over his. And it was better, deeper than any kiss we'd ever shared.

EPILOGUE | Five Months Later

"You saw it?" Carter asked, dropping a kiss on my cheek before sliding in next to me on the chaise lounge where I'd been enjoying some late afternoon sun on the back patio.

"Yeah."

Carter pulled the magazine from my hand and tossed it on the floor. I wound my arms around his neck.

"I missed you today," I said.

"And I missed you, Miss Platinum Performer."

I smiled and it kept widening until my cheeks ached. "I still can't believe the whole album sold that many copies."

He smacked a kiss on my lips. "I can."

He pulled back far enough to brush my long bangs from my forehead. His gaze was serious. "You are an amazingly talented woman, and I'm so lucky you're in my life."

I wiggled a little, unwilling to remove myself from his embrace, but the energy zipping through me needed an outlet.

"Your brother helped."

Carter scoffed. "You wrote nine of the ten songs. You sing some amazing vocals."

"And Cam plays mean lead guitar and harmonizes like an angel."

Carter scowled. "No talking about my baby brother like that. You love me more."

He snagged both arms around my waist and rotated onto his back and I sprawled over his chest.

"I do. Very much."

He smiled as he kissed me. "And I love you. We should do something about that," he said.

A tingle of pleasure swept up my spine. What had he meant by do something?

"How's your dad?" Carter asked.

The change in topics caught me by surprise.

"He's okay. He says the rehab facility taught him some important skills that are working."

"I'm glad he finally decided to go."

I nodded. "He has a couple of more weeks there. I can't believe I didn't know he was struggling with alcohol."

I frowned, hating that my father spent years using alcohol to numb the pain from losing my mother. And I felt so stupid for missing the signs.

"He hid it well." Carter ran his palms up and down my spine in that sinuous motion I loved.

"He did. After he gets out, who knows what he'll do. Not anything in music, which is for the best. The industry makes it too easy to get alcohol or drugs." I stacked my palms on Carter's pectorals and stared down at him.

"That's why I plan to keep you here, in my lair."

I laughed. Carter's lair was the house I'd bought months before. We'd spent weeks picking out the remainder of the décor together so now it was *our* house. We'd had to work around my recording sessions and Carter's meetings in San Francisco. He'd also spent significant time with his new illustration/animation team here in Austin.

"How'd it go with Sean today?" I asked.

This time, Carter's face split into a huge grin.

"Great," he chirped.

Such an unCarterlike noise, but something about that child had Carter acting more enthusiastic and excited than anyone else.

"I took him to that maker's space I told you about. We spent three hours working on a robot that can sweep floors."

Not my idea of fun, but it seemed right up Carter's alley. Sean was big into those STEM courses and tinkering with batteries and parts. Carter said the boy wanted to be a mechanical engineer. I could definitely see that in his future.

"I still can't believe the judge went along with my suggestion to let me step in to act as Sean's big brother."

Carter had gone through the application process with the group to make sure the entire process was legal. At first the judge had been hesitant, worrying that Dean would become more violent toward his children if Carter spent time with Sean. But, after Carter crafted a generous offer to buy Dean's company—one he knew Dean couldn't turn down since it was over the company's market value—Dianna sweetened the deal by suggesting Dean retain a larger percentage of the sale in exchange for relinquishing his parental rights.

The kids and Dianna were happy with the outcome and Dean recently relocated to Miami.

Carter still wished Sean was his son, but he seemed to enjoy spending time with the boy and he'd hinted a few times that he was more than ready to settle into domestic bliss just like his brother.

"Cam and Jen's wedding is coming up quick," Carter said, pulling me back to the present. I snuggled in closer, loving how good Carter smeller.

I nodded.

Carter raised an eyebrow as his gaze sharpened. "I don't think my baby brother should get married first. That's…well, it's bad form."

I chuckled even as I shook my head. "He's *five minutes* younger."

"Which is why I need to get married five minutes before him. So I can have the same amount of time with my beautiful bride as he gets with his."

"Wait." My breath caught. "Are you serious?"

"Sure am," he said with a grin.

"You want to get married."

He gave me a strange look. "Of course I do. In about six weeks. Think you can find a dress?"

Carter understood how hard I'd found Mindy's betrayal. Since Savannah's death—for much too long, she'd been my only female friend. But if we married the same time as Jenna and Camden, having fewer attendants wouldn't matter because we'd have our families there—the people we cared about surrounding us on the land that had been in Carter's family for generations.

And he'd set it up so that he took the blame. To protect my feelings.

"In six weeks," I whispered. "You, Carter, are sneaky."

He sat up, tugging me with him. He lifted me into his arms

and then turned, settling me on the chaise before sinking down onto his knee.

"I love you, Regan." He pressed soft kisses to both my wrists. "I always will. I want to knock you up and have lots of little singing babies with you."

I still struggled to catch my breath.

"And I want to kiss these perfect lips about a million times each day." He clasped my hands again. "I want to hold your hand through your next multiplatinum song and album and the Grammy awards I just know you're going to win. And I *really* want to watch you finally lose at Scrabble."

I laughed then. A deep belly laugh. This man. He was such a pleasure in my life.

He grinned before he let go of my right hand and dug in his pocket. He pulled out a blue box. I gaped. A Tiffany ring?

He popped open the lid. Tears filled my eyes. It was beautiful. A large diamond set in a swirl of sapphires.

"They reminded me of your eyes. Tell me you want all those things with me," he said with a crooked grin.

"No," I whispered. Before he could take it the wrong way, I cupped his strong jaw and kissed him long and slow and deep, letting him feel all my love and passion.

"I want to watch you reach your dreams with your business. And I want to hold your hand at the biggest tech industry events. And I want to destroy you in chess."

His eye lit up. "So, that's…"

"A yes, Carter. Of course I'll marry you. Yes, yes, yes!"

He whooped as he tugged out the ring and slid it on my

finger. He stared at my hand for a long minute, his eyes burning with a sensuality that tugged at my belly. Every woman should find a man who looked at her like she was his whole world. The feeling was heady and delicious.

He clasped me to him and kissed me with a touch of possessiveness I found sexy. Then he swept me up in his arms, carrying me inside.

I admired my ring as he strode across the living room.

"Why aren't you taking me to bed?" I asked.

He settled me at the dining room table. It was set with champagne and chocolate-covered strawberries, and a huge arrangement of all my favorite flowers in a range of the most delicate shade of pink spiraling out to fuchsia and a deep, rich red. I stared at them, realizing Carter had planned this moment. Then, I noticed the Scrabble board at the far end of the table.

I couldn't help but laugh again.

His eyes gleamed with wicked intent. "After I beat you here, I'm going to splay you out on the table and make sweet, sweet love to you, my fiancée."

I decided right then and there that I was going to win this game, *and* I was going to enjoy him making love to me.

I lost the game.

But I still won.

Because Carter was mine. And his loving was sweet and hot and perfect.

Just like our life together would be.

ACKNOWLEDGEMENTS

Daqri Bernardo of Covers by Combs created the delightful cover for this book and this series. You made something special, Daqri, and I thank you!

Thank you, Sarah Allan, for your detailed comments in the manuscript. I LOLed a couple of times. I really enjoy working with you.

Thanks to Charity Chimni for her time, understanding of AWS, and amazing proofreading skills.

And, as always, to Chris. You help me in so many ways. Thank you for all that you do (and for putting up with my crazy all these years).

ABOUT THE AUTHOR

USA TODAY Bestseller & Amazon International Bestseller.

Alexa Padgett's books have garnered awards from Kirkus Reviews, The Romance Reviews, and Readers' Favorites. Her newest novel, Deep in the Heart, has been added to several Goodreads Best lists.

Alexa spent a good part of her youth traveling. From Budapest to Belize, Calgary to Coober Pedy, she soaked in the myriad smells, sounds, and feels of these gorgeous places, wishing she could live in them all--at least for a while. And she does in her books.

She lives in New Mexico with her husband, children, and Great Pyrenees pup, Ash. When not writing, schlepping, or volunteering, she can be found in her tiny kitchen, channeling her inner Barefoot Contessa.

Austin by Morning

An Austin After Dark Book Three

CHAPTER ONE | Kate

I knocked my empty mug off my desk in my mad scramble through my papers, trying to find my ringing cell phone.

"Aha!" I called triumphantly. My burgeoning grin fell when I saw my brother Cam's number.

I picked up the mug and answered, "Hello?"

The mug's handle stayed on the ground. Dammit. It was my favorite—from a diner in Chicago—and I used it pretty much every day.

"I need your help, Katie Rose."

I slammed my head into the edge of my thick, wooden desk. I breathed out a curse and got up more carefully.

"I've asked you not to call me that, Cam," I said.

"Sorry. Old habits and all that."

"I'm twenty-six years old. You need to let go of the image of me as an incompetent brat."

"I never thought you were incompetent." He didn't say anything about the brat part. Right. I deserved that.

"Let's start again. What do you need, Camden?"

"My guitar's banged up. Can't play it today." Camden's voice was sheepish, and I'd bet he hung his head. Not that he was typically a sheepish or head-hanging kind of guy. A country music superstar, Cam and his ego typically matched. But his wife

Jenna made him that guitar, and he adored the instrument almost as much as he loved her.

Such shows of cuteness activated my gag reflex, but his love for Jenna was one of the reasons I hadn't completely quit talking to him.

"What did you do?" I asked.

"I didn't do a damn thing." His irritation crackled through the phone line. I sat up straight, tossing the pieces of my mug in the trash bin before I glared at my computer screen. I would have preferred to glare at Cam, but he was across town.

Convenient for him.

"Fine," I said on a sigh. "What happened to your precious?"

"She's standing right here next to me, looking as sparkly as her wedding and engagement rings."

Yeah, my brother had it bad. I bit back a smile but didn't try to stop my eye roll.

"*Camden.*"

"A roadie dropped my guitar. After he took it out of the case."

I gasped. "He took it out?"

"Wanted a closer look at the design Jenna made in the metal."

"Let me guess. He's no longer your roadie."

"He's working a different stage now," Cam replied, his voice dry.

One thing about my brother—he might be angry with the man responsible. No doubt he was livid, but he wouldn't want the guy to lose his job. Yet another reason I couldn't complete my justified anger of my dear big brother. He was kind. Noble. Good to Jenna.

The problem I struggled these past few months to get past was that Cam and his twin, Carter, went along with my mother to perpetuate the lie we were one big happy family.

The worst part in the situation wasn't the fact I was the only spawn of the no-account asshole our mother married. No, the *worst* part was that my family—the people who claimed to love me—wouldn't have told me the truth. Ever. If I hadn't overheard Cam and Carter talking…

That stuck deep in my chest and ripped at my heart each time I remembered the twisted mouth and shadowed eyes my mama turned my way when I asked her about the lie she kept pushing.

I shoved that memory away, just as I shoved all thoughts of my mother away.

Cam, my big brother who'd gone and married my boss, wouldn't let me take time to hide and lick my wounds. He said I'd work myself up into a fit of righteous anger.

Um… *Exactly.*

But Cam kept calling, kept dropping by and being sweet, which made staying angry with him difficult. Carter, Cam's twin, I'd pretty much forgiven since he wasn't even here most of the time my world imploded. Plus, he'd just gone through his own personal hell.

I had no such issue with my mama. We were *not* on speaking terms.

"I need you to bring me one of the other ones from the shop," Cam said, breaking me out of my reverie.

"Any one in particular? We can showcase the narrow-bodied mahogany or the bell-shaped Brazilian rosewood."

"Good. Yes, both of those. Jenna said there's another one in the back she's been working on."

"You expect me to carry three guitars into South by Southwest by myself?" I scowled. "That's over fifty thou in equipment, Camden. I'm capable of handling myself, but that seems excessive."

"Right. Fine. Then bring the two you think would be best," he said, his voice filled with exasperation. "C'mon, Katie Rose... er, Kate, sorry. I *need* a good guitar. I don't want to borrow my opening act's instrument. He's already a nightmare to work with."

He used the wheedling voice. The one I'd never been able to resist. Fine. I didn't want to resist it or Cam. I loved my big brother, even if he had hurt me deeply, and I wanted him to have a successful performance.

I glanced down in mournful silence at the pile of paperwork still in need of attention.

"I'll be there in an hour," I said.

"Thanks, darling. Honestly, you're the best."

"Too right. Now, be sure to play something I like."

"Right after all Jen's favorites," Cam promised.

Oh, she was *good*. Mainly because she hadn't put any effort into making him so sweet—he did that all himself because he wanted her happy. Much as I loved their interactions, I felt a short, sharp stab in my chest—much too near my heart. No time to think like that now.

"Bye." I hung up and stood. After a quick stretch, I pulled down my ruffle-fronted white silk blouse, re-tucking the front into my purple A-line skirt. I had great legs, and I liked to show those suckers off.

I slid my feet back into my black Manolo Blahniks—ninety percent off at last year's Nordstrom Rack sale, thank you very much. After I carefully placed both guitars in their cases and double-checked their clasps, I went to the front and shut off some of the lighting. I flipped the sign to "closed" and ensured the door was indeed locked, which it always was. Jenna had some trouble with an old…well, not flame, more like jerk-wad from her past. Since then, we didn't unlock the door until we knew who was on the other side.

After shutting down my computer, throwing my phone and charger into my purse, and digging out my keys, I, collected all my belongings and headed out to my car. I only had to run back in once—and then one more time to double-check I'd set the alarm and locked the rear door.

I looked back in longing one more time at the small, unassuming shop. My refuge, my baby these days. I'd much rather work.

With a sigh, I put the key in the ignition and wished for the patience to deal with this newest round of awkward.

———— ★ ————

I managed to get a decent parking spot, no doubt because today was the day before the festival began. I gripped the guitar case handles tight and let my gaze rove around the lot, hoping to see one of Cam's security guys hustling toward me. Normally, thanks to my brothers' overprotectiveness, I had my own security detail. Unlucky for me, Lou's daughter and wife were both too sick to function without his help.

So, I'd managed to spend the day alone, which I'd enjoyed

immensely until this moment when I had to carry two expensive guitars across a dark parking lot by myself.

I power-walked as fast as my stilettos permitted. Until I heard that voice.

I stopped at the very first note. His clear baritone licked over my skin and made me shake with a desperate need to hear—to feel—more of him.

I stood, trembling, shocked by my reaction.

My brother's voice regularly reaped international acclaim. I should be used to such beauty. With a small shake of my head, I gripped the handles of the guitar cases and strode with purpose toward Cam's trailer.

Until the unknown singer began the next verse. My chest tightened as he crooned the next few lyrics. Not straight-up country. It had more…soul, I guess, though I wasn't sure that was the correct word.

I hurried forward. A face…that voice deserved a face that I hoped would be as sexy.

Almost in a trance, I barely acknowledged Chuck, my brother's head of security, as I ran—hard to do in my stilettos—toward the stage.

"Katie Rose! You're a life saver."

Cam stepped into my path and I skittered to a halt, trying to ignore my hitched breath and my aching chest. Much as I wanted to shove the instruments at him, I couldn't. They were worth too much money.

"Who's singing?"

Cam's face settled into a scowl. "My opening act."

Jenna walked up behind him and slung an arm around his waist, pressing a kiss to his cheek.

"He's a nice man, Cam."

"Late. Demanding. Shouldn't I get to be the demanding one since I'm the headliner?"

"Demanding doesn't suit you. In this situation." Jenna smiled and Cam softened, just as he always did. Jenna turned to me with a beaming smile. "Thanks for doing this. I know it's way out of your way."

I shrugged. "I think I got the best of the ones we discussed. Where do you want them?" My body vibrated with the need to see the man singing, but I wouldn't leave until these instruments were secured.

"I'll use this one," Cam said, picking up a case. Jenna grabbed the handle of the other one and they turned in unison back toward his trailer.

"Come on!" Jenna called. "Cam's got great snacks."

The singing stopped. I cursed my brother—quietly. In my head.

"Just a sec." Now was my best opportunity. I peeked around the stage curtain and out at the man now scowling at his sound guy. At least I assumed he was the sound guy based on his headset and the conversation about too much bass coming through the speakers.

A musician I was not. But I sold Jenna's amazing designs and brought her more acclaim with each passing month. The Instagram profile for J. Olsen's proved my genius. People couldn't get enough of a beautiful young woman creating mega-star's instruments.

The singer brushed long blond hair back from his face. He

had a beard—full but not too long, a couple of inches, accentuating his jaw. His mustache covered part of his upper lip, causing me to shiver with distaste, but his lower lip was plump and pink. His nose appeared straight, if a tad long. A nice face, strong and masculine. At least what I could see of it.

He brushed his hair back again, then in annoyance, he pulled a hair tie from the thick golden mane and shook it out. He turned toward me and started the process of pulling all the pieces back. Blue eyes. Of course. He looked like a Viking. Well, his beard was too short for a full-on *How to Train Your Dragon* kind of warrior, but he was tall, athletic, and very sexy.

I'd never dated a blond man. Never dated one with long hair, either. Never thought shoulder-length hair on a man would be attractive. I was wrong. *So* wrong.

I shifted, planning to follow Jenna and Cam. Or, better yet, escape to my car and forget my brother or this blond god, who was almost near enough to touch. Then he glanced up and his eyes latched onto mine.

I gasped, shocked at the physicality of that look.

His face smoothed out as he continued to stare at me—just my face. He didn't drop his gaze to check out the rest of me, yet I still felt the heat from his ice-blue gaze steal over my skin.

"Thought we'd lost you, Kate," Cam said.

I huffed out the air I'd unwittingly held and shook my head at my brother, who placed his hand between my shoulder blades and led me away from the stage.

Good timing on Cam's part. If I stared at the singer much longer, I might have done something stupid—like run forward and fling myself at him. My cheeks flamed as my body cooled and logic returned.

Never had I wanted with such abandon. Sure, the man's voice spoke to me. Sure, he was attractive. So were many of the men I met through my brother.

I couldn't reconcile either of those with my deep-seated need.

And, if there was one thing I did not like, it was not being in control.

CHAPTER TWO | Rye

I scrubbed my hands over my cheeks and then over my bearded chin, willing my heart rate to return to normal.

All those auburn curls. A sassy pink mouth. That skirt flirting around her knees and just a hint of silky thighs. Holy hell. Lust slammed through me harder than a two-hundred-fifty-pound linebacker and knocked me as flat on my butt.

Camden Grace glanced back, a scowl surging across his face. Definite step-off vibe. Kate, he called her.

I wasn't sure how she fit into Cam's entourage, but he was protective of her. With me, the guy who showed up nearly an hour late and demanded to practice first. I understood Camden Grace's dislike.

I deserved his enmity.

Just as I deserved all the bad press surrounding my life this past year-plus. I glanced down at my scuffed sneakers and winced. I'd barely managed to leave the little house I'd rented for the next month. What I put on seemed so far down the list of details. Until now. I wanted to impress her. *Kate.*

I shoved my hands in my pockets and trudged back to my stool. With a sigh, I picked up my guitar.

"You ready for this next go?"

The sound engineer nodded so I started playing the song I

wrote five-and-a-half years ago. The one that took my life on such a different trajectory than I'd anticipated.

I sang the lyrics, still burning with Deirdre's eventual dismissal.

You promised me forever, but that turned out too soon
I wish in our time together we could get a re-do

People always assumed I was singing about a fictional woman who died too young.

I wasn't.

Sure. Before I wrote that song, Deirdre and I seemed to have everything going for us. We were in love, but life gobsmacked us, and Deirdre didn't cope well.

Or cope at all.

No, she didn't turn to booze or pills or any of that trite shit. No, my wife—correction, *ex*-wife as of last year—turned into a zombie from too little sleep and too much guilt. Which was why I needed to be smarter about this woman, Kate.

While I sang, I thought of how her long, burnished auburn ringlets might gleam in the stage lights, and how she rocked a prim dress shirt and flirty skirt better than any woman I'd ever seen. Even Deirdre. But that didn't matter.

Didn't matter that I was interested—didn't matter she was the first woman I'd wanted in years. None of that *could* matter.

I had a job to do—and I needed this gig to go well. I needed this show to go well to smooth over my months-late last album that was just now hitting the airwaves. I needed this show—no matter how much I didn't want to be there, didn't want to be opening for a country music star. I needed it to keep my cover for spending the next month in Austin without raising too many eyebrows.

I needed this show to take the heat off my wallet and my son.

Ike deserved more. He deserved every chance to see, to read the books he loved. And, yeah, while it was *my* dream, he deserved to play catch with me.

We'd never had that. Not when he struggled to focus around the growing black hole right smack dab in the center of his world.

Better to put the pretty Kate from my head. No one wanted to get involved with a man who had a special needs kid.

I'd learned that when my wife—*ex*-wife—walked out on us all those months ago.

———— ★ ————

I finished my last song and looked over at the tech. He gave me the thumbs up, so I hopped off the stool, already glancing at my watch.

Two hours and fifty-three minutes. If I hurried, I might be able to read Ike a story and kiss him goodnight. My favorite part of the day. Well, after the big hugs I received each day along with a yawned "good morning".

My kid was the rock-star. I just wish he could believe that.

I snapped my guitar into its case and hurried backstage.

"Good work there," Cam said.

I stopped. Spun toward him. While I wasn't a huge fan of his genre of music, I respected the hell out of his following—and the fact he wrote his own songs.

"Thanks. I appreciate you letting me go on first."

Cam raised an eyebrow even as his mouth settled into a scowl.

"Not like you gave me much of a choice."

Guilt built, causing my cheeks to flame. But I held his gaze. "I have somewhere I need to be."

Cam strolled closer. "You going to show up on Saturday?" he asked, his voice laced with something more menacing.

I dipped my head once.

"Cuz I don't work well with people who shirk their responsibilities."

I gripped my guitar case tighter. He had no idea about my responsibilities. But this little conversation made the likelihood of me seeing Ike awake tonight slim to none.

"You hear me?" Cam growled.

"Oh, I heard you. And the threat. All of it."

Cam's lips quirked up in acknowledgment of my unwilling-ness to back down. "Seems like you got a mighty big chip on your shoulder, Rye."

I shook my head. He didn't know the weight I carried on my shoulders. My son's future.

"I'll be here Saturday. I'll perform. I'll make sure the crowd's ready for you to hop up there and do your thing."

"Then, it's the fact I'm headlining and you're not? That's what's bothering you?"

Years ago, I had been all set to headline my own tour. Sometimes, late at night, I still tasted that excitement. But then Ike came—two months early and with a slew of health problems. Thankfully, most corrected over the last four years. Except for his vision.

"Nope. That doesn't bother me." Of course it did. While my

career made me enough money to support my son, I might never have the adulation or fame Cam had…or another woman to share it with.

Kate's wide gray eyes and glossy auburn curls flashed across my mind again, but I shut that down.

Cam continued to study me, his eyes narrowed as if he considered me little better than a gnarly bug.

"I'm going to head out," I said.

Cam sighed. "Fine. Do what you do."

"I'm leaving now, too," a soft, feminine voice said.

Cam and I turned. The redhead. Kate. Up close, I decided the name suited her. Her skin was creamy with a warm rose in her cheeks and all that flaming hair.

"You sure you don't want to stick around? Jenna's going to order up some 'cue."

Kate wrinkled her nose. "Much as I appreciate the offer—and I'm assuming you mean Stubbs—I'm not interested in being a third wheel."

Cam wrapped a companionable arm around her shoulder, but Kate's face stiffened near as much as her shoulders.

"You're never a third wheel. I like spending time with my sister."

"Half-sister," she muttered.

"You're my baby sister, Katie Rose. Always have been. Always will be."

She extricated herself, unaware of the hurt that flared in Cam's eyes.

"Tell Jenna bye. I'll be at the shop bright and early tomorrow."

Kate's eyes sought mine and that damn zing sizzled down my spine. "Can you walk me to my car?"

"Yeah. Sure."

Cam opened his mouth—probably to warn Kate not to go anywhere with me—but snapped it shut when Kate stepped away, giving Cam her back.

She strode in front of me. I glanced back up at her brother, whose eyes remained trained on Kate, a black scowl forming as the hurt in his eyes deepened.

I sighed as I followed.

"You don't get along with your brother?" I asked. Why, I couldn't say. But something in Cam's expression called to me.

Kate's jaw clenched tight. Her eyes narrowed. "I'll say this one time: my relationship with my half-brother is none of your business."

I raised my free hand in a placating gesture. "Fine. Just seems unfortunate that he's making such an effort and you're putting up roadblocks."

"You know nothing about me."

I shrugged. "Just what I see."

She stomped off ahead. I rubbed my hand along the back of my neck, considering my options. Apologizing would be the decent thing to do. Not that anyone considered me all that decent at the moment. Still, I didn't like the idea of the auburn-haired beauty being angry with me.

"Katie, hold up."

She spun around on those four-inch stilettos, hands jammed into fists on her hips. Her cheeks flushed crimson and her gray eyes sparked with fire. "My name," she said through gritted teeth, "is *Kate.*"

"Oh. Well, Kate. I wanted to apologize for pissing you off."

She dipped her chin in a regal nod before once again giving me her back. My shoulders slid forward and I gripped my guitar.

I shouldn't have gotten involved. I had my own shit going on—more than I could handle, really—and I did not need to further insinuate myself into someone else's problems.

I watched her for another moment before I blew out a breath. Just as I was about to turn away, a roadie slunk toward her, his eyes zeroed in on those killer legs.

I strode forward, my heart pounding. Damn, he had her crowded against a car. Not touching her—yet—but still enough to make me uncomfortable.

Quickening my pace, I made it to her side just as the man leaned in, pressing his hips to hers. In the next instant, the roadie howled in pain. As the man fell forward, Kate slammed her fist into his throat.

"Do not touch me," she growled at him.

The roadie groaned. "I'm going to press charges," he muttered, struggling to rise.

His face was still ashen. Good.

"Can't see why you would," I said, stepping protectively between the man and Kate. "Seeing as how you manhandled her."

The roadie staggered up, pulling a knife from his pocket. I cursed, low and vicious, as I dropped my guitar and seized the guy's wrist. I brought my other arm up in an elbow jab across his throat before grasping and squeezing with all my force. The roadie gurgled and groaned.

People were yelling behind me but I didn't dare take my eyes off the knife. Just as I anticipated, the guy tried to lunge toward me. I stepped my foot between his, throwing him off balance and using his own weight to slam his wrist into the top of the car beside me.

From the corner of my eye, I saw Kate cringe and squeal. She darted forward and grabbed the guitar case, making sure I didn't fall over it. The yelling increased in volume and now I could hear running footsteps.

With a grunt and gritted teeth, I slammed the man's hand onto the edge of the car. This time, the knife fell from his fingers. Voices and yells surrounded us. I glanced over, quick, to make sure Kate was okay. She clutched my guitar case to her chest, eyes wide and mouth gaping.

The air shifted and I managed to duck just before the asshole's fist landed against my face.

Two big men—bigger than me—came up behind the roadie and grabbed his arms.

I stepped back, chest heaving.

Shit.

Thanks to this guy, I might well not get to see Ike tonight at all. And if the jerk-wad tried to press charges, I might not get to see my son in the morning, either.